Liquid Avenue

Liquid Avenue

Phil Wernig

iUniverse LLC
Bloomington

LIQUID AVENUE

iUniverse books may be ordered through booksellers or by contacting:

iUniverse LLC
1663 Liberty Drive
Bloomington, IN 47403
www.iuniverse.com
1-800-Authors (1-800-288-4677)

ISBN: 978-1-4917-3180-2 (sc)
ISBN: 978-1-4917-3179-6 (e)

Library of Congress Control Number: 2014907548

Printed in the United States of America.

iUniverse rev. date: 04/26/2014

"I got drunk and puked
in the
Death Club"

—Liquid Avenue tee shirt

Chapter One

The vomit on my office door didn't bother me. I was used to it. In the cool heavy air at this time of the morning, it had already lost its acrid tang. Luis would be around in a couple of hours to hose it off.

I slipped my key into the deadbolt lock, nudged the door open and flipped on the lights. The florescent overheads were dim and always hummed for ten or fifteen minutes until they warmed up. The lamp on my desk threw off a more welcoming glow and a far better light for bookkeeping. The clock tacked up on the wall with its long rat's tail electric cord trailing to the floor past brown stains seeping through from the kitchen on the other side reported that it was 3:25 AM. The club had been closed for about two hours.

While I waited for the overheads to warm up, I adjusted the wall clock two minutes ahead to agree with my watch, a far more steady timekeeper. A note in Jimmy's handwriting waited for me on my desk. As usual, it was illegible. Jimmy had no doubt scrawled it sometime after 1:30 AM. The only word I could make out was "beer."

For about the hundredth time, I wished we had an answering machine in the office so people could leave me messages I could decipher. We used to have one attached to the extension phone on the portable banquet table crowding the office on the other side of my computer printer. The device was virtually worthless because all the calls were from hopeful bands looking for booking. That was Dan's bailiwick. He had given up working in the office, preferring instead to stay home with his wife and their newborn kid. The answering machine was always swamped with unattended pleas, its red "message waiting" light flashing painfully, as if its belly were swollen from having to hold all those pleas. Dan had taken the machine home with him so he could ignore them in peace.

My first duty was to brew a pot of coffee. I snagged the canvas bag and the purple parka tucked between the stained wall and my desk, went back outside the office—really just a shed attached to the main building—marched a few steps across a small parking lot to the back entrance of the club, pulled up the ring of keys attached to my belt on its retractable chain, fitted the key, and pulled open the service door. I snapped on some interior lights and passed through a short aisle to the hallway that led outside to the dining patio. The bathrooms were on the left side of the hallway, under a storage loft; to the right was a door with a scratched tin sign reading "Employees Only." Inside a tiny break room with a few folding chairs and cans of sand that served as ashtrays, three battered gym lockers with doors that did not close all the way leaned against one wall for the convenience of staff that wanted to park their belongings. I stashed my own stuff in my office.

The employee time clock was fastened to the wall with its rack of employee time cards stationed next to it. I pulled mine, punched in, and slid it back into the rack. It was 3:35 AM. I did not need to adjust the clock's opinion of the time to agree with my watch. I had set it myself eight months ago and, unlike the crappy clock in my office that lost two minutes a day, the employee time clock could track time like a Greenwich Observatory astronomer.

Retracing my steps, I went back down the hallway past the aisle and pushed through a pair swinging impact doors into the kitchen.

The *Cocina Habana* had been closed since midnight. The proprietors, Margarito and Elena, never left a mess. The warm aroma of congealed lard, cayenne pepper, and fried plantains hung over the oven and grills, but the pots and pans had already been scrubbed and stored, the cutting boards washed, the knives and ladles mounted on their wall pegs, and the garbage neatly bagged in plastic and set out by the service door for Luis to truck to the dumpster. The *cocina*'s owners had left a clean pot for me. I knew where to find the coffee, the water, the sugar, and the cream.

I got the coffee going and headed into the main area of the club. Pale, nauseating light filtered through thick uncirculated air, a misty vapor of urine, stale spirits and cigarette smoke. The floor, as always, was strewn with sawdust, shredded napkins, shattered plastic cups, broken bottles, pools of beer, and mushy puddles of puke. Along the baseboards, cockroaches scuttled among grease-soaked crumbs, blackened butts and crushed foil crack pipes. Against the far wall, past the dance floor, behind the bar, a four-foot cluster of migraine blue neon tubes that were never unplugged spelled the club's name: *Liquid Avenue.*

As I shuffled toward the bar, I noticed among the two dozen small sturdy tables bolted to the floor a figure curled up against a wall. I knew her. She was one of the seven reasons why I was in the club at this ghastly hour.

It was Lyss Nelson, Tommy's wife. Her back was to me, but I recognized her grass green cotton print dress and the shapely legs tucked beneath it. She was sleeping off another evening of alcoholic blitz, not for the first time. I liked Lyss; I even fancied her a little bit, although I hate drunks and I had rarely seen Lyss sober. She was married to one of my three bosses, but that didn't seem to mean much. Tommy had a girl friend; it was hardly a secret; Elizabeth was in the club all the time.

Six of the seven reasons had names. Lyss and Tommy Nelson, Elizabeth Strennis, Dan Pensacola, his wife Alicia, and Randy Garch. They were all on the payroll. None of them

3

actually worked in the club. Tommy, Dan, and Randy were the owners, partners in Liquid Avenue and other ventures, and my bosses.

The most compelling reason I was there every morning at 3:30 AM did not have a name because it was an inanimate object. It was the safe. It contained the previous evening's take. If I didn't get to it before the other six reasons did—each had the combination—there might be nothing left in it to pay the bills. My canvas bag was for the money and the rolls of sales receipts from the closed-out cash registers.

I left Lyss to her dreamless slumber. It would be fruitless to try to wake her. Her drunk was no doubt abetted by opiates, most likely codeine. I would have covered her with a wrap against the chill if I had one. She would be okay. She was feeling no pain.

I was the one who needed protection from the cold. The safe was not too conveniently located in the walk-in refrigerator where the beer was stored. Whatever the ambient temperature in the club, it was always arctic in the cooler. That's what my purple parka was for. I pulled it over a wool sweater. My fingers trembled as I dialed the knob on the safe; my breath made clouds. There were several plastic pouches and two paper sacks waiting for rescue, stuffed with cash and eager to be counted. I felt warmer.

A single glance at the depleted beer inventory explained Jimmy's illegible note. It was Friday morning. To be ready for tonight, we would need more bubbly mead.

The coffee was ready in the *cocina*. I poured a generous serving into a large paper cup, dosed it with cream and sugar, grabbed the canvas bag with my free hand, went around the corner to the service door and hit the crash bar with my hip.

In the parking lot I had a visitor. "Hi, Anthony. How's it going?"

A woman in a shabby coat that just reached the top of her thighs stood in the shadows, hugging herself. Her legs were bare beneath cutoff jeans and ended in tattered sneakers.

She was a regular apparition. "Good morning, Carla. Care for a cuppa mud?"

"Sure. Sounds good."

Carla turned up once or twice a week. She had been coming by Liquid Avenue for about a month now. I had never seen her in the daylight. At this hour her business was slow. Most of her clientele staggered out of the club after midnight, probably the same ones who chucked up undigested dinner on my office door. She provided a service for the inebriated gentleman looking for something to top off his evening.

"Could you hold these for me, please?" I handed her the canvas bag and my cup of steaming coffee, fussed with the keys again, and let us in. In the kitchen, Carla took a paper cup, half filled it with coffee, took it to the rim with cream, and slipped a handful of sugar packets into her coat pocket. We let ourselves out.

"Say, Anthony. Do you think you could help me out?"

This was part of our ritual. Other street desperadas had approached me in this parking lot, but I had always turned them away empty-handed. There was something different about Carla. I couldn't put my finger on it; probably didn't want to. I thought I detected a trace of British accent in her diction, which made her seem a cut above the others. She was so sweetly pathetic. I knew I could trust her. That's why I had no worry that she might dash off into the darkness with my canvas bag. I handed it to her again, reached for my wallet, and plucked a double sawbuck.

Carla took the twenty; I took the bag. She stepped forward and gave me a hug.

"Thanks, Anthony. You're a doll."

She faded into the clammy dark and I went back into my office.

We'd had a decent haul for a Thursday night. I was still toting it up when I heard the hose outside scrawling over the shed and my office door, and then sloshing the parking lot. That would be Luis bathing the dumpster and the cracked asphalt with its two parking spaces lined with barely discernible white paint. I glanced at the clock. 5:05 AM. Luis was as reliable as sunrise.

Some minutes later there was a pounding on my door—always locked when I was doing the daily tally. An urgent voice called out.

"¡Señor Tony! ¡Señor Tony!"

I opened the door for Luis. He stood on the wet cement, baseball cap in hand.

"Está Señora Lyss."

"Yo sabo, Luis. I saw her. She is sleeping."

"No, Señor." Luis shook his head sadly. "¡Ella es muerta!"

Chapter Two

Liquid Avenue occupies the corner of East Haley and Anacapa Streets. Even in the best possible light, East Haley is a scrofulous neighborhood. One block west, prosperous State Street runs north from Santa Barbara's harbor and Stearn's Wharf through fifteen blocks of well-tended commerce. Tourists flock there for the retail shopping, the sidewalk cafes, the flagstone-lined *paseos*, and the Spanish Colonial look, ideal for snapshots. East of Anacapa, the "look" fades, like the edges of the colonial era daguerreotypes framed in the local museums. During the day the drab shops, decrepit hotels and decaying residences wear a sepia tone, as if color will not stick to them. At night, what little vitality they display drains away altogether.

Luis had been right. Lyss Nelson was definitely *muerta*. The Santa Barbara Police Department had concluded that her vitality had been drained deliberately. She had been strangled.

By sunrise, Liquid Avenue was a crime scene. The yellow police tape was everywhere. Black-and-white squad cars blocked East Haley and Anacapa Streets. An ambulance and a police van sat in the parking lot Luis had just washed. A forensic team had examined the victim, photographed the body from every angle and lifted fingerprints from everything within a ten-foot radius of poor Lyss Nelson's inert remains. Now they were making their careful way among the club detritus in a methodical search for clues.

Luis and I had identified Lyss and given statements to the first officers at the scene. Reporters from the *Santa Barbara News-Press* and television news stringers had not been admitted yet, but they were keen to speak to us and take photos of their own. Dan Pensacola and Randy Garch had been notified and were on their way to the club. Tommy Nelson had not yet been located.

Elena and Margarito, arriving to open the *Cocina Habana*, had been allowed to enter the building although the police instructed them to refrain from prepping the kitchen for business. They were, however, permitted to make coffee for everyone.

"You were right. This is delicious!"

Detective Imanaka took another sip from her cup of *café Cubano*, her lower lip protruding slightly as she savored the fresh brew from the kitchen. We sat in the covered patio adjacent to the club, the only place, other than my office and the employee break room, where there were chairs. There were tables too for *Cocina Habana's* daytime customers.

"You should try the food here sometime, if you have a taste for Cuban." I managed a wan smile. "It's truly excellent."

"So, what's the deal here? You have this little restaurant by day and a nightclub by night?"

"Liquid Avenue sells alcohol. It helps our insurance rates if we also sell food. We, I mean the owners, Nelson, Garch and Pensacola, rent this space to Margarito and Elena Capra for their restaurant so we can offer food to our nightclub customers. They are open for business from lunch until midnight."

"I get it." Detective Imanaka nodded. Her lower lip rubbed against its upper sister. The detective's whitish face was round and flat, her eyes brown under dark brows. She looked down at her notebook, resting on the table. "So, the building is open from lunch time until after sometime after midnight?"

"Yes."

"And when do the people who work here arrive?"

"Luis is always first. He's the custodian. He always comes in at 5:00 AM. Margarito and Elena are here at 10:00 to get the restaurant up and running for lunch. Jimmy Nelson, the club manager, arrives around 11:00. The bar opens at 4:00 in the afternoon. The club opens at 8:00 PM. That's when the hostess and the bouncers arrive. The band—we have different bands in here all the time—will start playing around 9:00. Jimmy closes out the cash registers between 1:00 and 1:30."

Detective Imanaka recorded these facts in her notebook. Her pale white hand had long, tapered fingers that moved with unhurried precision. Her script, as it appeared from my side of the table, was impeccable. She looked up.

"Isn't there someone you're forgetting, Mister Trapp?"

"Please call me Anthony."

"Of course." She smiled. "Call me Rachel." Any dentist in the world would have been proud to claim her spotless teeth as his own handiwork. Rachel Imanaka was a very attractive woman. "Isn't there someone you haven't mentioned, Anthony?"

I frowned. Who had I left out? "I don't think so, Rachel."

"What about you, Anthony? You didn't mention yourself."

Oh, my God! My face burned with embarrassment. Did that make me seem guilty or just stupid?

"Geez, I'm sorry, Rachel. You're right. I forgot that I'm an employee too. It's just that I'm almost never here when the club is open for business. I usually come in before 3:30 in the morning. Today I was in at 3:25. I take the previous night's money and paperwork from the safe, count it in my office, and prepare the daily bank deposit.

I watched Rachel scribe all of this into her notebook. Her lips massaged each other. Peering at her notes, she said, "It sounds like you handle all the cash."

"Yes," I agreed. "I don't do the *cocina*—their operation is all their own—but I account for everything in the club that comes through the door and the registers; everything that winds up in the safe."

Rachel raised her head and drilled me straight in the eyes. "Why do you come in so early, Anthony?"

Was this a good time to tell her that the owners only trusted me because they couldn't trust each other? Should I mention that they nearly went bankrupt only a year ago because no one knew where all the money went, they bounced checks to all their vendors, they fell six months behind on the club's rent and almost got evicted, and they were four quarters in arrears on their payroll and sales taxes? For some reason, maybe because I had just realized that Detective Imanaka was not really as attractive as I thought, I was not entirely forthcoming.

"I like to come in early because it's easier to count the money and reconcile the sales receipts when there are no distractions. Later in the day, people will be coming in and out of the office. It's so much easier to do the rest of my job when the money is out of the office and safely in the bank."

Detective Imanaka had stared at me intently throughout my explanation. Her lips rubbed each other again. She nodded curtly. "That makes perfect sense."

She wrote a few more lines in her notebook, then she closed it, reached for her coffee cup, and took a long swig. "That is really good coffee." She grinned. "I'll take you up on your advice to try the food here sometime." She stood and so did I. She reached across the table and we shook hands.

"We'll need to have the names of everyone who worked here last night, including the band. Will you be able to give that to one of my officers, Anthony?"

"Certainly, Rachel. No problem."

We walked back through the hallway into the club together. The detective stopped to indicate a ladder fixed to the wall between the two bathrooms. "Where does that go?"

"There's a loft up there for storage. Accounting records, holiday decorations for the club, paper plates, cups, napkins and so forth."

She nodded again. "I'll have someone check that out."

There was still a knot of uniformed people gathered around the murder site, but I could see that Lyss Nelson's body was gone. Before she rejoined her colleagues, Detective Imanaka paused. "It was a pleasure to meet you, Anthony. I may need to talk to you again later to nail down some details. I hope you won't mind." She showed me the unblemished smile again.

"No, not at all, Rachel. Anything I can do to help."

"Oh, yes. One more thing. Do you happen to know where we can find Tommy Nelson?"

Chapter Three

"Those fuckers worked me over pretty good, Tony, but I didn't give 'em anything. I've had worse. Much worse."

Randy Garch stood by my desk, watching me finish preparing the bank deposit. His voice was raspy, more gargle than speech. His rusty red hair, shaved at the sides above his ear level, piled up on his head with smelly tonic like a bowl of greasy orange peels. His blue eyes flamed with indignation.

"They got me under the lights and smacked me around with their batons. I should call my lawyer. Here, look at these marks!"

Randy pulled a white, v-neck tee shirt up over a hairless sagging belly and pointed to a faint brown streak on his sternum. He had shown me this bruise last week. On that occasion he reported that his spotter had dropped a 300-pound barbell on him that he was bench-pressing at the gym. I had seen the police interviewing Randy at the far end of the club near the bar. The brightest light on hand for their interrogation was the blue neon *Liquid Avenue* sign, which might have put Randy in harm's way for a headache but hardly for intimidation.

I regarded my boss, reared up to his full five feet and five inches of outrage. "What did they ask you, Randy?"

"They wanted the names of my bouncers. Can you believe that? I told 'em it was none of their fucking business. That's when they started playing rough. As if they could scare a Vietnam vet. I was tortured by the Viet Cong at Dien Bien Phu. I still have cigarette burns on my balls!"

He didn't offer to show me the burn marks, for which I was grateful, and I didn't volunteer to parse his sentence for historical unlikelihood. According to his own declaration some months ago, in connection with his dread of air travel, Randy had never been west of Honolulu. I had already given the names and addresses of the bouncers to the police, along with that information for everybody on our payroll.

"You have any idea where Tommy is?"

"How the hell would I know? That fucker still owes me thirty grand. When I see him I'm gonna put my fist up his ass. All I wanna know is, is the club going to be open tonight? I need to tell Trigger and Peanut if they're working or not."

"I don't know yet, Randy. I'm still waiting for Jimmy to tell me how much product he's ordering so I can go to the bank."

It was nearly 2:30 PM. I had already had a long day. Police were still in the building. Jimmy Nelson was checking the inventory of booze and beer. The *Cocina Habana* was not open yet, although Margarito and Elena had been in the kitchen since this morning. The Liquid Avenue bar was supposed to start serving at 4:00.

When Detective Imanaka asked me if I knew Tommy Nelson's whereabouts, I had told her truthfully that I did not. But I had withheld something. I had no reason to. The detective was going to find out anyway.

I had not seen Tommy since I handed him his paycheck on Wednesday, two days ago. If he wasn't home, I wouldn't know where he was nesting. Even his brother Jimmy wouldn't know. But Elizabeth Strennis would.

Tommy and Elizabeth were an item I couldn't add up. She was a specimen; all the boys agreed on that, including me. Green eyes, olive complexion, a mass of brunette curls erupting from her head, pouring over her shoulders like lava. She wore nothing that failed to emphasis her figure; her long sculpted legs seemed longer still in her attachment to flesh-hued hose and high heels in primary colors. Elizabeth was fond of necklaces and bracelets. She always wore several of each that made her movements jingle like nickel-plated wind chimes.

Every woman in the club hated her. Elizabeth did not enhance her popularity by being on the Liquid Avenue payroll with no duties other than to hang on Tommy's arm and order drinks at club expense. On our books she was listed as a "hostess." She had a real job as a bank teller. What she saw in a jittery, skeletal, self-centered, inarticulate web spinner like Tommy Nelson mystified me.

Tommy had married Lyss two years ago, in Long Beach, just before Dan Pensacola had sold the original Liquid Avenue bar he owned there and partnered up with Nelson and Garch in Santa Barbara. Lyss had also been a Liquid Avenue "hostess." In her employee personnel file, I had a photocopy of a passport for Lyss Wattenwill. She was Swiss. She was 38 years old, blonde with light blue eyes. She was neither stunning nor plain. In appearance and demeanor she occupied the descriptive space called "fine"—"fine" like my Movado watch, incidentally, also Swiss. On those occasions when she had appeared in my office—like everyone else, she was always looking for Tommy—she was very nice, soft-spoken in clear English undercut with native German. She somehow whetted my appetite for link sausages; maybe that's because I liked to look at her legs.

I do not know how Lyss tolerated Tommy's paws on Elizabeth when they were all in the club together. Little wonder she found solace in alcohol and opiates. Word had never reached me of any jealous unpleasantries. I reckoned her diplomatic neutrality must be bred in the bone. After all, she was Swiss.

"Jesus Christ, Tony. I feel so bad about Lyss."

Dan Pensacola strolled into the office nursing a cup of *café Cubano*. He pulled out the chair parked under the folding banquet table stacked with binders, reference pamphlets from the IRS and the State of California with payroll tax withholding guidelines, a case of green bar paper for my printer, and a storage carton containing assorted office supplies.

A pang of guilt scalded me. "I saw her lying on the floor this morning. I thought she was asleep."

"How could you have known? Lyss bombed out under the tables every other week." Dan sipped and we observed a respectful silence.

"You just missed Randy."

"Missed him? I was hiding in the kitchen until I was sure he was gone."

"He complained about police brutality."

"Is that all? He didn't complain about high taxes, racial impurity, and all the people around here who speak Spanish?"

"I'm sure he was getting to that. He wanted to know if we're open tonight."

"Yeah, we're open." Dan sighed and sipped again. "It doesn't seem decent, does it? We just had a death in the club. We should lock up for at least one night."

Dan and I both knew we could not afford to close the doors on a Friday night. "I wish I could say Lyss would have wanted us to carry on, but that would be insane. How's Alicia taking it?"

"She freaked out. She didn't want me to come down here. I had to tell her the police would come by the house if I didn't come down to the club."

Dan took another sip and sigh. His chair creaked. Dan is a heftier man than I, two years younger according to his personnel file. It was easy to understand why Alicia would feel threatened by the homicide at the club and uneasy about a home visit from the police. She had once been a Liquid Avenue cocktail waitress. Now she and Dan had a newborn at home. I wondered whether Dan, at age 41, had picked the right time to become a first time father. He seemed to wear the role well. Nothing seemed to ruffle him much. He was expert at avoiding his partners.

"The police got the names of the band from you?"

"Yeah." The chair squeaked again as Dan leaned to put his empty cup on the table. "It was easy. Last night we had the Discordians."

Clark Gary and his outfit was our virtual house band. They often took the stage on less busy nights when Dan did not book a more expensive ensemble. The Discordians had been a One Hit Wonder about ten years ago. The AM radio stations played their song twenty times a day for a month and then it dropped with their album into the sale bins at Licorice Pizza and the Wherehouse. They were available locals. They played for whatever we could collect at the door.

"Jesus, I feel bad about Lyss." Dan was up and headed for the door.

I had to ask. "Any idea what's become of Tommy?"

Dan shrugged. "That's the question of the day, isn't it?"

Chapter Four

Who killed Lyss Nelson? *That* was the question of the day.

With all the intensity rippling through the club, the disruption of routine, and the upsetting presence of police on board, I had not had time to digest the most chilling fact. Someone had come into my workplace and killed a woman I knew.

Who? Why? These were interrogatives for Detective Imanaka. I was left to chew on the indigestible awfulness of it, a horrible gristle of mortality seasoned with shock.

Another worry suddenly asserted itself. What could Lyss have done to deserve death? There seemed to be a random aspect in the murder of this harmless, helpless woman. Could this be the strike of a serial killer? Was Deejee in danger?

For the first time all day, Lyss Nelson's murder felt personal and therefore alarming. Darlena Giordano had worked in the club last night. Suppose the killer had taken her instead of Lyss? Would he be back for more victims?

Deejee was scheduled to work tonight too. Should I talk her out of it, persuade her to spend the night at my place instead?

I returned from the bank at 3:30 with cashier's checks for today's deliveries of liquor and beer and went into the club to hand them off to the manager. Nelson, Garch and Pensacola enjoyed credit with nobody. We had to pay for everything with guaranteed funds. The vendors, the landlord, the State Board of Equalization, the Franchise Tax Board, the Internal Revenue Service—all had exhausted their patience with the rubberized payments presented to them in the past. Only Liquid Avenue employees would accept company checks; they had no choice.

I had postponed calling Rita. She was in the field anyway, and would not have heard about the nastiness at Liquid Avenue. I planned to call her as soon as I was home.

My long day refused to come to an end. I heard the jingling coming through the office door. As I turned, Elizabeth Strennis shouted, "Was it you who gave my name to the cops, Tony?"

"Yes."

"What? Why the fuck did you do that, asshole? Do you know that they actually came to the bank and pulled me into the vice-president's office to ask me questions? Do you have any idea how embarrassing that was?"

"I gave them everybody's name, Elizabeth. I'm the bookkeeper. They came to me for the time cards and the personnel records. They've been here all day asking questions. That's what they do when they're investigating a murder. What I didn't tell them was that you have a relationship with Tommy."

"Tommy treats me nice, that's all. Who says we have a relationship?"

Anybody who saw them together at Liquid Avenue would have said that they had a relationship. Few would have guessed that Tommy was married to Lyss. Jimmy Nelson would have said they had a relationship. Randy Garch and Dan Pensacola would have affirmed it. Even Margarito and Elena would have said so. I was probably the only one who had not. Tommy Nelson himself would have said so if he had been around to answer questions.

"So, Elizabeth, where's Tommy?"

Elizabeth jingled as she turned abruptly to look at something in the parking lot. She reached into her purse, extracted a pack of Benson & Hedges, got one between shiny dark brown lips, and put a cigarette lighter in front of it. "If I knew that, why would I tell *you*?"

"If you knew that, why *wouldn't* you tell me? Tommy's not a killer. What does he have to hide?"

I had put a dumb question to a mute witness. Tommy had plenty of things to hide. I had no doubt at all that Elizabeth knew where he was. She perched on the edge of the table, still gazing through the office door into the parking lot. Her chocolate brown dress called attention to a freckled cleavage delicately sprinkled with glitter. Her hemline rode up a few inches above her knees. On her feet, a pair of yellow pumps shone as bright as tropical birds.

If Deejee ever knew I coveted this girl she would drop me like a 300-pound barbell.

"Okay, Tony. I believe you." Her lungs expelled a cumulus of smoke that broke up as it reached the door. "No harm; no foul." Elizabeth flicked the cigarette through the open door and followed it out into the afternoon sun.

It was time to drive a stake through the heart of this evil day. I locked the office, found my way to the employee break room and punched out. It was 3:50 PM. I always parked my Volkswagen Rabbit across Anacapa Street in the public lot. It was not a rule, but it was understood that the two parking spaces behind the club were reserved for the landlord, the owners, and the mysterious silver Rolls Royce with darkened windows that eased in every Monday morning to collect Randy, spirit him off to an undisclosed destination, and return him an hour later. Randy loudly declined to identify the occupant of this handsome carriage, referring to him only as "Pops", but proudly declared he was connected to the Mafia. The vanity plate on the Rolls tied it to a highly visible industrial laundry service.

I considered stopping for supper, but I had calls to make so I had the Rabbit sail me straight to my apartment on West Valerio Street.

Darlena's phone number did not belong to her. The line led to her grandmother's home and my chances of reaching Deejee on it were no better than 50-50. I tried it anyway and caught Darlena after the second ring.

"Deejee, it's Anthony."

"Trapp! I bet you have some verbs to cough up about the killing. You coming by the club tonight?"

"Sorry, Deej. I've had enough of the club for today. I'm calling to see if you want to pull out tonight and hang here instead."

She laughed so sharply I had to take the phone away from my ear. "Are you delirious? Jesus, Trapp, I can't wait to get there! A Friday night after a murder? Could it ever get more exciting than that? I'll make more tips tonight than I made all month. Christ on a stick! The atmosphere will be incredible!"

"Aren't you worried it could be dangerous? I was sick all day thinking it might have been you."

"Me?" Her laugh crackled the line again. "You think I'm as stupid as Lyss? When I heard someone got herself killed, Lyss was my first guess. I just wish it would've been Elizabeth."

"Okay. Keep your eyes open, though. Try to keep yourself surrounded with other people. Are you sure you won't need some company after work?"

"Trapp, baby. Relax. Sometimes you're absolutely the square root of zero. If I need company, I'll get Peanut to come home with me. Tell you what. Let's get together Sunday afternoon. We'll score some rock. Have us a party."

The thought of Deejee taking one of Randy's bouncers home with her squeezed acid drops on my peptic ulcer. Was Darlena tumbling around between the sheets with that bald headed, steroid ripped hominid?

The phone clamored, I grabbed it.

"Hello, Anthony."

"Well, howdy, Doc. I was about to call you."

"We just got back to the hotel. I'm bushed. I could sleep for ten hours. I've got one more meeting tonight before I get to put my head on a pillow. Before I go downstairs for dinner with the guys, I wanted to hear a warm friendly voice talking about something other than drilling for shale oil."

"You got the right number. Today was worth talking about."

I told Rita about the murder, Detective Imanaka, and the general disturbance that had rolled into Liquid Avenue. It loosened my coils to speak to someone with a head squarely on her shoulders.

"God, Anthony. What a fucken nightmare! Are you sure it's safe to go back to work? I wish I could be there for you."

"Thanks, Doc. I miss you too."

"I have to be here another week. You know, if things get too hairy, you can come up and stay with me. I'll be glad to send you the plane fare."

"That's really sweet, hon. I appreciate the offer. What's there to do in Anchorage, anyway?"

"We could always talk about drilling for shale oil."

Chapter Five

Who killed Lyss Nelson?

I had the morning edition of the *News-Press* in front of me over breakfast at Carrow's. The article on the murder at Liquid Avenue ventured no speculation on the "who" or "why" of the case, but it did provide some details on the "how":

". . . Detective Rachel Imanaka stated that the victim had been strangled to death while already unconscious due to intoxication. Ligature marks on the victim's throat indicated that the assailant throttled her with a length of fabric, possibly a scarf or a stocking. The killer apparently concealed himself in a storage loft during the nightclub's business hours and attacked the victim later after the patrons had left and the building was closed.

The medical examiner established that the victim died sometime between 2:00 AM and 4:00 AM . . ."

I closed the paper and peeked at my wristwatch. 2:55 AM. I would be punching in at the club in half an hour. Was Deejee entertaining Peanut while I sat here poking my eggs with a fork? Did they score some rock; have them a party?

I stared at my ham and scrambled, trying to remember why I thought I was hungry.

Had the killer been waiting in the loft yesterday morning while I was there? Was Lyss already dead when I saw her curled up under the tables, presuming she was asleep? Would I have saved her life if I had tried to wake her? Suppose the murderer had been lurking in the shadows, his weapon twisted in his cruel thick hands, waiting impatiently for me to clear off? If he had decided to wrap it around my neck instead, I could be the corpse Rachel Imanaka had described to the press with those cold implacable facts.

Maybe Rita had been right and I was a fool to brush off her sensible advice. How could I be sure the killer wasn't in the loft right now? How did I know I wasn't attending my last meal?

"Can I hit that coffee for you again, Tony?"

My waitress interrupted my grim reverie. I looked up at her heavy, weary face, lined at the corners of her eyes and mouth, too much makeup lending her features a padded depth, like a stage actress stepping away from the footlights into the wings. She was calm and familiar. Since she worked this graveyard shift regularly, I knew her both well and not at all. Her stolid presence dissipated my worries.

"No, thanks, Jean." I glanced at my watch just to make a theatrical gesture. "Time to jump in the pool and start paddling."

My worries seemed no more threatening or substantial than cobwebs when I arrived at my office door and drew the keys from my belt on their retractable chain. A black and white police car sat in the parking lot. Two uniformed officers waved at me. Moments later, on my way back to the rear entrance service door with my canvas bag to let myself in, I went up to the car.

"Would you gentlemen care for some fresh coffee?"

The officers followed me into the club. I switched on all the lights and they patrolled, peering under the tables and into the shadows as I pushed through the swinging doors into the *Cocina Habana* to start brewing. My coffee was nothing like the *café* that Elena and Magarito made with the spices that made it *Cubano*, but it was bound to be better than the joe the cops took out of the all-night donut shop.

Credit belongs where it's due. Deejee had called it. Judging by the heft of the swollen money pouches and paper sacks from the safe, Liquid Avenue had enjoyed a record night. Murder was good for business.

It was Saturday morning. I had until 1:00 PM to get all the cash tallied and ferried to the bank. Since there was so much of it, I needed to bear down.

Counting money is tedious. I guess most people imagine it would be fun to be paid for riffling through piles of currency, sorting it into stacks by denomination, and rubber banding it all into the exact bunches the bank prefers. Thank God I did not have to roll up coins. The club did not accept coins or credit cards. All prices were rounded to even dollar amounts, a convenient dodge the Board of Equalization swallowed only on the condition that we post signs stating that sales tax was included in all the prices.

I had fudged my job description slightly when I told Detective Imanaka that I "reconcile the sales receipts." For proper accountability, the money should equal the amounts rung up in the cash registers and recorded on those rolls I collected every morning from the safe. I had given that up long ago because it was never even close. There was no system of tickets issued for the cover charges taken at the door either. It was simply impossible to determine whether cash was disappearing into employee pockets, or, to be more realistic about it, how much.

Added to that, the owners, their wives and girlfriends, and Jimmy Nelson had access to the safe. The whole operation invited thievery. Nelson, Garch and Pensacola didn't care. As long as everyone got their paychecks, the club had enough money to buy inventory, and the company satisfied long-standing obligations to its former creditors, Tommy, Randy and Dan were satisfied.

It was no way to run a business, which is why the owners nearly went bankrupt before they hired me. Which is why I was in the club every single morning at an hour of the day when respectable people were hugging blankets and having dreams.

I heard Luis with his hose in the parking lot. I didn't have to look at the clock to know it was 5:05 AM. There was a pleasant side to counting money. It evoked a trance-like state, like chanting with monks or staring at rotating spirals. In the absorption, time passed unnoticed. I didn't think about Deejee and Peanut.

As soon as I wrapped up the day's chores and pointed the Rabbit at West Valerio, I did.

What was it about Darlena Giordano? She wasn't as pretty as Rita. She certainly wasn't as smart, in the formal education sense, or as accomplished. She wasn't as even in temperament. I already had a great girl friend. Why was I tangled up with Deejee?

I suppose it was *because* she was so unlike Rita. Some of Deejee's anatomy was downright ugly. Her hands and feet were thick with blunt nails. She was short-waisted, with heavy thighs and small breasts that she downplayed by wearing trousers and blouses that buttoned up to the neck. Her hair was honey blonde.

Darlena's facial features were unnervingly mutable, according to her mood. She had the half-mast bedroom eyes, I had to give her that. They were light brown, the shade of under-done pancakes. Her teeth were over-sized, covered by thick lips that specialized in pouting.

Jealousy does not obey reason, but it puzzled me that I resented the idea of Peanut's talons clutching Deejee's body. Until yesterday, I had never had a beef with him, had barely ever spoken to him, even when he came by the office every Wednesday to pick up his paycheck. Now I hated the bastard.

As for my own rapturous clutching of Deejee's body, well, that was still in the future.

Chapter Six

How long had I been dating Deejee? About three weeks now, if dating was the word for it. We had opposite work schedules; I tended to be asleep when she was awake and vice versa. So far we had managed only four get-togethers, all on afternoons when she was not scheduled to be at the club that night, all but the first one at my apartment, each more intense than the last.

Deejee didn't know about Rita. Rita didn't know about Deejee. For the time being, I thought it best to keep it that way. Rita's schedule was unusual and subject to change, though she was by no means the night crawler that I had become since Dan Pensacola hired me to untangle all the crossed wires that shorted out Liquid Avenue's finances. Rita had been in Alaska for the past two weeks, so it had been easy so far to keep her in the dark about Darlena Giordano.

I couldn't get the picture out of my head of Deejee and Peanut sucking crack through some filthy glass pipe and getting up to God only knew what. I knew what I wanted to get up to with her and that became the frame for my fervid envy. Squirming restlessly on my couch, I had a strong urge to do something active, like hopping into the Rabbit and cruising by Deejee's place to see if I recognized any cars I didn't approve of. The problem was, I didn't really know where she lived.

It was true that she had an address in her personnel file at work, a house up on the Riviera by the Mission. Deejee had told me that she did not actually live there. It was her grandmother's home, a convenient permanent address for mail and a phone, to establish residency for official purposes. She had recently moved from Chicago; she was staying with friends until she could find affordable housing. That was certainly believable. Affordable housing is an evergreen hassle for lower income Santa Barbara dwellers.

I could run the Rabbit by Peanut's place; I had his address on file too. I would learn little or nothing from drive-by surveillance there. Deejee didn't own a car. Every time we had got together, I had picked her up at the club and dropped her off later at a restaurant or a bar or some place where she was hooking up with friends.

I had nothing better to do on a Saturday afternoon than fret. I could call Rita. She might be reading or writing geological survey reports in her hotel room. She was always glad to hear from me. But we had talked just yesterday and I could hardly share with her why I was so possessed with itchy feelings that it was all I could do to stay seated and stop pacing my tiny apartment like a jail cell.

There was one thing I could do that went well with sitting still. I could smoke dope.

Last week Bogo had replenished the wooden cigar box holding my stash with two ounces of Colombian marijuana. The box squatted comfortably in its space among the books, videos and music cassettes that crammed the four brick and board shelves of my library. That box had served as curator for my cannabis for over fifteen years. No matter what mood I was in, it was a pleasure just to open it. The accumulated fragrance of a decade and a half of pot enclosure had worked its way into the cedar and sent invisible tendrils of sweet aroma into my nostrils the moment its lid was lifted.

A few minutes later I had twisted a sparkler and put it to work. A few minutes after that I was staring at the blank television screen four feet in front of me, propped on a dusty dresser in faded tan paint, considering which video to pop into the VCR. Behind the TV, Venetian blinds hid the parking lot from my ground floor view. They were even dustier than the dresser. To my right, an accordion-folding vinyl door screened my bedroom and bathroom.

My telephone perched on a desk that abutted the rear of my small gray fabric sofa. Like my office, I had no answering machine for it. I did when I first moved here, but when it fritzed and quit on me, I didn't replace it. Rita had gently nagged me to buy a new chatterbox so she could leave me communiqués, but I had discovered that I liked being hard to reach. Relationships introduce confinements. I enjoyed having a bit of wind in my sails.

It was a condensed living quarters, but I didn't have to waste a lot of time cleaning it and it was, by Santa Barbara standards, affordable. My apartment complex was the last address on West Valerio where it dead-ends at the 101 Freeway, picking up again on the other side of the interstate. My apartment was situated about sixty feet from the concrete wall topped with cyclone fence that separated me from the incessant traffic swooshing by at all hours. With my door or windows open, the noise could be deafening, somewhere between an onrush and an uproar. My windows were closed all the time. If I paid attention to it, the continuous sound of eighteen-wheeled semi-trailers and bulky sedans whizzing past would be unbearably irritating.

Eight cartons of books and vinyl LPs slumped against the wall that made a corner behind my desk. How many books and records did I own? I had no idea. I had been schlepping these items from place to place since my marriage melted into puddles years ago, not because I hoard and fear to purge, but because I collect and relish completeness. The virtues of integrity offset the onus of transport.

Still, I had no immediate plans to revisit the collected works of Cornell Woolrich and Roger L. Simon. And when was the last time I listened to The Electric Flag's *A Long Time Comin'* or Elton John's *Tumbleweed Connection*?

My stereo components lived on the top shelf of my library with a modest pair of speakers the size of cereal boxes at each end. The videos shared a shelf with some of my favorite escapist fare. My eyes drifted over the books, methodically organized by author: Ambler, Bester, Effinger, Greene, Heinlein, Le Carre, MacInnes, Stapledon, Vonnegut. The paperbacks made collective bookends for movies and series I had taped from TV: *The Ipcress File*, *Our Man in Havana*, *The Sandbaggers*, *The Spy Who Came in From the Cold*.

Indecision stymied me. I switched on the TV to settle for whatever was there. *Mystery Science Theater 3000*. Perfect. I rolled another mind baton.

I was hungry. And I was sleepy. I pushed myself off the couch and trod the five steps to my refrigerator for a snack. The clock reported that it was 6:30 PM. It was nearly bedtime. On a Saturday, I typically dropped into the sack around 7:00 PM so I could be up at 2:00 AM to shave and shower, and get down to Carrow's for breakfast. The club would be busy again tonight. Tomorrow morning there would be a lot of counting.

In my ashtray, four cindered roaches accounted for my afternoon. The day had passed rather agreeably as soon as I numbed my wicked worries about Deejee and her bouncer. Cloying vapors moved aside gently as I made my way to bed.

Chapter Seven

The patrol car held a space in the parking lot again. I was pleased to see it. I was not so much fearful about homicidal maniacs hiding in the storage loft as I was relieved to know the police had been posted last night to protect Deejee and everyone else. The officers followed me into the club; I brewed coffee for us.

The cash counting on Sunday morning is more casual than any other day of the week. The banks are closed. The club would be open tonight, but there would be no deliveries of inventory, no need of cashier's checks, and no pressure. I could take all day to do my tallies if I wanted to.

Today I didn't want to be casual. Deejee and I were having our fifth get-together this afternoon. I wanted to get all the business done as soon as possible.

Another thing about Sunday was different. Since the bank was closed, I had to take the money home with me. There were still those reasons with names that had access to the safe. I was not enthusiastic about storing a bag stuffed with cash in my apartment, but it was safer than the safe.

Today was special in still another way. At 2:00 AM this morning, those of us who have a special relationship with chronometers, such as the Movado I wear on my wrist, the rat's tail clock on my office wall, or the timekeeper in the employee break room, gained an hour from Daylight Saving Time. I always felt more in step with the world after I had made the requisite adjustments.

By the time I finished my chores, the squad car was no longer in the parking lot. Luis had finished cleaning up the club. The *Cocina Habana* was open for lunch. I considered calling Deejee to see where and when I would be picking her up for our date. It might be a little early for her. I didn't know how late she stayed up after her shift at Liquid Avenue. It would be best to let her call me.

Anyway, I had shopping to do. My fridge and my cupboards needed provision. Today I was entertaining a guest.

The Volkswagen took me home first. Plopped on the passenger seat next to me, my canvas bag looked like a carry all for gym socks, jock straps and sweaty shorts. Only a super burglar with X-ray vision could have divined that it contained over eight thousand American dollars. My mangy white Rabbit was not the sort of conveyance that attracted vandals, but why take unnecessary risks?

In my apartment, I shoved the bag under my bed. Was it really safe here? It was so long as nobody knew.

I went back out to fetch supplies.

From the market, I took loaves of sourdough and sweet pumpernickel, a variety of sodas, including my favorite Vernor's ginger ale, two six packs of Heineken beer, potato chips, corn puffs, pretzels, shortbread cookies, bran muffins, chocolate and vanilla ice cream, an apple pie, a spinach quiche, raspberry kefir, and produce for making salads and sandwiches. I visited the deli for choice cuts of beef, ham and turkey as well as Swiss and cheddar cheeses and condiments.

I had my pantry stocked and my fridge full of promise by 12:15. Was it too early to give Deejee's phone a try? I did so. Six rings went unanswered, so I gave it a rest.

I tried again at 1:15. Same result. It looked as though I would be waiting for my date to initiate contact. Visions of

Deejee wrapped in Peanut intruded. I wanted to banish those unwelcome intruders. So I called Rita.

I reasoned that Rita would not be working in the field on a Sunday afternoon, but there was no answer at her hotel room in Anchorage. I tried calling the hotel's front desk and reached a very courteous clerk who seemed bored and pleased to have a caller to chat with. After I gave her my name and told her I was calling from Santa Barbara, she wanted to compare notes on the weather. She said that she had seen Doctor Barron leaving the hotel earlier, but her guest had not mentioned when she might be returning.

At 1:30, I decided to stop punishing myself. I reached for the trusty cigar box, rolled myself a sin cylinder, and unwound. I snapped on the television. A football game spread out on the screen. That would do.

By 4:00 the game was over, I had smoked two more puffers down to their gnarled nubs, and I was still waiting for Deejee's summons. My head lolled on my shoulders. I lay back on the sofa.

The phone rang. It had seemed like a matter of seconds, but it was after five o'clock. I had been asleep for over an hour.

"Trapp." Darlena's voice raked through a noisy background. "I'm at Mel's. How soon can you come over and get me?"

"Mel's?" The haze in my head burned away slowly. Mel's was a bar near the corner of Mission and De La Vina Streets. "Five minutes, I guess."

Mel's was five short blocks from my apartment. Deejee could have walked there in ten minutes. I rolled the Rabbit into a vacant space on De La Vina across the street from Mel's. Two figures promptly popped out of the doorway and trotted across the street.

Deejee pulled open the door on the curbside, folded down the passenger seat, and climbed into the back. Another woman settled herself into the passenger seat. The introduction was brief.

"This is Mary," Deejee announced from the back seat. "She's gonna score some rock for us."

One thing I had learned about Darlena Giordano. She was spontaneous. When she had an urge, she liked to run with it. The first time we had done anything together, she had come to my office to pick up her paycheck just as I was leaving for the day. Exhaling a blast of mentholated cigarette, she asked me for a ride to Summerland. We went into an apartment where three guys in tie-dyed tee shirts were lying on their backs listening to Pink Floyd at maximum volume. I did something with Deejee that I had never done with Rita in our three years together. We dropped acid. One of the guys in the tee shirts gave Darlena two tiny squares of blotter paper with a Mister Natural imprint. Deej and I walked down to Lookout Park, where we turned left and made tracks in the shoreline all the way to Loon Point, halfway to Carpinteria, and back. Deejee snapped a photo of me with a Polaroid camera she liked to tote around in her voluminous shoulder bag, and then persuaded a surfer to photograph us together, arms around each other's waists, against a backdrop of sandy, ice plant-covered slope. We watched the sun sink into the Pacific dragging the chromatic spectrum with it from white orange to burnt red to gem blue. It was, I thought, a magical and promising beginning.

"Pleased to meet you." Mary was holding out a hand for me to shake. Her complexion was richly dark, like coffee beans. Her palm was lighter than the back of her hand by several shades. Her eyes were as dark as blackberries.

"I'm Anthony. Pleasure's all mine."

I gripped a firm hand with long fingers. Mary's teeth were small and stained under a flat nose with wide nostrils. Contrasted against her smooth brown skin, her smile gleamed. She reached for the volume dial on my car stereo where I had a tape running quietly.

"You mind if I turn that up?" She cranked the dial. "That's Thelonious Monk. I love this man! The way he uses those whole tone scales makes his melodies sound tilted, as if they were trying to slide off the keyboard. When I play his songs, I can never get them to sound like he does. That's genius, Tony. Pure genius."

Chapter Eight

"Miles Davis, Rahsaan Roland Kirk, Taj Mahal." Mary was on her knees, going through my collection of tape cassettes in shoeboxes on the floor under the bottom shelf of my library. "Bud Powell, Melvin Van Peebles—Tony, are you sure you're not black?"

"Keep looking, Dolly Hard On." Deejee was rummaging through my refrigerator. She retrieved two bottles of beer. "He's got hillbilly shit in there too."

Deejee pulled open a drawer, located a bottle opener and pried the caps off the two sweating Heinekens. She handed one to Mary. "Dutch beer. See what I'm saying? Trapp couldn't be any whiter."

"Listen, Tony. I need to make a call." Mary stood. "Do you mind if I use your phone?"

I was on the threadbare gray couch, screwing up pot sticks. I hooked my thumb over my shoulder. "Help yourself. On the desk."

Deejee flopped on the sofa next to me. "I'll have one of those." She reached across my lap to pluck a joint from the stack of slim white logs I was preparing for our burning, pushing her chest against my shoulder. Today she was wearing a cinnamon halter-top over her customary blue denims. Her warm breath and exposed flesh exuded fragrances—alcohol, coconut and musk. She had been drinking Mai Tais. "Mary's going to hook us up with some rock."

I broached a sensitive subject cautiously. "Did you have any luck scoring any with Peanut?"

"Peanut?" Darlena touched the tip of the joint protruding from her glossy lips with a cigarette lighter, inhaling deeply.

"You said the other day that you were going to get some crack from Peanut." I concentrated on my rolling so that my expression would not betray my jealousy. "How did that go?"

Deejee didn't answer because she was holding her breath. So was I. She exhaled slowly, adding another aroma to the heady mix enveloping us.

"That fucking clown!" She barked harshly. "You can't count on him for anything. He said he had a connection. I waited for him at the pier for over an hour and he never showed up. What an asshole. I was shivering out there like a wet Chihuahua."

Relief gushed through me so strongly that I exhaled too, even though I wasn't smoking anything. All my anxious envy had been pointless. Locking limbs with Peanut? Deejee didn't even like him! I felt like the nervous patient hearing from his doctor that the puzzling rash in his thatch isn't herpes after all.

I smiled broadly. "I'd like something to scratch my jones," I said, reaching for the sparkler in Deejee's paw.

"What, you guys are fuming and not sharing?" Mary joined us on the couch. She too was redolent of rum and coconut. Maybe Mel's was having a sale on Mai Tais.

The three of us polished off the first twisted cigarito and started another.

"The guy I need to talk to isn't home yet." Mary passed the smoldering puffer to me. "Instead of pestering his people with a hundred calls, I left your number with them so he can call us when he gets in."

Mary had given my phone number to some crack dealers without asking me if that was okay? I was about to ask how she had my phone number to give until I remembered that it was displayed in a plastic sheath right on the dial.

"Better keep rolling, Trapp. There's no telling how long we'll be waiting. How about some TV?"

Three stoners sitting on a sofa four feet from a television should not have to wrestle with indecision, but we did. I would have opted for movies, but the ladies had other ideas. Since they were my guests, I let them wrangle.

I kept tubing the brain apostles. We kept sucking them down. Smoke crowded the ceiling.

Before long, we were out of beer. I wasn't quaffing it myself. I am not a drinker. That was one of the reasons my bosses at Liquid Avenue trusted me—interesting because I am certainly a toker, which was not a secret to anyone.

"I think we need a beer run," Deejee advised us, closing the refrigerator door. "And I could go for a Big Mac and a pile of fries."

I had forgotten about my provisions chilling in the fridge and encamped in the pantry. "Hey, I could make us some sandwiches."

"No way, Trapp. I need the grease."

"And I'm up for a bucket of McNuggets," Mary offered.

"It's settled, then. Trapp and I will jet out for suds and eats and you can hang here and wait for the call. We can be back in twenty minutes."

It was irksome to have my hospitality spurned, but, I had to admit, none of the supplies would go to waste. I myself owned an appetite, especially when there was maryjane around the house.

What troubled me was leaving Mary alone in my apartment with over eight thousand dollars in a canvas bag under my bed. True, we would be back in less than half an hour and Mary did not know the money was there. I had no reason to suppose she would go poking around in my belongings, but what if she did? I had known her only three hours. How well did Deejee know her? Mary or anybody else for that matter could get pretty far with that bankroll before anybody caught up. It would be a bit ticklish trying to explain to Dan, Randy, Jimmy, Tommy—if he ever turned up—or the police how I managed to be so careless, to say nothing of the employees expecting paychecks and all the other people Liquid Avenue owed money to.

For a moment, I considered taking the bag along with us, so as to err on the side of caution. What would be my explanation for that? Sorry, Mary, I have to take this with me because I don't trust you. We just met. Besides, I'm white and you're . . .

Jesus Christ! Did that thought actually cross my mind? Am I truly a racist and unable to admit it even to myself?

I found it far easier to roll the dice with someone else's stake than to remind Mary, probably for the millionth time, that American white guys are never really color blind. I left the bag behind. When Deej and I returned with the beer and food, the bag still slumbered undisturbed under the bed.

Darlena disappeared into the bathroom. I took a seat next to Mary, who handed me a joint.

"No joy from the phone?"

"Not yet." Mary smiled. "Don't worry. Lloyd is not the brightest bulb on the block, but he does return calls."

Deejee returned from the bathroom with her Polaroid. "Hey, Dolly. How about getting a glossy of Trapp and me?"

Mary obliged. Deejee draped her arm around my neck, pulled my mug up next to hers, and we grinned like a pair of baboons when Mary cued us.

"Say Limburger."

The phone rang. "'Bout fucking time." Deejee spoke for all of us. It was after 9:30 PM.

Mary picked up the receiver. "Yowdy, my man. Where you at?" She listened for a moment. "Oh. Yes. He's right here." Her disappointment was as plain to see as the cannabis cloud swirling around the light fixtures. "It's for you, Tony."

"I give up, Anthony." Rita spoke sharply. "Who was that?"

It was unusual for Rita to be calling at this hour. She knew that I was ordinarily asleep by now. The hotel must have told her I had tried to reach her that afternoon.

"Oh. Well, that was Dolly. I mean Mary. One of my people from work. I mean, she's a friend of one of my people from work."

I knew that Alaska was a cold place at this time of year, but until that moment I never realized how much of the chill could come through a long distance telephone line.

"Dolly. You mean Mary. I don't remember your ever mentioning that you had 'people' from work. Actually, I had the impression that you didn't really like any of the people you work with."

"Well, I don't really. I mean, I don't usually. They're just here blowing a little grass is all."

"They? Dolly and Mary and who else?"

I was too fumigated for this conversation. "Just us. Just the three of us. Just smoking dope. That's all." Good thing no one handed me a shovel. I had already dug a deep enough hole. "So . . . how's it going?"

"I don't know, Anthony. You called me."

"Oh, yeah. Yes I did. I just wanted to talk, hear your voice, see how things were going. That's all."

I was tiptoeing. I did not want Deejee to hear me pouring sweet talk on my girl friend any more than I wanted Rita to suspect I was folding down the bed for a new customer. My reassuring tropes sounded hollow, even to me.

"You sound pretty weird to me. I'll cut you slack this time since you just had a murder in your workplace. Are you planning to send your 'people' home soon?"

"Absolutely. The party was just about to break up anyway."

"All right then. Tell Dolly and Mary I said 'hi'."

Deejee and Mary stabbed me with stares as I took my seat on the couch.

"Season of the witch?" Darlena jibed.

"My sister," I lied. "Rita. She lives in Alaska."

The phone went off again.

"I better get that." I expected a few more frosty remarks from Doctor Barron, but a man's voice asked, "Is Mary there?"

Deejee passed me the smoldering reefer as I rejoined her on the sofa while Mary took the phone. "How many other 'sisters' you got, brother?"

"Just the one, Deej." My mendacity needed polish. "She's older so she still thinks she can boss me around."

"Next time you talk to her tell her that's my job now."

"Saddle up, cowpokes," Mary announced. "We're in business."

Chapter Nine

The seedier side of Santa Barbara tends to lie east of State Street, so it surprised me when Mary had me turn the Rabbit rightward at Carrillo Street, and aimed us west in the direction of the prosperous Mesa. We ducked under the 101 Freeway overpass, broke left on San Pascual into a secluded residential neighborhood, and rolled to a stop on Sutton Avenue, a half block cul-de-sac with only two homes on each side of the street.

The girls climbed out. "Wait here," Deejee instructed. "We'll be right back."

I waited. Sutton Avenue at this hour on a Sunday evening was the Zen of quietude. I had parked under a street lamp, one of those old fashioned fluted concrete pillars topped by a milky glass hexagon with a brass beanie. Mary and Darlena had been admitted through a front door occluded by a tall box hedge as impeccably manicured as an English butler. All the other automobiles in sight were in driveways. My Volkswagen was the only one parked on the street. In the classy understated light of the 1920s lamp, the Rabbit looked shabby and underdressed, like the drunk cousin that stumbles in uninvited at the formal dinner.

The girls had disappeared into the house on the corner. All the homes on Sutton were two stories tall and set well back from the street. Each was fronted by a lush immaculate lawn trimmed in flowerbeds. The residents must have pooled their resources and hired a golf course groundskeeper to maintain this look. If this was how drug dealers lived, I was in the wrong line of work.

On the phone Rita had said she would cut me slack "this time." Her pointed barb referred to my last line of work and the blunder I had made that knocked me out of it.

Fifteen months ago I was an employee of Golden Sunset Publications, Inc. GSP published four periodicals: *Dynamic Look*, a monthly fitness magazine; *Otolaryngology Praxis*, a monthly trade magazine for ear, nose and throat doctors; *Golden Voices*, a monthly literary vehicle; and *Bargain Bin*, a weekly throwaway rag with classified ads for used cars, yard sales, church rummage affairs, dating services, and flea markets. Guess which one I edited.

GSP was owned and operated by Jennifer Mitchell, a 50ish widow who was downstream of the original publisher's estate when he died and poured it into her lap. Jennifer knew only one thing about the magazine publishing business, but it was the most important thing to know: it's all about advertising.

Dynamic Look, edited by Julie Mendenhill, was the company bread winner, its pages packed with ads for gym equipment, nutritional supplements, workout apparel, running shoes, and books by fitness gurus, with minimal editorial content supplied mostly by the aforementioned gurus.

Oto Praxis kept the ear, nose and throat docs up to speed with the latest methodologies for diagnoses and treatments and lavishly illustrated ads for pharmaceutical products. Its editor, Harvey Hasridian, the highest paid employee on the staff, was a retired otolaryngologist who culled the editorial pieces by abstracting from scholarly medical journals and soliciting contributors who worked in the field. This magazine alone could have floated the whole company because it had little competition and the drug companies spared no expense in pursuit of their markets.

Golden Voices carried no advertising. It was the love child of the late Gerard "Mitch" Mitchell, who had a weakness for arty literature and a yen to promote young, unpublished writers. The contributors were not paid, of course, but the magazine, having no advertising, produced no profits from its meager subscription rates. Kathleen O'Keenan piloted this vessel. Hers was the job I really wanted.

My baby was *Bargain Bin*. It was all advertising with no editorial content at all. Julie, Harvey and Kathleen made no pretense of accepting me as an equal. Since I had no contributors to schmooze and edit, no advertising sales reps to manage, no subscribers or circulation to boost, I did it all myself: budget, layout, interaction with the printers, and coordination with the circulation department and distribution network. I answered to a weekly deadline, rather than the more leisurely monthly cycle the other editors adhered to, so the pressure on me was continuous. Nevertheless, the other editors regarded me as little more than a paste-up artist. I was paid the same salary as Herb, the assistant warehouse manager.

My bachelor's degree in English from the University of California had never kicked open any doors for me. I can't bitch about it. Even some of my college professors had warned me that it wouldn't. One of my advisors had talked me into taking a couple of business administration and accounting courses contrary to my inclination. If I had not done so, I would have had no marketable skills from my college education.

Light flickered briefly in my rear view mirror from a car passing along San Pascual, the first traffic I had noticed since I parked the Rabbit. It was a black-and-white cruiser from the Santa Barbara Police Department. That figured. This was a sweet neighborhood. No doubt it was patrolled regularly. I wondered how often the SBPD swung by my neck of the woods on West Valerio. Now that I thought about it, considering all the cannabis I torched there, I hoped they didn't. The pot reek permeated my apartment and seeped through all available apertures in the doors and windows. It was a wonder that none of my neighbors had ever complained to the building manager.

Suddenly I felt exposed, sitting by myself in the only car parked on a well-patrolled street in a nice neighborhood on a Sunday night. I was still pretty buzzed. Suppose the cops noticed me still sitting there the next time they drove by? I was breaking no law that I was aware of, but they would be well within their purview if they decided to pull up and ask me what I was doing there.

Where the hell were those women? It was after 10:00 PM. I had been cooling my jets for over forty-five minutes. Something must have gone wrong, unless Deejee and I had variant interpretations of the phrase "be right back."

This crack dealer—was he dangerous? Was he some demented maniac with an unbridled temper and an itchy trigger finger? Is that why Mary and Deejee had not invited me to go into the house with them? Could he possibly be involved with the murder of Lyss Nelson? How did I know the poor girls were not lying bound and gagged on a cold garage floor with a homicidal creep standing over them casually flicking his razor sharp switchblade with a calloused thumb?

Now the minutes slowed to a crawl. I checked my Movado watch about every 30 seconds. My heart jumped when lights danced in the rear view mirror again, but it was only an innocuous sedan drifting past on San Pascual. Mist had begun to gather in the street lamps. This close to the harbor it was more chilly and damp than further inland. I wished I had the purple parka with me that I kept next to my desk at work.

Thinking of work, when was I planning to go to bed? In about six hours, I would have to be at the club again. That thought stiffened my resolve. I had to go see what was up.

A new Oldsmobile Cutlass Supreme rested in the driveway shined from recent waxing. A late model Buick Regal slumbered in front of it. At the head of the parked parade, a handsome Volvo 240 sat in front of the garage door. I walked past the auto show quietly and approached the hedge that sheltered the front porch. As I drew near, a clamor rose inside the house. Someone shouted, "Oh, yeah!" Another shrieked, "All right!" People were cheering.

I took a deep breath and pushed a doorbell under a plaque that warned "No Solicitors, Please". The door swung open almost immediately.

"Hello," said a pleasant looking woman in a Los Angeles Kings hockey jersey. Her resemblance to Mary was unmistakable. "Hey, we're awfully sorry about the noise. The guys were getting carried away."

"Oh, no," I hastened to explain. "I'm not here about any noise. I wondered whether Mary is here."

"I'm so sorry." She looked crestfallen. "You missed her. She and Lloyd left about half an hour ago."

"How about Deejee?" I asked. "Did she leave with Mary?"

"Deejee? Oh, you must mean Darlena. Yes, she's here. Would you like to come in? It's getting cold out there." She extended a dark hand with long fingers that ended in ruby pearl nails. "I'm Anne. Please come on in."

"And I'm Anthony," I smiled. Anne stood in a foyer. As she stepped aside to let me in, I could see into the living room where the cheering came from. A cluster of faces that spanned the palette from caramel to baker's chocolate was illuminated by tasteful floor lamps and blue radiation from a large television screen. They were spread among a plush sofa and three corduroy armchairs. A coffee table positioned in front of the sofa sported bowls of pretzels, chips, dips, and bottles of Budweiser on cork coasters.

"Hey, everybody," Anne announced cheerfully. "This is Anthony!"

Heads with bright smiles turned my way. "You're just in time." One fellow stood and offered his hand in greeting. "The Kings just scored and sent it into overtime! I'm Don. Can I get you a beer?"

"Sure. Thanks. Do you happen to have a soda instead?" I was not very thirsty, but it would have been rude to say "no" to the cordial offer. Don returned with a bottle of Vernor's ginger ale.

"Hey, this is great. I love this stuff." I inquired, "I was looking for Darlena."

"She's back there in the den." Don pointed to a door on the other side of the room. "Right this way."

He escorted me across the room, knocked on the door, and pushed it open. "Darlena? Company!"

Chapter Ten

It was surpassingly modest for Don to have referred to the room I entered as a "den". It was nothing less than the most impressive game room I have ever seen.

Immediately in front of me a ping pong table stood ready for action. To my left, against a wall paneled with cork and walnut laminate panels, there was a pinball machine and three other electronic arcade games of the type designed to dazzle ten year-old kids with bells, buzzers, whoops, screams, rifle fire and ray gun blasts, with an assortment of ferocious monsters, demons, and space aliens to destroy while the machines sucked quarters out of their pockets. In the middle of the room, a solid table hockey setup beckoned. To my right, a poker table sat in the corner, surrounded by six padded chairs, with a Tiffany lamp depending from the ceiling directly over it.

Sliding glass doors that led to a covered patio interrupted the right wall. Against the far wall, a 36" x 48" poster of Wayne Gretzky beamed at me, while pennants and other paraphernalia of Los Angeles pro and college sports teams were pinned up all over the place and a gallery of framed glossy 8" x 10" photos I could not make out from where I stood paid court to Gretzky.

The piece-de-resistance in this paradise of competition pleasures dominated the far side of the room. The only two occupants of the game room were busy at it, chalking their pool cues and studying the configuration of numbered balls scattered on its green felt surface for geometric possibilities. The billiard table itself was a magnificent polished oak masterwork that looked like it weighed a half-ton and belonged in a high stakes Las Vegas lounge.

Deejee loaned me a glance, as if I were borrowing precious concentration time at a usurious interest rate. "Hey, Trapp. What's up?" She leaned over the table, lined up her shot, and released the cue with a smooth stroke, followed by a sharp crack, a two-bank carom, and the dunking of the six ball into a side pocket. She grinned at her opponent. "Your ass is mine, Fudgesickle."

I strolled over with quiet respect. When I play this game, I am satisfied if I can make solid contact with the cue ball. If it knocks anything in, I think of it as Divine Providence.

The other player was a tall, lean 30ish man with a long face and large brown eyes. He stuck out a hand for me to shake. "I'm Pete. I see you like Vernor's. So do I."

Deejee poked another shot and a corner pocket swallowed the seven ball. "You could just pay up now, chump, if you want to end the humiliation."

"You got the stick. You do the trick." Pete ambled around the table with the feline grace of a man who played his hoops above the rim. "I got all night, Buttermilk."

The pool players were intent on their contest and it sounded like money was on the line, so kept my questions to myself for the time being.

I examined the photo gallery to see who was hanging with the Great Gretzky. None of them were strangers to Southern California sports aficionados. Kirk Gibson, Orel Hersheiser, Jim Everett, Todd Marinovich, Jim Abbott, Wally Joyner, Rogie Vachon. Every one of these glossies was autographed. This was a place were games were taken seriously. I could have a lot of fun here.

In fact, I might have been having fun here for the past three quarters of an hour instead of chilling on the street and letting paranoid spiders build fanciful cobwebs in my head. I wondered why I had not noticed Mary and Lloyd leaving. They must have slipped out through those sliding glass doors and found their way to San Pascual by way of the back yard.

I had drained my ginger ale and was thinking about going back into the living room to beg for another when a faint roar went up from beyond the cork and laminate walls. Apparently the game had ended in favor of the Kings. Maybe the Great One himself had put the puck in the net to seal it and send everyone home happy.

I wanted to go home happy too and the sooner the better. Deejee and Pete were still measuring their shots, chalking their cue tips, and trading jibes. It was time I dropped my quarter in the slot.

"Um, do we know when we are expecting Mary?"

"Nope. We don't." Deejee eyeballed the table. "You need to learn some patience, Trapp. These things don't always answer to your watch."

Patience? I scarcely needed my Movado to ratify my perseverance. I had been waiting all day to play with Deejee. Now I patiently watched her play with somebody else.

"Well, you see, the thing is, I have to be at the club in about six hours. I don't think this adventure is going to happen for me tonight."

Deejee sighed and shouldered her cue stick. "Okay, Trapp. There's no reason you should have to hang around. I can get a ride home from Lloyd when he and Mary get back." She stepped up, put her arm around my waist, and planted a wet smack on my cheek. Faint traces of musk and coconut still clung to her cinnamon halter-top. She whispered, "Love you, baby. I'll catch up with you at the club in a couple of days, okay?"

It was not okay, but it did send me home with a swelling south of my belt buckle that reminded me why I was dancing with Deejee in the first place.

My apartment seemed cold and empty when I closed the door and faced the debris. Big Mac wrappers and French fry baggies littered the floor. On the kitchen counter, stale beer bottles and two greasy buckets of fried chicken batter crumbs added a rancid flavor to the cloying aroma of marijuana mixed with mentholated cigarette smoke. I would clean up this mess tomorrow. Tonight, I needed some z's.

Monday morning I slept in and skipped breakfast. The rude coffee I cooked up in the *cocina* carried me through until the proprietors arrived. Margarito and Elena's *cafe Cubano* was always a welcome guest on my palate. This morning it was especially soothing. My throat was raw from yesterday's excesses. Last night's take at the club had been light—typical for a Sunday night. I would not have to be here all day counting it. Not enough liquor had been sold to require restocking the inventory, so I would not need to wait for Jimmy to order deliveries that would need cashier's checks. I could get the banking done early, take the afternoon off, and catch up on my sleep.

A voice like a rake dragged across a gravel path broke my musings. "Hello, Tony. Has Pops showed up yet?"

"Not yet, Randy."

"Jesus, Tony. Did I ever have a bad night. Must have been something I ate. I was up all night barfing up green and yellow chunks of mucous. It smelled like a dead body. My ulcers are killing me. Those doctors at Cottage Hospital didn't know what the fuck they were doing the last time they stitched up my stomach. My lawyer's going to sue them for stupidity. Hey, do you have any Maalox or Pepto Bismol or something?"

I too had an ulcer that I medicated with milk when it troubled me. Nevertheless, I had no more empathy in me for Randy's duodenum than I had admiration for Hitler's mustache.

"I'm sure Elena has some Alka Seltzer in the kitchen."

"Fuck that. I don't want to talk to those greasers. It was probably their food that made me sick in the first place. Oh, good. Here comes Pops."

Randy's regular date with the silver Rolls Royce spared me further vivid descriptions of his health problems. When he returned in an hour, Randy would be in a much more mellow mood and he would be carrying a small paper sack with fake identifications for his bouncers to sell to underage customers so they could drink in the club. These ID's would never fool anybody in the light of day, but, in the event that the police or undercover agents from the Department of Alcoholic Beverage Control braced these kids, the bouncers could always claim they had only seen the ID's briefly under a flashlight and blame the customers for presenting false identities.

Randy's bag also contained other goodies of a pharmaceutical nature. I never asked exactly what they were. The less I knew about them the better.

By noon I had all the banking done, locked the office, and had the Rabbit take me home to confront the mess at West Valerio. A white business card tucked between the door and the jamb above my doorknob waited for me. On its back, in blue ballpoint, it read:

> "Sorry I missed you! Please call or
> visit me at my office at your earliest.
> —Rachel"

Its flip side was more formal:

> Detective Rachel Imanaka
> Santa Barbara Police Department

Chapter Eleven

The Santa Barbara Police Department was an inviting two-story white building with a red tile roof on East Figueroa Street surrounded by oak and sycamore trees. I climbed broad concrete steps to the entrance, passed through a lobby to the front desk and asked for Detective Imanaka. Within a few minutes, Rachel came out to greet me.

"Hi, Anthony! Thanks for coming in. I knew I could count on your cooperation."

Rachel smiled brightly. My first appraisal was right. The detective was a very attractive woman.

"Sure thing, Rachel. I'm happy to help."

She escorted me to a small room with pleasant light drifting in through matched rectangular windows placed high on one wall. The ceiling and all the walls were painted uniformly beige. We sat in sturdy chairs fashioned of metal with seats and backs of padded vinyl in baize. We rested our arms on a metal table topped with baize linoleum. A tape recorder, a microphone, and two empty ashtrays occupied the tabletop.

Rachel grinned. "You are welcome to some coffee, but I'm sure you'd be disappointed. It doesn't stack up against the great coffee you served me at your club."

"Good advice, Rachel. I'll pass, thanks." I did not imagine I would be here long enough to put it to the test.

"You know, I'm a little embarrassed about the formality here. You've come in voluntarily. I really appreciate it. This whole setup," she waved her arm inclusively at the table and the room, "is all about correct procedures. Frankly, it's more for our benefit than yours. After all," a shy smile warmed her lips, "we have rights too, just like you do. I hope you don't mind."

"No. It's no problem. I understand."

"Thank you. Let's get this under way, then. Shall we?" She reached a pale hand to the recorder and pressed a button.

"I'd just like you to know that you don't have to answer any of my questions. You don't have to say a thing. You can leave at any time."

I nodded. "Yes. Thanks."

"I'm recording our conversation just in case anything should come up later in a court of law. If you would feel more comfortable having a lawyer in the room, we'll be happy to wait until you bring one. Or, if you prefer, we can borrow an attorney from the Public Defender's office just down the street. He or she could be here in no time at all. You understand, right?"

"I understand perfectly."

"I knew you would. You are very cooperative, Anthony. You're saving us all a lot of time."

I was pleased by the compliment. My time was valuable too. I was very much in favor of saving as much of it as possible.

"Please state your full name."

"Anthony Solomon Trapp."

"What is your present address?"

"Four Twenty-Nine West Valerio Street. Apartment Five. Santa Barbara, California."

Including the city seemed pointless, even as I said it. I hoped Rachel would not think I was fooling around or wasting anyone's time. By her expression, I judged that I had said the right thing.

"Who is your employer?"

"I work for Nelson, Garch and Pensacola, a limited partnership. They own and operate Liquid Avenue, a bar and nightclub located at Two Hundred East Haley Street. I'm the bookkeeper."

Rachel nodded to show me I was doing fine. "What is your regular work schedule?"

"I work every day, Monday through Sunday, beginning around 3:30 AM until about 1:30 PM. Sometimes I take a lunch break at 10:00 or 10:30. Sometimes not."

"Did you work at Liquid Avenue on the morning of Friday, October 23rd?"

Rachel knew very well that I had worked that morning, the day of the murder. But then, she had told me that these questions were mere formalities.

"Yes, I did."

"Did you go anywhere before you went to work?"

"Yes. I had breakfast at Carrow's on West Carrillo Street."

"Do you remember what time that was?"

"I was probably there about 2:40 AM and I left a little after 3:15."

"Can you recall when you arrived at work?"

Rachel had seen my timecard. Was this formality really necessary?

"I arrived at my office at 3:25 AM. I punched in at 3:35."

"Can you account for the discrepancy between the time you arrived at your office and the time you clocked in?"

Discrepancy?

"Sure. First I opened my office behind the main building. There was a message on my desk that was barely legible, so I took a few minutes to decipher it. My office clock loses a couple of minutes every day, so I adjusted it as usual. I took the collection bag and the jacket that I keep next to my desk. Then I went into the club to punch my timecard."

"Is that your normal routine?"

"Almost invariable."

"What did you do next?"

"After I clocked in, I started a pot of coffee in the *Cocina Habana*. While it was brewing, I went to the safe to collect the previous night's money and sales receipts."

"Did you do or see anything unusual on the morning in question?"

Unusual? Like a dead body lying in the sawdust with the empty beer bottles? I reminded myself that these questions were mere formalities.

"Yes and no. I saw Lyss Nelson lying under one of the tables near a wall. That was not unusual; I had seen her there before. I took it for granted that she was passed out. It was unusual that she was dead, but I didn't know that until later."

Rachel's lips rubbed each other. "It didn't occur to you to take a closer look, to see if she was okay?"

"It occurred to me, but I didn't because, as I said, it was not unusual for Lyss to drink too much at the club and then sleep it off."

"Wouldn't anybody at the nightclub call a taxi to take her home?"

"Usually her husband, Tommy, uh, Thomas Nelson would be there. I think the people who work in the club believe that would be his responsibility."

"To the best of your knowledge, did Mister Nelson accept that responsibility?"

"To the best of my knowledge, he never did."

"Was Mister Nelson present in the nightclub on the evening of Wednesday, October 22nd or the early hours of the morning in question?"

"I don't know whether he was. I myself was not present, so I can't say for sure."

"Not present, you mean, until 3:25 AM."

What was the detective getting at?

"Yes, that's correct."

"Did Mister Nelson clock in or clock out on the evening of October 22nd or the morning of October 23rd?"

"No. Mister Nelson, that is, Thomas Nelson, is one of the business partners. He receives a straight salary. I specify his name because his brother, James Nelson, the club manager, is an hourly employee and does punch the clock."

"Did you see anyone else after you clocked in?"

"No. Not until Luis Alvarado, the custodian, knocked on my door to inform me that Lyss Nelson was dead."

"What time was that?"

"I am not absolutely certain, but it was about 5:15 or 5:20."

"And then what did you do?"

"I called you. I mean, I called the police department."

The light in the rectangular windows had faded; the sun had moved along. The detective was not smiling. Had I said something that bothered her?

"Do you recall an interview that you had with me, Detective Rachel Imanaka, on the morning that you called the police?"

"Yes, I do."

"Do you remember that I asked you at that time if you knew where we, I mean the police department, could find Tommy Nelson?"

Had that been part of the "interview"? I had not seen the detective write that down in her notebook.

"Yes. I remember that was the last thing you asked me after we left the patio."

"Why did you not tell me at that time that Tommy Nelson was having an affair with Elizabeth Strennis?"

She had me cold. I had left that out because I felt some absurd loyalty to Elizabeth, that I was somehow "protecting" her by leaving her out of the investigation.

"Elizabeth told me that Tommy treated her nice. She denied that she was having a relationship with him."

"When did you have that conversation with Elizabeth?"

"It was later, when she came to my office to complain because you, I mean, the police department, had questioned her at the bank."

Did that get me off the hook for my omission? Rachel said nothing. She held me in a gaze distinctly lacking in warmth. In fact, the whole room seemed to be cooler than it had been earlier. The detective's lips rubbed each other. She leaned forward and switched off the tape recorder.

"All right, Anthony. That's all for now."

Her chair scraped the floor noisily as she stood. I stood too and we shook hands.

Detective Imanaka walked with me through the station's lobby to the front entrance. She placed a hand on my shoulder.

"As you know, Anthony, we are investigating a very serious crime. You are one of our most important sources of information. When I ask you questions, your answers become evidence. It would be a very good idea for you to give me completely truthful answers."

We stood in the open doorway to the station. Warm sunshine splashed the concrete steps leading down to East Figueroa Street.

"We'd be very grateful if you could arrange to stay in Santa Barbara for the time being. Or at least let us know if you have any business that takes you elsewhere. Thank you very much for coming in."

"You're welcome, Rachel."

The Santa Barbara Police Department was investigating a murder, a very serious crime. Every step I took toward the street felt heavier as the full awareness embraced me that I was their most serious suspect.

Chapter Twelve

Who killed Lyss Nelson? Now the question was personal and the police were not the only ones who wanted it answered. I could safely cross myself off the list of suspects. Who else belonged on it?

Could it have been Tommy Nelson? In the movies and mystery novels the husband is always at the top of the list. Was that true in real life? How would I know? This was my first real life murder mystery. I had no idea where to begin. Tommy's disappearance seemed damning, but as far as I knew there was nothing necessarily suspicious about it. Tommy was an owner. He came and went as he pleased. Sometimes he had Lyss or his brother pick up his paycheck, and I wouldn't see him for weeks.

The police had told the press that the killer had waited in the storage loft until the club was closed. Tommy could let himself in and out any time he wanted to. He hardly needed to hide in the loft. He certainly knew that Lyss occasionally passed out in the club from the booze and the pills because he was the one who let her sleep it off there. But why would he kill her in the club and then take to his heels? Nothing would be more certain to pull the cops into his wake. I didn't think much of Tommy's brain wattage, but he wouldn't have been that dumb. He was a low budget weaver of ill-conceived enterprises, not a cold-blooded murderer.

Then there was the question of motive. What would he have to gain by throttling his wife? Did she have money? They were married. He would already have access to it. Did she have a life insurance policy that named him as beneficiary? Too obvious. Was Lyss blackmailing him? What could she have been holding over his head? Tommy was an openly philandering jackass with more vices than a Turkish sultan. He owed money all over the lot—just ask Randy. Did he want a divorce from Lyss that she would not give him? Please. In 1990s California, legal marriage was no more binding than toilet tissue. Either partner could dissolve it without resorting to murder.

That thought brought Elizabeth Strennis into the picture. Suspect Number Two. Was Lyss an obstacle to her designs for Tommy? When she had bellowed at me in my office, Elizabeth did not seem overwhelmingly enchanted about the public perception of her relationship with Tommy. Could she have been protesting too much? Of course, if Elizabeth was truly entwined with Tommy and wanted Lyss out of the picture, it still obtained that divorce was easier than murder.

What about the other Nelson brother? Jimmy was a cipher to me. I made him Suspect Number Three because I knew nothing about him. That didn't make it easier to fill in the blanks. Tommy had the money to be a partner in Liquid Avenue. Jimmy apparently did not. Was that a clue? Had something lurid gone down between the brothers—maybe Jimmy had been in love with Lyss, but Tommy had somehow wrested her away? That didn't make sense either. In that case, wouldn't Jimmy have killed Tommy instead?

How about Randy Garch? Yes, I fancied Randy for Suspect Number Four, mostly because I wanted more suspects on my list. Randy liked his tough talk, but he was all gas and no mileage. Could he have gone off on Lyss in one of his intemperate rants and started a quarrel that got out of hand? A quarrel about what? That thirty thousand bucks he claimed Tommy owed him that he was always growling about? Something personal about his beloved bouncers? Except for his pal Pops in the mystery Rolls, I was not aware that Randy had any other friends. Maybe Lyss said something insinuating about Randy's manhood. And that would make him strangle her? Really?

I was groping here. I almost sympathized with Detective Imanaka. I had a very short list and already I was out of suspects.

Dan Pensacola? Maybe there was something in the past between Lyss and Dan's wife Alicia from the nights when they worked in the club together. Something that didn't surface for a year and was a problem now that Alicia had a kid? Did not compute.

Luis Alvarado? Why? Because he was Mexican? I was already nervous that I might be a closet racist. Was I also an inveterate xenophobe?

Randy, Dan, Alicia, or Luis would never need to hide in the storage loft with homicide in mind. They could let themselves into the club any time they liked. Building security was not a great concern for the owners. There were no alarms, still less video cameras. For insurance purposes, Dan had taken bids for building alarm systems, but decided against because their cost was greater than any reduction they might bring in the insurance premiums.

Anybody who was clever with a lock could access the building when it was closed. Thanks to the identification card scam of the bouncers, anyone over the age of fifteen could be admitted to the club when it was open.

What was it Sherlock Holmes always said? Eliminate the obvious? Eliminate the falsehoods? I forgot what Holmes always said. I would have to look it up. The killing at Liquid Avenue had to be the work of a random psychotic. Nothing else tallied with the facts.

There were not many people left to add to my list. Margarito and Elena? The bouncers? The bar tenders and cocktail waitresses? Clark Gary and the Discordians? Deejee?

Thinking of Deejee, I should try to get in touch and let her know the police had found me interesting and this might not be the best time to be experimenting with crack.

I still had a mess to clean up at West Valerio from the night before. Before I got started on it, I parked at my desk and made a couple of phone calls. I gave Deejee's number eight rings that went unattended. No surprise.

I was still bristling about my interview with Detective Imanaka and I wanted to share my pique with someone. Also, I wanted to take Rita's temperature and see if she needed placatory noises from me about my entertaining a couple of women in my apartment. I called Anchorage, but there was no answer from Rita's room.

For some reason that upset me. According to my watch—the fine Movado Bold Rita had given me for my birthday two years ago—it was 4:30 PM. Was Doctor Barron still at work? Probably. I was not in touch with her daily schedule, so I was ignorant of how these conferences played. That was my own fault, actually. Rita would have been pleased to give me details on her ins and outs, but I had never asked. She was always there for me. Now that I was eager to talk to her, I was irked that I couldn't.

I turned my attention to tidying up the apartment. It was cool outside, but it wouldn't hurt to open the windows and let some fresh air sweep away the lingering traces of last night's smoke festival. It was a lucky break for me that I had not been home when Rachel Imanaka had dropped by. It would be the prudent course for me to be more cautious about my illicit drug use while I was a murder suspect. Mary and Deejee and I had consumed most of my cannabis inventory. Notwithstanding my present standing with the Homicide Squad, I would have to get in touch with Bogo pronto and put the wheels under him to secure me another batch of weed.

I finished straightening up my nest, put together a dinner plate from my well-stocked larder, and plunked myself in front of the TV to relax. The phone went off.

Excellent. That would be Rita. I felt the flush of relief. I was keen to hear her voice.

"Trapp!" Deejee barked. "Mary scored some rock. How soon can you get out here and pick us up?"

Chapter Thirteen

"Here" turned out to be Trigo Road in Isla Vista, spitting distance from the University of California campus, a thirty-minute Rabbit hop from West Valerio at this time of day, the busy time for traffic on the 101 Freeway.

I was not in the mood for this. After a short night's repose, a brittle day at the office, and a nasty shock at the police station, I was counting on a tasty dinner, a relaxing puffer, and a long night's rest to soothe my nerves and ready myself for tomorrow, Tuesday, the day I always devoted to payroll preparation.

Then there was the matter of caution regarding the police that I had just promised myself I would take seriously. I took the caution with both hands and tossed it into the wind.

"Took you long enough," Deejee greeted me as she climbed into the back seat.

"Yowdy, Tony." Mary said, taking the front bucket. "What you listening to?" She cranked the volume knob on my cassette player. Art Tatum flooded the small compartment. "Oh, yeah," she nodded. "You're listening to God."

The traffic was no better heading back into town, but it carried us to Sutton Avenue where we deposited Mary. Deejee took her place in the front seat.

"McDonald's," she directed. "I'm starving."

"I have provisions at my place," I suggested.

"I bet you don't have steaming hot fries, a case of Corona and a carton of Kools at your place."

She was right. We made the necessary stops.

"Listen, Trapp. You don't have a heart condition, do you?"

In the poetic sense, I did. Watching Darlena origami a square foot of tin foil into a slapdash pipe, however, I guessed why she was asking.

"No. Healthy as a hobbit. Is that stuff really that dangerous?"

"Mother's milk is dangerous if you get carried away with it. I just don't want you to keel over and croak on me."

We were perched on my sofa. Deejee, in Levis, sneakers and a soft gray Chicago Bulls sweatshirt, concentrated on placing tiny crystal slivers into the bowl of her just-crafted pipe. Her cigarette lighter hovered over it; she inhaled.

A metallic tang floated from the bowl, as unlike the heavy sweet aroma of marijuana as kerosene is unlike patchouli incense. Deejee refilled the pipe with the meticulous care of a lab technician.

"Okay," she said, handing me the device. "Your turn. Take it easy now."

I took it easy. A smokeless puff went into my lungs. I held it, passed the pipe back to Deejee, leaned back into the couch, and exhaled.

"How do you feel?"

I felt anxious. I did not want to say so and be ungrateful or disappoint Deejee's anticipation. She was peering at me intently, as if I were about to explode. Her bedroom eyelids paused at half-mast. Her oatmeal colored skin glowed softly under a thin layer of makeup. Her always glossy lips looked inflated.

"I feel . . . potent."

Deejee grinned with pleasure. Faint stains on her sizeable front teeth reminded me of mud under melted snow. "It's good, baby, isn't it?"

She tilted in my direction and her lips brushed my cheek under my ear. "Didn't I tell you?" Her breath fumed with beer and fried potatoes. She straightened and went back to work on the pipe.

After we had exchanged it three or four times, I got restless. I thought about waking the television or loading a cassette into the tape player, but those distractions didn't suit my mood. I was antsy enough to clean my apartment but amorous enough to sit tight on the sofa and measure Deejee's state of mind. How receptive would she be if I turned physically playful? This was our sixth occasion together but we had not yet traveled that path. Watching her dropping slivers into the blackened tin foil, I found it hard to read beneath the Chicago Bulls logo on her chest.

Emboldened by the pipe, I tried my luck. "Say, Deej. Could you go for a foot massage?"

Like a pawnbroker in the examination of a dubious gem, her focus stayed on the object under scrutiny. She did not look up. But she did accede. "Sure. Why not?"

From my bathroom I fetched a towel and a bottle of Johnson's baby oil. I squatted on the carpet in front of her and unlaced her sneakers. A familiar stench swarmed up that I knew well from my days at Greenlake and in the Navy, a smell that would have been quite at home in the locker room of the Chicago Bulls. I peeled off a pair of damp socks, applied oil, and unleashed the pent up energy through my fingers.

"That feels awesome," Darlena sighed, momentarily giving the pipe a rest.

Deejee's feet were not her best feature. Like her fingers, her toes were short and blunt, with chipped silver polish on the nails. Her arches were not pronounced, her soles rather flat. By comparison, Rita's feet were exquisite with high arches and long tapered toes. She loved it when I massaged them for her. As a professional geologist and college professor, she spent a lot of time on her feet. Our mutual enjoyment of what I was up to now was one of those little rituals that lovers with a comfortable history behind them can rely on for reassuring rapport.

I remembered that I had tried to reach Rita a few hours earlier and had missed her. And that reminded me why I had called her.

"By the way," I told Deejee, "The cops had me at the station this afternoon. They think I killed Lyss Nelson."

Deejee's laugh cracked the peaceful tranquility in the small apartment like a bolt of summer lightning.

"Ha! You? The cops think *you're* a murderer? Christ on a stick, Trapp! You're about as menacing as a daddy longlegs spider in a bathtub. *I'm* more the murdering type than you are. My God, the cops are stupid."

"As a matter of fact, the chief detective on the case came here to see me. She left her business card."

That remark put an end to our peaceful tranquility and my earnest attempt to get to Deejee's heart through her feet. She sat up abruptly, pulling her legs up on the couch.

"What? The cops were here? Why the hell didn't you say so? You think they might come back?"

Darlena was restless too. She pitched herself off the sofa and went to the closed blinds behind the television, peeling up one of them to monitor the parking lot.

After that, restlessness permeated the apartment, a palpable disquiet that seemed to slosh around in the room like water jostling in a toilet bowl. Deejee moved from the couch to the blinds every few minutes to check for police patrols. At one point she became convinced that she had dropped a sliver of crystal in the carpet and we both spent half an hour on our hands and knees combing the pile for it.

I was much relieved when she suggested that we call it a night.

"Tell you what, Trapp. Give me a ride down to the club. Monday's a slow night, but maybe Jimmy will let me on the floor so I can pick up some tips."

As the Rabbit ferried me home from Liquid Avenue, I recapitulated my day. Randy had been annoying, as always. The weekend money in my collection bag had made its way to the bank without incident. Rachel Imanaka had put the hairs up on the back of my neck. Deejee had not been entirely sympathetic to learn that I was a murder suspect, had introduced me to the least charming inebriant I had known since I stopped drinking alcohol in my 20s, and had been by turns edgy, pushy and indifferent.

And I had failed to connect with Rita. Was it too late to call her now? It was 9:15 PM here. What time was it in Alaska? Wasn't it the "Land of the Midnight Sun"? Or was that just summertime? Why didn't I know these things?

There was one more thing. Crack is not the best drug to fool with if you want a good night's sleep. It was far past my bedtime, but I still felt amped. And paranoid. I actually cruised my parking lot twice before I slid my Volkswagen into its customary space in front of my apartment.

I poked through the broken buds and loose crumbles in my stash box, scraping together enough for a brain apostle. It was definitely time to give Bogo a call. Not tonight. Tonight was for sleep.

My sleep was fitful, as restless, disconcerting and unsatisfying as the day had been. I reviewed my roster of suspects. None of them seemed up to the task of murdering poor Lyss Nelson. I passed into slumber trying in vain to remember that damned quote from Sherlock Holmes.

Chapter Fourteen

Tuesday was one of my favorite days at the office. Everybody, from the exalted owners to the humble bouncers, liked to get paid. Everybody knew and respected that Tuesday was the day I made that happen, so I was left alone.

As Deejee had observed, Monday was a slow night at the club. That was why I always prepared payroll on Tuesday morning, when I didn't have to invest inordinate time counting the previous night's take.

From an accounting point of view, after the maintenance of the general ledger, putting a payroll together was the most important and responsible thing I did. All the vendors and government agencies with whom I had negotiated debt payment agreements might disagree, but payroll was my personal point of pride. My predecessor in the job did not take payroll seriously, particularly the withholdings and employer contributions to FICA and SDI. The Internal Revenue Service and the California Employment Development Department had the power to close the doors on Pensacola, Garch and Nelson, but they saw the sense in making monthly payoff arrangements rather than prosecuting a corporation that had no assets to seize other than bar furniture and empty beer bottles.

In spite of inadequate sleep, I had a belly stoked with Carrow's pancakes and scrambled and a sense of purpose, so

I was not in as surly a mood as I might have been, all things considered.

Over breakfast, I had tried and failed to add murder suspects to my mental list. I was undecided which possibility was the more frightful: whether Lyss Nelson's killer was somebody I knew or somebody I didn't. After punching my time card in the employee break room inside the club, I paused at the ladder leading to the storage loft where the murderer had sequestered himself, tightly gripping the silk scarf or the nylon stocking, whatever it was, testing its strength and his own resolve. On my way to the safe with my canvas collection bag, I glanced anxiously at the spot where Lyss's body had lain last Friday morning. There was nothing there but table shadows cast by the bright blue Liquid Avenue sign behind the bar.

How could any human being kill another? What emotions engage the mind and control the actions? Fear? Rage? Revenge? Hatred? Self-righteousness? Determination? The conviction that no other course is possible? Could a killer genuinely relish the act itself, watching the death throes and knowing an irreplaceable life was being extinguished?

I had joined the Navy fresh out of Greenlake Preparatory Academy because I feared I might be killed in the Vietnam War. Back in '66, the draft was sweeping up young men my age who did not proceed directly from high school to college. The Selective Service draft was the shortest path to involuntary enlistment in the Army or the Marines, the service branches most likely to drop me in the jungle face-to-face with people I had no argument with for the purpose of killing them or being killed by them. I had no inkling why the United States was going toe-to-toe with a remote Asian country full of Buddhist farmers and nobody I met could explain it to me any better than they could explain their belief in God. All I knew for sure was that I didn't want to die before I had lived.

I emerged from the club with jangling keys and my fresh cup of coffee when the apparition approached me in the parking lot.

"Hi, Anthony."

"Good morning, Carla."

She was shivering, poor thing, in her thin shabby coat and bare legs. It was closing in on winter; the usual morning mist was cooler, wetter, more penetrating. I wondered if she had to stay up all night huddling in a doorway somewhere just to keep warm.

"Cuppa joe sound good?"

"You're a saint, Anthony."

In the *Cocina Habana*, Carla topped her coffee with cream and filled her pockets with sugar packets. I wished there was something edible I could give her, but Margarito and Elena did not leave things lying around when they closed up and I was too much intent on getting to my payroll to heat something for her. I pulled two twenties from my wallet. I didn't want to insult her by suggesting that she use some of that to buy herself something to eat. It was no business of mine how she made her money, still less how she spent it.

Looking out over the service counter toward the bar end of the club, blue splashes sat on the tabletops while dark patches clung to their legs. The dance floor and the bandstand were awash in blue neon, a murky lagoon where empty beer bottles seemed to float on the surface. I remembered that we were in a dangerous place.

"Did you hear about the murder here last week?"

"Sure, Anthony. Everybody on the street heard about it."

"I hope you have a safe place to stay until the police catch the killer."

"That's awfully sweet of you."

Under the lights in the kitchen, I could see Carla more clearly. Her hair was a tangle of rattan colored knots that might be infested with many strains of pox. Her rheumy eyes were puffy. She wore makeup that was streaked, clotted and uneven. Her teeth were brown and mottled, as if she had been chewing on Snickers bars that had never entirely rinsed away. Who knew when she had last bathed?

"On the street, we look out for each other."

Clutching our coffee cups, we pushed out through the back door into the chilly parking lot. "I don't mean to pry. I'm just worried about you, is all."

"Do the police have any leads?"

"So far their best suspect seems to be me. They're still looking for a guy named Tommy, the husband of the woman who was killed. He disappeared right after the murder."

"This guy Tommy." Carla looked thoughtful. "Is he the owner of the nightclub?"

"One of them."

"I think I know where he is."

She pointed across the parking lot to a three-story building on the other side of East Haley Street, down a few doors from the corner. It was a transient hotel called The Addison, a place where rooms could be rented by the hour and they didn't ask you personal questions if you paid in cash.

"Last week there was a guy in the lobby there who said he owned the nightclub across the street. No one believed him because he was joysing China White. He said his name was Tommy. He might still be there."

That was worth checking. I thanked Carla for the tip, locked my canvas bag in the office, and walked across the street. In The Addison's lobby, three armchairs that looked like poor relations of my sofa were stationed around a low table strewn with magazines. Each chair held an occupant. All were asleep.

I rang the chime at the front desk. A wall clock over a pigeon hole array labeled with room numbers ticked off the seconds leading up to 4:15 AM. My second ping on the chime roused the desk clerk, a prim fellow in his 50s who wore a bow tie and an overdose of Old Spice after shave. A badge on his coat identified him: "Kent".

"Good morning. Do you have a guest here by the name of Tommy?"

"We have a lot of guests here. They have a lot of names."

I couldn't tell if this martinet was following the rules or fishing for a bribe. In either case, I didn't have any small talk to spend on him. I drew from my wallet the business card that had been left on my front door yesterday. There was a pad of notepaper on the desk with *The Addison* printed at the top. I used a ball point pen attached to a chain to copy Detective Imanaka's name and number on it, tore it from the pad, folded it and handed it to the clerk.

"Kent, please make sure Tommy Nelson gets this. This lady has some news for him."

Chapter Fifteen

Any of the three owners could sign company checks. Dan Pensacola, being the most responsible among them, was the one who customarily autographed the payroll. When I was finished with the daily banking and had all the paychecks ready for signature, I called him to see when he was coming.

"Hey, Tony. Glad you called. Alicia is having a tough day with the kid, so I'm staying home until the club opens tonight. Would you mind running the checks out to my place so I can sign them here?"

I had never been to Dan and Alicia's home. I found the address on Virginia Road in Montecito easily. It was less than fifteen minutes from the corner of Anacapa and East Haley, but it might as well have been in a different universe.

Montecito is famous for being a preserve of the wealthy. Some of the estates are so beautifully secluded by towering trees, sandstone walls and spacious grounds that you wouldn't know there are mansions tucked away in there. You can drive around for hours and see nothing but stands of ash, pepper, sycamore, and eucalyptus.

Not all of Montecito is so customized for privilege. Near the commercial strips on East Valley Road and Coast Village Road, there are more middle class neighborhoods. Dan and Alicia's place on Virginia Road, running alongside the 101 Freeway, was one of these.

The Pensacolas lived in a ranch style house with an attached garage. Next to the garage and within the property fence there was a separate dwelling that might be a "grandma" house or a rental unit. As I neared the front door, I heard a child squalling inside.

"Welcome to *mi casa*." Dan pulled open the door with a mug of coffee in hand. "Can I get you something to wet your whistle?"

"That coffee looks good, thanks."

Inside the house, the squalling registered several orders of magnitude higher on the decibel meter. "Sorry the wife couldn't come out to say 'howdy'. She's back there dealing with *that*." He canted his head toward rooms that abutted a hallway. "Let's take our business next door."

Carting my coffee in a mug identical to Dan's in one hand, a manila envelope with the paychecks in the other, I followed my boss out the kitchen door into a patio. He held a gate open for me.

"Those your wheels?" Dan waved his mug at my grimy white Volkswagen, asleep on the graveled edge of Virginia Road. "You could be overdue for a raise."

We marched to the separate structure on the other side of the garage. It might once have been a "grandma" house, but Dan had converted it into a showroom. There was only the one room, a large trapezoidal shape of about 600 square feet, with an adjoining bathroom. An office arrangement sat in one corner, with a desk and chair, a file cabinet, a personal computer, a desk lamp, and a telephone with the answering machine that used to be in my office attached to it, its red "message waiting" light still winking impatiently. Next to the desk, an inviting sofa beckoned, fronted by a coffee table with ashtrays and coasters. The room's center harbored four large wooden pallets, each draped with heavy tarpaulin covers that stood four to five feet high. On the walls, nearly every square inch displayed neon signs, all of them lit.

The room was a pandemonium of exotic shapes and carnival colors. Several of the signs blinked tiny bulbs in rhythmic sequences that spelled words or actively illuminated the designs with carefully timed on/off switches or crawling scrolls.

"What do you think?" Dan could scarcely contain his pride. Some men collect cars, coins or stamps. Rita congregated mineral specimens. I gathered up books and music. My boss collected neon signs.

"Unreal." My jaw must have dropped. I made an effort to form syllables with it. "Incredible. These are magnificent! Where on earth did you find them?"

"Everywhere on earth. Well, at least everywhere I've been. Some of these are from England, France, Italy, Japan. Most are from the States. As you can guess, some of them are pretty old, a few from the 1920s. The ones under the tarps are still crated because I don't have enough room to hang them. I've been collecting neon since I was teenager. My chemistry teacher told me that neon is one the 'noble' gases. How neat is that? Have a look around."

Dan seated himself at his desk with the paychecks and started hancocking them while I drifted from sign to sign like a museum tourist.

"You keep these signs lit up all the time? Your electric bill must be monumental."

"Spoken like a bookkeeper. I only fire up the signs when I'm in here. Still, it runs up the meter. Alicia complains about it, but we both agree that this room has probably saved our marriage."

I halted before a sign that was distinctly arresting. In bright cherry red letters it read *Hotel and Dining*. The script formed by the tubes was the same as the *Liquid Avenue* sign in the club.

"This looks familiar."

"Good eye." Dan grinned from his desk. "That's the bottom half of our sign in the club. That's from a hotel that opened beside one of the canals in Venice, California in 1923. Get it?"

"You know, I always thought you had our sign made special for the club."

"It's the other way around. I got into the liquor business because I already had the perfect sign for a watering hole. It would have been cheaper to have one made. I bought *Liquid Avenue Hotel and Dining* at an auction about fifteen years ago for four grand.

"I was using the 'Liquid Avenue' half of the sign for the bar I owned in Long Beach. One day Tommy Nelson walked in and pitched me on the idea of a nightclub. He had money to invest from his recent marriage, but no experience in business. It was actually Lyss who bankrolled our nightclub version of 'Liquid Avenue'.

"Oh, by the way. Tommy finally surfaced. He called this afternoon."

That pulled me away from the entertaining signage over to the sofa. I put my mug on a coaster and sat. "What did he have to say for himself?"

"He's been on a smack bender at The Addison since last Wednesday. All this time everyone's been looking for him, he was right across the street."

"Does he know about Lyss?"

"The cops told him."

I tried to picture Detective Imanaka breaking it to Tommy that his wife had been murdered in the club as she was Mirandizing him. It occurred to me that, if Tommy was off the table, I was even more appetizing as a suspect.

"I suppose Tommy's stay at The Addison alibis him for the murder."

Dan had finished with the checks. He slid them back into the envelope and handed them to me, taking a seat next to me on the sofa.

"You didn't really think Tommy killed her, did you?"

I sighed. "No, I didn't. Tommy's not the most outstanding citizen in the Tri-County area, but he's not a maniac."

"Alicia is my alibi," Dan grinned again. "What's yours?"

"Mine? That's a bit of a problem. I don't have one. Detective Imanaka questioned me at the station yesterday. She's placed me at the scene at the guilty time. If she comes up with a motive, I'll be looking for a lawyer."

"And I'd be looking for a new bookkeeper. Let's not have that. I like the way things are going now." He pinched together between his thumb and forefinger the two checks for himself and his wife. "These are good, right?"

"Golden."

"Good answer."

Chapter Sixteen

It was heartwarming to have a vote of confidence from one of my bosses. I still wanted that from my girlfriend in Alaska, so as soon as I got home, I called Anchorage.

Once again, there was disappointment at the other end of the line. Rita was not in her room. I rang the front desk and connected with the same polite clerk I had spoken to on Sunday afternoon. We talked about the weather again. She agreed to give Doctor Barron a message for me.

My next call went to Bogo. The marijuana marketplace was always iffy, but Yevgeny Bogol was a trusty and resourceful supplier. He was not home, so I left my message on his answering machine.

I had no further appointments or assignations scheduled, so I gave myself the rest of the day off. I opened my cedar stash box that now contained little other than its promising aroma. I stirred the bits of leaf with a fingertip, decided I had enough to scrape together a pinwheel reefer, snagged the Zig Zag rolling papers, and twisted one.

A few puffs later I was recapping my day. Tommy had turned up. That was good and bad. Good because the suspense was lifted. He had not killed his wife. Bad because, like Detective Imanaka, I had to cross him off my list, which brightened the spotlight on me.

I had got the weekly payroll out of the way. The checks were safely locked in my office. Tomorrow everybody would be dropping by to pick them up.

Dan had invited me to his home and showed me his neon treasures. I knew as little about him as I did about Tommy or Randy. I had still never met his wife, even though I issued her a paycheck every week.

My phone cried. That must be Rita.

"Tony. It's Gene. Got your message. How much shopping are you planning on?"

"A couple of oh-zees, if you can get them. That last batch, the Colombian, was excellent."

"Don't hold your breath for that. I'll see what I can find. Will you be home tonight?"

I knew more about Yevgeny Bogol than I knew about the guys I worked for. No surprise there. Bogo and I had sucked weed and swapped stories many a time over the past seven years. Until today, I had never so much as shared a cup of coffee with Nelson, Garch or Pensacola.

You would never guess from hearing him talk that Bogo was born in the Soviet Union. His English was as absent any trace of his native Russian as if he'd hailed from Omaha. He was raised in Hollywood, matriculated from Hollywood High School and, as I did, attended the University of California. I went to Santa Barbara to read literature. Yevgeny went to Davis to study veterinary medicine. His father had been an equine vet who worked for Hollywood Park racetrack.

Bogo had dropped out of school. He had brains in triplicate, but by the time he turned 21, he was already making as much money as his dad—and equine veterinarians are the best-paid animal doctors in the trade. Bogo became a track tout, a handicapper. He knew all the breeding stables in North America, all the breeders and big time trainers. He kept pedigree charts of all the successful studs and their offspring going back to Swaps. He knew all the important tracks and the conditions produced on them by various kinds of weather. He had files on dozens of jockeys, past and present. Having been raised by a horse doctor at a racecourse, and having studied veterinary medicine, he could tell how a horse was feeling and how it was likely to perform by the most cursory examination.

As a lifelong observer of horses, Bogo knew better than to bet on them. At the racetrack there were no certainties other than the compulsion of humans to undertake risk for the endorphin rush.

Yevgeney's first wife, a Russian girl he had known since elementary school, had committed suicide while he was in college. According to Bogo, he had been so prostrate with grief that he had spent most of his life trying to recover from the shock. In the hope of recapturing the magic of his early romance, six months ago he had married a Russian mail order bride from Novosibirsk with the same name as his first wife, Natalya.

Should I marry Rita? Where did that thought come from? Thinking about wives, I guess, and what they meant to Dan and Bogo. Even Tommy Nelson had done well with his marriage before its grim conclusion. Lyss had come with a dowry.

While I had lied to Deejee about my relationship with Rita, I had told the truth about the difference in our ages. Doctor Barron was five years older than I. We had been together three years; in fact, our anniversary was just around the corner. That was long enough to gauge how serious we were about each other. We used to live together at her place in the Samarkand. She had asked me to leave after my stupid fuckup at Golden Sunset Publications.

It was really all about Kathleen O'Keenan and *Golden Voices*, the literary monthly she edited. I wanted that job very much. I sweated over *Bargain Bin* day in and day out just to get it to the printer on time every week. The other editors seemed to spend endless hours on expense account lunches with their contributors or in amply provisioned conferences with advertising sales representatives. Julie Mendenhill and Harvey Hasridian were nice enough. Since I didn't give a Mulholland damn about personal fitness or otolaryngology, we planted no burrs under each other' saddles.

Kathleen, on the other hand, was as nasty as body odor. She never missed a chance to remind me how much more she knew about serious writing than I did. She had the advantage in lording it over me because we had gone to the same school, and even though she was younger than I, we had taken some of the same courses together. She had gone on to acquire a master's degree, whereas I had settled for the bachelor's.

"Well, I believe Shakespeare wrote for the money." I argued with her in the warehouse over stacks of the latest issue of *Golden Voices* being readied for shipment. "He just happened to be a genius."

"Only an ignoramus believes that the country-educated glove maker's son from Henley Street wrote the plays and sonnets that appeared under his name."

We were working with Herb, the assistant warehouse manager, applying address labels to the magazines. Herb was slicing the sheets of pressure sensitive labels on a heavy paper cutter; I was sticking them to the magazine covers; Kathleen was counting labels to ensure that all her subscribers were included.

"The writer, whoever he was, was intimately familiar with Montaigne and Bacon, to say nothing of Marlowe and Kyd. Your obsession with Shakespeare shows how shallow you are about the brief literary renaissance of the English oppressors. If you had a Celtic soul you might know something about real lyricism."

"How shallow you are." Herb scolded me after Kathleen left us to load all the magazines into trays for delivery to the post office. "If you had a Celtic soul, you might have noticed that you've got some of these mailers out of zip code order."

"Who do I have to fuck to make that girl work for some other publisher?" I complained. "You know that 'O' in her last name? That wasn't there when she was in school. The closest she's ever been to Ireland is East Minneapolis."

My musings were interrupted by a soft knock on my door. Shit! Could that be Detective Imanaka, come to take me into custody now that Tommy Nelson was off the hook?

A furtive peek through my blinds gave me full view of a young man in a navy blue pea coat with a distinctive rainbow-colored knit wool cap. It was Bogo. That was good and bad. Good because he was not Rachel Imanaka. Bad because he was bringing me something that was guaranteed to amplify my paranoia.

Chapter Seventeen

Like me, Bogo was not a drinker. We sat on the sofa together nursing Vernor's ginger ales. We were also sampling the new batch of cannabis buds my supplier had delivered.

"Not as good as the last stuff," Yevgeny noted, "but better than a sharp stick in the eyeball, right?"

"Better than a sharp stick," I agreed.

We were listening to Reno and Smiley, some of the "hillbilly shit" that Deejee had assured Mary would be found in my shoeboxes of cassettes.

"Bluegrass," Bogo murmured, exhaling a volume of cloud. "It's all about heartbreak, isn't it? Hard times, bad luck, lost love, good dogs long gone, and faith in Jesus."

"Not to mention great singing and fabulous musicians."

"It's the despondency that grabs me. It's like reggae. All the white kids in their fashionable dreadlocks are dancing to it, but if you listen to the words, they're singing about hunger and despair and running from the law."

"I know the feeling." My own exhalation dispersed in front of me. "Not the 'I shot the sheriff' feeling, but the law breathing down the back of my neck feeling."

"That murder in your nightclub, huh? Did you know that girl?"

"Yeah. She used to come by the office to pick up her hubby's paycheck. I saw the body. I'll probably never get that out of my head."

"I found Natalya's body. No matter how much of *this* I smoke," Yevgeny gestured with the tubelette he was holding in his fingertips, "I'll never get *that* out of head."

"What happened to her, Gene? How did all that go down?"

Bogo took another drag, held it, let the vapors exude slowly. "Seems like I knew Natalya all my life. It was as if our relationship had been orchestrated by fate. Halfway through high school we knew we were going to get married. We tied the knot right after graduation.

"But she was already losing it. I knew something was wrong. One minute she'd be laughing her ass off, the next she'd be sobbing about losing a toy or something when she was a little kid. Sometime around our second year at Davis, some switch flipped inside her and she went totally manic. She just couldn't stop talking, humming to herself all the time, or just making incoherent noises. We tried to get help for her, but nothing worked—therapy, meds, exercise, diet. Near the end, she was visibly swirling down the drain. She stopped eating, didn't seem to know who I was, spent most of her days just burbling and picking up shit off the floor and putting it in the fridge.

"She had lucid moments, but those were the worst because all her guilt came gushing out about how bad she felt about being a burden on me. One night she went out to the garage, took sleeping pills and sat behind the exhaust pipe with the car running. That's how I found her.

"I swear to God, Tony. My first emotion was relief. I thought her death was the best thing for both of us. I've always felt weird about that, but it's true. Natalya was beyond my help, beyond anybody's help."

The silence that followed invited my thoughts. "You know, I felt weird too that I didn't do anything for Lyss Nelson. When I saw her body, I thought she was asleep. I considered covering her with something, but I figured it didn't matter. As it turned out, it didn't. But I still feel weird about it."

Reno and Smiley had run out of tunes, so I swapped their tape for something more moody. I popped in Miles Davis, *E.S.P.*

"You going to her funeral?"

"Funeral?" Lyss Nelson had been dead for five days now. No matter who killed her, something had to be done about her remains. "I doubt it. So far no one has said anything about it."

While I was fussing with the music, Bogo had busied himself with prepping another holy roller. He handed it over, a thin wisp of smoke trailing its red tip.

"Natalya's funeral was worse than finding her body. All those women sobbing about how sad it was that she was so young, as if that somehow made it worse. Everybody coming up to me to say how sorry they were. It was sickening. No matter what, I'm never going to another funeral again."

We listened in silence as Wayne Shorter rode his tenor over Herbie Hancock and Ron Carter. I attached a roach clip to the dwindled reefer.

"This is what I noticed more than anything, Tony. After Natalya died, nothing changed. I thought the whole world would seem different, but it didn't. Food tasted the same. Freeway traffic was as annoying as ever. The horses still ran at Hollywood Park. The world just kept on rolling and it didn't make any difference at all that Natalya was no longer part of it.

"A week after the funeral, I was having breakfast at a pancake house in Westchester. I started flirting with the waitress. When I realized what I was doing, I was disgusted with myself. My wife was barely cold and I already had a hard on for another woman. It was as if my marriage had never happened, as if Natalya had never existed.

"That's what will happen to me too, and to all of us. After we die, the world just keeps on going without us as if we had never existed." He waved the roach clip and a small trail followed it. "*This* helps me a lot with that."

"How is your present wife doing?"

"Novo-Natalya? She's glad to be here. She never stops talking about the Barabinskaja back home, but she's found plenty of comforts in her new country to compensate for what she left behind. Mostly she's found them at Robinson's and Bloomingdale's."

"So you found true love and wedded bliss through a dating service?"

"True love?" Yevgeny's laugh made him cough. "What the hell is that? We get along. The sex is okay. She wants to have kids and I don't, so she will probably go back home or leave me for someone else here as soon as her English improves. It doesn't matter. I wasn't looking for love anyway. I think I was looking for a ghost."

"Do you think I should marry Rita?"

He laughed again. "If you need to ask me, you probably shouldn't. Tell you what though, if you don't, I can give you the number for a reliable dating service."

Chapter Eighteen

Wednesday. Payday.

I was up a little earlier than usual. I like paydays. Almost everybody in the company stopped by my office on Wednesdays. It was the only time I ever saw most of them.

"There was an Asian woman in here yesterday morning asking about you."

Jean, my waitress, refreshed my coffee cup. This morning Carrow's kitchen had worked up a platter of powdered French toast surrounded by rashers of bacon for me, done crisp the way I like them.

"That would be Detective Imanaka. She was checking my alibi for last Thursday morning, wasn't she? I hope she didn't put you through any bother."

Jean might have been smiling or frowning. It was hard to tell. Her makeup was so thickly applied that her facial expressions tended to look frozen, like a mannequin's.

"No. The cops were here last week to check your story. This lady was asking about what you like to read when you're eating. And I don't think she was Japanese. She said her name was Chin."

Chin? I didn't know a Chin. Jean must be mistaken. It had to be Rachel.

"For what it's worth, I told her you like to read the paper."

This morning's edition sat on my table. "Well, that's certainly true." I never knew the police investigated the reading habits of their suspects. When I had lunch or dinner here, I often brought mystery or spy novels for company. I was glad that, at this hour of the day, I always read the newspaper.

"You don't think I'm a killer, do you, Jean?"

"Tony, I've been working the graveyard shift at a chain restaurant two blocks from an interstate highway for eighteen years. If God tells me on Judgment Day that I never once served a murderer, I'll tell Him flat out that He's a liar."

I liked the idea of a liar god. I thought about that while I was counting last night's Liquid Avenue proceeds in my office. Was the Judeo-Christian deity into mendacity? In mind's eye, I rippled through the pages of the Old Testament. Had God lied to Abraham? Job? I couldn't remember. I recalled the Greek pantheon. Surely there were some gods in there that fudged the truth. Wasn't there a lot of underhanded rivalry among the Olympians? What did Homer have to report in *The Iliad*?

"Wrong again." Kathleen O'Keenan had reprimanded me one morning over bagels at GSP. Her eyes that she insisted were green even though they were plainly brown were narrowed, as if a headache was about to encroach on their Celtic lyricism with pedestrian concern. A snogget of cream cheese lay pasted on her chin. I made a point of not mentioning it.

"Homer was not a person. Homer was a personification, a famous name applied to a tradition of oral poetry in a pre-literate society. Obviously you slept through your course on the classics."

I had slept well enough after Bogo left last night, although Rita had not returned my call. She was probably out in the field. In fact, Rita's enjoyment of the great outdoors was one of the glaring differences between us. She loved camping, wilderness treks, roughing it. I was more bookish and sedentary, inclined to my favorite television shows and watching sports more than playing them.

It was perfectly reasonable that a geologist would delight in the wild. That's where the rocks are. Rita was a shale expert; her doctoral dissertation—far too abstruse for my level of scientific appreciation—concerned the various locations and biochemical compositions of the world's shale deposits.

"If you look carefully," she said, handing me a sliver of clay and a magnifying glass, "you can make out the minute strata in this diatomaceous earth."

On our first weekend together, we had driven up to Lompoc. We were poking around the cliffs on the beach near Point Arguello, a few miles south of Vandenberg Air Force Base. Rita wore khaki shorts, hiking boots, a UCSB Gauchos tee shirt and a broad-brimmed straw hat. Her bare arms and legs gleamed with Coppertone suntan lotion. Her bright blue eyes were robin's eggs half blanketed by heavy lids.

"The microscopic critters that formed this material lived in a pond that dried up here two hundred and thirty million years ago, about the time that Africa and South America were separating along the Mid-Atlantic Ridge."

She put a sandy hand on my arm to steady it so we could admire the fossils under the glass together and contemplate the staggering length of time they had lain buried side-by-side on this sunny beach. Just offshore, the Pacific Ocean swept south toward Point Conception, a visible current that stretched across to the horizon. It felt as if the shore itself was running northward. A touch of mustard and sweet pickle relish rode on Rita's breath from the hot dogs we had just eaten for lunch at a café in Lompoc. She was the most beautiful woman I'd ever been with.

My office door was open now. Liquid Avenue employees were in and out. Randy Garch had been first to arrive.

"You wouldn't believe the migraine I had last night," he rumbled. "I thought my skull was going to explode."

I had no trouble believing it. I had smelled his hair tonic. While he was there, Randy picked up Trigger's paycheck for him. His bouncer carried the Christian name Lawrence Czerniak.

Peanut strolled in behind Randy. I thumbed through the paycheck envelopes for David Selkirk, the name his parents had bequeathed him. Peanut perched carefully against the table with my green bar printer paper, listening quietly to Randy's complaints. He was tall with a torso that angled up from his hips to broad shoulders a helicopter could land on. He wore an extra large cable knit sweater that draped loosely over his massively developed chest. Acne dotted his cheeks below a freshly shaved scalp.

Until Sunday afternoon, I had been fiercely jealous that this fellow was getting sweaty with Deejee. After Randy left, he stepped forward to receive his pay envelope. "Thanks, man," he mumbled. "Hey, you doin' okay? I heard the police had you over to the station the other day."

"Yeah. I'm all right. It was just routine stuff. Thanks for asking."

Peanut stared at the floor. "That was unreal, Friday, after the murder, with the cops here and everything. Poor Lyss. She was always so courteous. Old World dignity or something. I liked her."

"Me too," I agreed.

"Have you heard anything about a funeral for her? I'd like to, you know, pay my respects, unless it's family only or something."

"No. I haven't heard anything. Maybe Jimmy knows the arrangements."

"I asked him. He hasn't heard anything either." He shuffled toward the open door, paused, and turned back to me. "Poor Lyss. You know, between you and me and these four walls, I always thought she could have done much better than Tommy."

Chapter Nineteen

I paid my respects to the *cocina*. Returning to my office, *café Cubano* in hand, I stepped carefully over the hallway leading to the patio. Luis was methodically sloshing a mop back and forth like a windshield wiper. The aisle gleamed and exuded the heavy scent of Pine-Sol. Luis had set up a "Slippery When Wet" sign to warn the unwary.

Shortly before noon, I heard the jingling of bracelets coming through the office door. Today Elizabeth wore a raspberry silk blouse, dark blue Calvin Klein jeans that made melons of her butt, and a pair of fire engine red high-heeled pumps. She had brought a playmate. He was of medium height, exceedingly thin, with the complexion of a scrubbed kitchen sink. He was as full of nervous energy as a whippet. He was my third boss, Tommy Nelson.

"Check this out, Tony. You won't believe it!"

Tommy leaned over my desk and pushed aside some paperwork and the stack of pay envelopes to clear space. He placed a translucent plastic container in front of me, opened it carefully, and tipped it over slowly into his hand. Like a blackjack dealer, he arranged in ranks a set of shiny pasteboard cards. When I bought cards like this as a kid, they came with bubble gum and featured baseball players. These cards carried the images of the celebrated Dream Team, the assemblage of

American professional basketball stars who had recently swept through the Olympics Games in Barcelona.

"In reality, these are going to be worth a fortune! I guarantee it."

The roster seemed complete. They grinned at me in pristine lithography. Magic. Bird. Jordan. Barkley. Malone. Ewing. Drexler. Pippen. Mullin. Stockton. Laettner.

"Some day I will leave these to my kids."

Behind Tommy, Elizabeth tittered.

"I got these from Dean. They're super special, very rare. They come from Portugal."

Dean D'Amato was a partner with Tommy and Randy in a shellfish exporting venture called D'Amato Delicacies. Dean owned a boat with diving equipment. He pulled up sea urchins from the Santa Barbara Channel and sold them to entrepreneurs in Honduras and Panama. Now and again he was in my office making long distance calls to vendors in pidgin Spanish. From what I could gather from his end of halting conversations, he had no problem selling his catches, but much difficulty getting paid for them. This occasioned a certain amount of friction with his investors Nelson and Garch, who spent about half their business time trying to locate him and the other half berating him in parking lot shouting matches.

I turned over Christian Laettner's card. Its backside displayed his college career statistics and brief biographical data. An imprint at the bottom from the publisher and distributor of this treasured memento declared "Candace Confectionary Enterprises, Copyright 1992". It might have come from Portugal.

"Can I get my paycheck? I have to get back to work."

Elizabeth stood by Tommy's side with her hand out. I extracted her envelope from the stack while Tommy scooped up his super special basketball cards and replaced them in their plastic cradle.

"See you later, Babe."

Elizabeth and Tommy put smooches on each other that left traces of lipstick on Tommy's cheek. She headed for the door, jingling like a sleigh ride.

Tommy's weekend bender joysing China White at The Addison had done him no harm that I could see. He always looked as though he could stand a little more time in the sun. His manner had always been twitchy and talkative.

"So, where are we with everything?" He pointed at the company checkbook parked on my desk. "What's the bottom of the line?"

"This week the checks are good," I said, handing him his. "There's enough inventory for tonight. Jimmy will be coming in later to let me know if we need deliveries. We're up to the minute on our settlement obligations. I have to run down to Ventura this afternoon to drop off a payment at the Board of Equalization."

"That's good." He nodded solemnly. "We have to keep the municipalities happy. Otherwise we'd be in the deep end at the end of the tunnel."

I considered uttering a few words of condolence on his loss and inquiring about the interment arrangements for Lyss, but, having seen his exchange of cordialities with Elizabeth, it didn't seem appropriate.

Tommy settled into the other office chair. "Jimmy's in the club?"

"Counting the beer."

"We had an argument once when we were in high school. Jimmy was so far on the dark side of the moon about it that we didn't speak to each other for a week.

"It was about abortion. I said the municipalities have no business telling anyone what they can put into their bodies or take out of them. Jimmy said nobody can fuck with God. If God puts a baby in a woman's belly, it's not her business anymore. It's God's business.

"In reality, Jimmy was an altar boy. We went to Fermin Lasuen in San Pedro. Franciscan padres like at the Mission here.

They got into his head. He joined this club of zealots that was always out picketing the Planned Parenthood clinic. I tried to talk him out of it. He took a swing at me when I said that babies are nothing but God playing with Himself."

One of our cocktail waitresses, a robust looking redhead called Brandilyn Archiver, strolled in. I had never heard her string two words together. She didn't do so now.

"Check." Brandi said.

While I riffled the envelopes for Archiver and Brandi stayed busy keeping her thoughts to herself, Tommy got up and drifted out the door, presumably into the club to see his younger brother. I had never pictured either of the Nelson boys contemplating multi-layered moral questions, never mind generating hard feelings about them. Leave it to Catholics to put up their dukes over doctrinal disputes. Did Tommy entertain these ruminations while he was joysing smack?

The subtraction of Brandi's envelope from the stack dwindled it down to three. One of those belonged to Darlena Giordano. I looked forward to seeing her.

I had my back to the door when the flash that threw a millisecond shadow over my desk, followed by the brief whine of a Polaroid mechanism spitting up a photo, announced her presence.

"Gotcha!" Deejee proclaimed.

She shook the snapshot to get some drying air on it and laid it on my desk. She draped her arm around my shoulder while we examined the image of the back of my head.

"You have a gift for catching me at my best." I noted. "Maybe you should do this for a living."

"Catching you at your best isn't as easy as it sounds, Trapp."

Deejee planted a soft kiss on my cheek just under my ear. There was an unusual amount of kissing going on in the office today.

"I guess you must have heard the news about the concert?" Darlena helped herself to the pay envelopes, took hers, and dropped the remaining two on my desktop.

"What concert?"

"You haven't heard? Why am I not surprised? Bob Dylan. At the County Bowl. Sunday afternoon. Listen, you've got to get us a couple of tickets!"

Dylan was another of those music makers represented in my shoeboxes of cassettes. I had never had the pleasure of seeing him perform in person. I had not followed his career since the '70s, but seeing Dylan with Deejee at a venue as sweet as the Santa Barbara County Bowl was an opportunity too good to miss.

"Yeah, sure. That sounds great! I'll get us some tickets."

Deejee pecked my cheek again. "I knew you were the man, Trapp. Call me when you get those tickets."

As soon as Deejee left, I picked up the phone to reserve a pair of seats at the Bowl. A terse fellow, who identified himself as "Charles", informed me that tickets for this particular concert were available only at the box office on a "first come, first served" basis.

"If I were you," Charles told me, "I'd get here early. We open at 4:00 PM."

That dovetailed my schedule nicely. I had time enough to get to the bank for cashier's checks, then down to Ventura and back before the County Bowl box office opened. I locked the office and went into the club with the last two paychecks to ask Jimmy to hand them off.

The brothers were on the *Cocina Habana* patio, sipping *café Cubanos* and laughing about something. It was my guess that they had not taken up the abortion issue again. It seemed unlikely that they were discussing funeral arrangements for Lyss.

I crossed Anacapa Street, found the Rabbit moored in the public parking lot, and started paddling.

Chapter Twenty

Ventura is twenty-five miles south of Santa Barbara, a very pleasant drive when the traffic is light that zips along the 101 Freeway past Montecito, Summerland and Carpinteria, and then runs adjacent to the grand Pacific Ocean tickling the shores of Rincon with its ever present gaggle of surfers bobbing in gentle swells.

Detective Imanaka had advised me to "stay in Santa Barbara" and to "let us know if you have any business that takes you elsewhere." Did my errand violate her directive? I had a regular appointment at the State Board of Equalization every Wednesday afternoon to deliver a cashier's check for past due sales taxes my employers had negligently ignored. This was one of my favorite chores, not really work at all. I would punch up the volume on the Rabbit's sound system to stuff my ears with tunes and let my mind munch on conundrums.

Abortion? Why had Tommy Nelson broached this topic only minutes after his proud display of objects intended for the future enrichment of his "kids"? Tommy had no children that I was aware of, at least none that required court-ordered support subtracted from his paycheck. So what was really on his mind?

Was Elizabeth pregnant? If that were so, it would be a fact of considerable interest to Detective Imanaka. Lyss could be an intractable problem if Elizabeth was carrying Tommy's child.

Suppose Tommy had suggested terminating the pregnancy and Elizabeth had assumed Jimmy's attitude about the matter?

Tommy had an alibi for the night of his wife's murder, but Elizabeth didn't. If she had a motive to push Lyss out of the pathway to Tommy, that might divert police interest in me.

I had to find out whether Elizabeth was pregnant. Since that was something she might be hiding from Detective Imananka, it was unlikely that Elizabeth herself would be forthcoming. I would never get a straight answer out of Tommy. I would have to find an indirect method of inquiry.

"I admit it, Tony. It always surprises me when you make these payments. Your employers don't keep promises, but apparently you do."

Judy Crenshaw was the affable, attractive director of the Tri-County branch of the State Board. She was another reason why this regular Wednesday assignment was not really work for me. Judy was right up there with Rita in the department of pulchritude. Her wide oval eyes wore that shade of brown that made yellow dresses look demure. She usually conducted our business seated at her desk, but last year, on the day I had successfully negotiated the installment plan for paying off Nelson, Garch and Pensacola debts, she had walked me to the door in heels that emphasized the fine articulation where her calves tapered into her ankles. Ever since, I had fancied taking her dancing, or better yet, walking barefoot with her on the sand dunes where California Street met the sea.

"Keep the payments coming," Judy smiled, "and I'll let you guys stay in business. Be sure to tell your bosses that *you* are the reason I haven't closed the doors on them."

Was that nugget of flattery flirtation or just good business? I thought about it driving back to Santa Barbara. Judy didn't wear a ring on her spoken-for finger. Why had I never asked her out? For one, our business relationship was intimidating. She had the authority to put an end to the skullduggery at Liquid Avenue, which would have me beating the bushes for another job. It could be risky dating a lady with so much power over my personal livelihood. It would not do to disappoint her.

For another, there was Rita. I was still on the choke chain with her, and I had not done any straying until recently, when I met Darlena Giordano. And that didn't count as straying until something happened, although I doubted that Rita would share that view.

Now I headed back to Santa Barbara with clear intent to make something happen. "You've got to get us a couple of tickets" Deejee had instructed me. That could help make something happen, couldn't it? I had neither of my two Bob Dylan cassettes with me or I would have been playing them to warm me up for buying tickets to his concert this Sunday.

In my time in Santa Barbara I had attended so many concerts at the County Bowl that there ought to have been a seat there with my name on it. A splendid venue for music performance, the Bowl was nestled among oaks, acacias and jacarandas in a deep ravine set back in the foothills under the Alameda Padre Serra where Milpas Street, running north, makes a sharp left curve and becomes East Anapamu Street heading west.

The Bowl seats forty-five hundred souls in a concrete amphitheater with acoustic properties that would have pleased Athenian audiences from the Age of Pericles. I had seen blues and pop artists there as various as Paul Butterfield, Bonnie Raitt, Sonny Terry and Brownie McGhee, Boz Scaggs, Jethro Tull, the Allman Brothers, and Yes. I'd heard Ali Akbar Khan, Bob Marley, Weather Report, Return To Forever, Bob James, and Tom Scott.

I checked my watch at the first stoplight on Milpas. It was 3:40 PM. I was going to be early for the Bowl box office opening, as Charles had advised. That was good. I would have a little time to kill, but at least I would not be standing in line, something I hate with a passion akin to my hatred for elevator music.

At the next stoplight, the traffic was unexpectedly thick. By the time I reached the left hook at the top of Milpas, I saw why.

The line of prospective concert goers slung out from the Bowl box office all the way down the sidewalk on East Anapamu as far as I could see. The cars crept along with taillights winking red every other second. As I stopped and started, stopped and started for another fifteen minutes amid dappled shadows where sunlight filtered through tall cedars that made a quarter-mile canopy over the street with interlocking branches, I tried to estimate the crowd. There looked to be fewer than 500 people, but it was going to be a long wait to get to the box office. I had counted on resting the Rabbit in the Santa Barbara High School parking lot conveniently located alongside East Anapamu, but there was no parking anywhere in sight. I had to go all the way to Olive Street, three-quarters of a mile from the box office, before I found an empty space to squeeze into. I leaped out, locked up, and dashed for the end of the line.

Santa Barbara is not a major metropolis. I have lived here twenty-three years, so it never surprises me when, in a random crowd of local residents, I run into somebody I know.

"What's the haps, Tony?"

A tall pale fellow with squinty blue eyes wearing a gray fedora like a shamus in a noir flick from the '40s was ambling up Anapamu Street from the box office.

"Howdy, Clark. You get some tickets?"

"Got two for me and the missus."

"What's it look like at the box? Are they going to sell out before I get there?"

Clark Gary, the leader of Liquid Avenue's house band, the Discordians, knew a thing or two about the sale of concert tickets. "Hard to say. This event will sell out for sure. They have a four-ducat limit at the window, but there's no way of knowing how many season tickets or pre-sold corporate and group commitments the Bowl has in hand. Then there are the seats taken by the radio stations and record stores for their promotions. And, of course, the speculators. For a Dylan concert, they and their accomplices will grab as many seats as possible to scalp at the door Sunday afternoon. I think you'll be okay. There's only five or six hundred people ahead of you."

"Are you guys at the club tonight?"

"No. Tonight you've got the Pleasure Drones. Dan booked us for tomorrow night, same as last week. Oh, by the way, I was real sorry about Tommy Nelson's wife. We were there, so the cops talked to everybody in the band. Did you know her very well?"

"She used to come by the office to pick up Tommy's paycheck. Lyss was a sweet lady."

"Tommy must be pretty torn up."

"He seems to be coping with his grief."

I had been shuffling forward slowly for over an hour. The box office had swallowed and digested about half the line. It was good to have someone to chat with.

"I never met Dylan," Clark offered. "But back in '75, when I was with an outfit called The Glamour Rats, we opened a show for him in L.A. during his *Blood on the Tracks* promo tour."

"I have that one. 'Crickets talking back and forth in rhyme.'"

A blonde guy in jeans and a windbreaker, who was directly in front of me and had not uttered a peep since I'd been there, now turned and said, "I'll look for you in old Honolula, San Francisco, Ashtabula. You're gonna make me lonesome when you go."

Clark laughed. "Dylan fans. Gotta love 'em."

He himself had to go, but it didn't make me lonesome because I now had somebody else to chat with for the remaining hour it took to get to the box office window and score a couple of tickets for Deejee and me.

Chapter Twenty-One

It had taken two hours of marching in slow motion with the parade of concert lovers on East Anapamu Street, but I had succeeded. I was keen to show Deejee our tickets. To save a few minutes, I stopped at Carrow's for dinner rather than running back to West Valerio.

While I waited to be seated and as I was trailing the waitress down the aisle toward my table, I peeked furtively at the other customers. Every time I came in here now, I was on the lookout for a lone Asian woman who might be the inquisitive Ms Chin. Not that I would know her by sight. In fact, there were three ladies this evening that fitted the vastly vague description of "Asian woman", all at the same table, all under the age of twenty. What would I say to someone I might accost innocently slamming down her French dip and fries? "Excuse me. Is your name Chin? Have you been asking questions about me?"

I let myself into the club through the service door a few minutes after 7:00 PM. Wednesday is not an especially busy night, but there seemed to be a good crowd. I was very rarely in here at this hour when the Liquid Avenue sign behind the bar actually looked welcoming. The Pleasure Drones pushed dancers around the hardwood floor under a spinning disco ball, and the waitresses carefully wound their way among the patrons balancing drink trays. I didn't see Deejee, but I did spy a redhead I had seen earlier in the day.

"Hiya, Brandi," I greeted her. "Is Deejee on board tonight?"

"Break."

She indicated that area of the club with a curt nod and I made my way back to the door with the nicked "Employees Only" sign. Deejee, parked on a folding chair, nursed a mentholated Kool, with one leg in Levis resting on the other. She wore a green frock with purple dots and enough makeup to stock a Robinson's cosmetics counter. The unforgiving flicker of the break room florescent ballast did not flatter her, but in all fairness, she would be more than presentable to the inebriated customers in the reflected sparkles tossed around by the disco ball.

"Trapp." She exhaled fog gray fumes. "Did you score us some tickets?"

I was pleased with myself for the investment of time and tedium I had lavished on the Dylan tickets. I brandished them, grinning like a bandit. Deejee put out her palm. I placed the two pulp rectangles on it.

"Good work, baby. I knew you'd come through."

I expected Deejee to give the tickets an appreciative glance and hand them back, but she casually dropped them into her voluminous bag with the Polaroid camera and everything else she hauled around with her.

"The concert starts at 1:00. Should we make a plan to meet somewhere, grab a bite, get good and baked for the occasion?"

"Absolutely. But not now, baby. I have to get back on the floor."

She punched her smoldering cigarette butt into the sand can, stood, stepped forward to wrap an arm around my waist, and kissed me near my mouth.

"We'll get together before Sunday."

"One more thing, Deej. How would you feel about doing a bit of detective work for me?"

She had one hand on the break room door. A sly pucker ticked the corners of her generous lips. "Detective work? Don't tell me you're getting devious, Trapp. I'm already attracted to you."

"I need to know if Elizabeth is pregnant."

"Strennis? Pregnant? You mean, by Tommy?" Deejee sat down again on the folding chair, shook out a cigarette from her pack of Kools and lit it. "That's interesting."

"If she is, she's probably keeping that from the police."

"I'll bet."

"So she won't likely be volunteering any information about it."

"Strennis is too stupid to keep anything from me, Trapp." Darlena smiled broadly. "I have ways of making her talk."

I followed Deejee out the door as she returned to work. My eyes ran up the ladder attached to the wall leading to the storage loft, as they always did now whenever I passed it. It was only six nights ago that a killer had cooped up there with vile designs. Unless the killer was Elizabeth Strennis, who would not need to hide anywhere if she planned to murder Lyss.

It was after my bedtime. I was too excited for immediate sleep. I pulled out my cedar cigar box and tubed a brain apostle from the buds I'd bought from Bogo. As I vaporized it, I considered.

This business with Elizabeth Strennis was a possible lead that Detective Imanaka did not have. Maybe I was better at solving mysteries than I gave myself credit for. As Sherlock Holmes said, "Eliminate the . . ." Eliminate the what? I still couldn't remember. Maybe I didn't need to.

Deejee's interest in the case was a promising turn. She was happy with me for getting the Dylan tickets. We were all set for a Sunday afternoon date. She had spoken some encouraging words, including mentioning in passing that she was "attracted" to me. I liked it when she called me "baby."

I wasn't playing music or watching television. My windows were closed, but in the background, framed by the relative quiet at this time of night, the 101 Freeway made its presence felt in the ebb and flow of thundering wheels racing by. I felt drowsy.

My phone rang. That had to be Deejee. She must have already gotten the poop from Elizabeth. That was fast. Maybe there was a future for us in the detective trade.

"Hi, Anthony. I hope I'm not calling too late."

"Hello, Doc. It's always a pleasure to hear your voice."

"Sorry I wasn't able to get back to you sooner. It's real busy up here. We're getting ready to wrap things up and head home. The front desk clerk said you called."

"Yes, I did. I was a little twitchy because the cops don't have any better suspect than me for that murder at the club last week. I called to get some sympathy."

"Jesus! You're a murder suspect? What the hell is wrong with them? You're not a killer. You don't always make the best choices, but you're not a bad guy. When I get home, I'll go talk to the cops and tell them you don't go in for murder because you'd probably screw it up."

"I appreciate your support, darling. I miss you."

"That's good because I need a favor from you. I'm arriving at Santa Barbara Airport Sunday afternoon. Will you be there to pick me up?"

Chapter Twenty-Two

I'd been right about the crowd at the club last night. It was busier than usual for a Wednesday. The splash of vomit on my office door suggested it. The cash from the safe verified it. While I was counting the money, I gave some thought to my problem.

It was good to hear from Rita. I was so glad my girl friend had finally got back in touch and had not mentioned any lingering aftertaste about catching me entertaining a couple of women at my apartment last Sunday that I had readily agreed to be at the airport to collect her this Sunday afternoon when her flight kissed the tarmac at 4:15 PM. My problem was that I was going to be at the Dylan concert with Deejee from 1:00 until whenever.

Now that things were heating up with Deejee, I had more reason than ever to keep her in the dark about Rita. Since Rita was the bird in hand, I certainly needed to be guarded about Darlena Giordano. There were no guarantees that Deejee and I would ever share the yoke, but it was an absolute that Rita would drop me off at the nearest exit if she knew I was tangling with anyone else.

The situation was delicate, but not impossible. I was confident that I could keep the romantic tracks parallel and clear of intersection until my lust for Deejee either blossomed or blew over. In the meantime, I was sure I could resolve the double booking on Sunday afternoon if I put my wits into it. After all, I had nearly solved Detective Imanaka's crime for her. The more I reviewed all the angles, the more clear it was that Elizabeth Strennis had strangled Lyss Nelson to ensure that Tommy would stay accountable for the child on the way.

Tallying the take and weighing my dilemma carried me past 8:00 AM when I realized that I had another problem.

I opened my office door. Puke still clung to it. In the misty marine layer hovering over the parking lot this morning, the trash spilling out of the club from last night was gathering dewdrops. Where was Luis?

I went into the club where undisturbed detritus waited patiently for the custodian's attention. For the first time in my tenure at Liquid Avenue, Luis had not turned up for work.

That merited a call to the club manager. I had never had occasion to call him at home, so I had to look up Jimmy's number in his personnel file. There was no answer, so I went up the chain of command. I called Pensacola.

I could hear Dan's child crying in the background. "No Luis? That's not good. Let me get busy on this end. I think I know where Jimmy is."

With my boss taking charge, I was free to return to bookkeeping and scheming for Sunday. There was nobody else on the bill with Bob Dylan. That would mean the concert would not last more than two hours. I could be out of the Bowl by 3:00 and have more than enough time to reach the airport by 4:15. All I had to do was cook up a good excuse to persuade Deejee that the rest of our date should be postponed. Or, I could enlist someone to pick up Rita at the airport with apologies and explanations of urgent business that summoned me elsewhere.

Of course both of those alternatives presumed that Rita and Darlena were trusting and slow-witted, neither of which applied to either of them. I made a mental note to be more careful about making dates when I was smoking dope.

Shortly after 9:00, Jimmy let himself into the office.

"Dan told me about Luis. He's calling around to get us some temp help. Meanwhile, the Capras will be here in an hour to get the *cocina* started. So it looks like it's up to us to get the club cleaned up."

"Us? You mean me too?"

Jimmy allowed himself a tight smile. "What's the matter, Tony? You're not afraid to get your hands dirty, are you?"

It was an "all hands on deck" situation, so I rolled up my sleeves. Jimmy took the hose and attacked the parking lot. I went into the club, grabbed a 50-gallon trash bin, and scooped up the empty beer bottles. Luis always took these to the recycling center, but today I was in no mood for civic responsibility. Everything was going into the dumpster. With both of us bearing down on the project, it took Jimmy and I two hours to get the building cleaned up and mopped down. The affair taught me an important lesson: physical labor was not my strong suit. I was born to be an office worker.

I was still putting the bank deposit together at 11:30 when Dan came in. He took the other chair and sighed. "Bad news. Luis was arrested last night for Lyss Nelson's murder."

"What? Luis killed Lyss? I don't believe it!"

"Neither do I. Neither does his lawyer. I just talked to him."

"That's nuts. Sure, he was here. So was I. Why would he kill Lyss?"

"The lawyer said Luis Alvarado was wanted by the Mexican police for killing a prostitute in Tampico. That's where he comes from."

"Jesus. Really? What did he have against Lyss?"

"Remains to be seen. Shocking, isn't it? Just when I thought this business couldn't get any nastier. Alicia says I should sell the club and get into something more respectable."

I wasn't happy to hear that. I was also troubled by the disloyal flush of relief I felt. The cops had the killer, so I was no longer an object of their attention. I liked Luis, but it complicated my feelings about our custodian to imagine him wrapping a stocking around a woman's neck and choking her to death. I felt tainted working for a company that had a murderer on the payroll.

"I have a friend with a restaurant in Canoga Park. He wants to lease the vacant building next door, remodel it as a bar and run the two operations together. Alicia's been pressuring me to consider it."

We let the silence that crowded the office speak for itself. Dan's chair squeaked. After the two hours of physical toil, I was content to sit and let my batteries recharge.

"What the hell am I doing with my life, Tony? I used to love booking the bands, discovering young talent, giving a stage to the up and comers. I'd go to my office, get my neons going, drink coffee, smoke weed, and listen to demo tapes. Now I'm not even sure I like music anymore. I'm in the business of getting kids drunk. It's easy money, but it's indecent.

"I have a kid myself now. Last week I remembered something my dad told me when I was a kid. 'There's no honor that can't be corrupted,' he said. 'But there can always be decency. That doesn't cost anybody anything.'"

Dan's chair squeaked again. He stood. "Maybe I'll feel better if I go sit with my neons. I have to find us a new janitor. Let me know if you need anything."

Chapter Twenty-Three

Dan had spoken of "decency" and "respectability" in connection with what I was doing for a living. Rita had used vocabulary like this in her occasional expressions of disappointment with my latest employment situation.

I was obliged to think of it as a "situation" rather than as a career or even as a steady job. Dan Pensacola admitted that he was contemplating selling out. Where would that leave me? Out of work, is where. I had no ties to Tommy Nelson or Randy Garch, even if they had the means to buy out their partner and keep the nightclub going, which was doubtful. In the absence of Dan's good will, I'd be looking for another job. At least I knew for certain it would have to be an office job.

After the regrettable mistake that had cost me my position as editor of *Bargain Bin*, GSP's assistant warehouse manager Herb Worthen had introduced me to Robert Bellaire, a CPA friend of his wife Sen-Jie. Bellaire did the accounting and tax filing for Pensacola, who was shopping for a new bookkeeper after he learned that the previous one had got the company in dutch with every agency of government Liquid Avenue answered to.

Herb and I were in the warehouse with Kathleen O'Keenan, prepping the latest edition of *Golden Voices* for circulation. The subject was Goethe.

"*The Sufferings of Young Werther* was the most important literary work of the eighteenth century," Kathleen declared.

"I doubt that," I objected. "In 1776 alone, Adam Smith published his *Wealth of Nations* and Edward Gibbon rolled out the first volume of his *Decline and Fall of the Roman Empire.*"

"Your infatuation with English writers indicts your ignorance, philistine." she sniffed. "Read the book. It inspired everything from the French Revolution to the music of Beethoven."

"I thought the French Revolution took more from the writings of Voltaire and Rousseau than Goethe." If there were going to be arcane literary *bons mots* tossed into the salad, I wanted to get in my *deux centimes.*

"Thinking about writing isn't what you're paid for, is it, Bargain Boy?"

As soon as the door had closed on Kathleen's faux-Irish derriere, Herb snorted, "Raggedy Ann O'Keenan, poster child for PMS."

I sighed. "Have I ever mentioned how much I wish Jennifer would let me play musical chairs with our literary editor?"

Herb was wrapping shipping tape on a carton set on the workbench in front of him. "Did you read this one yet, Bargain Boy?" He plucked a magazine from the carton. Thumbing the pages, he found the text he was looking for and read aloud.

"'Romance' by Denver Lang.

"'You say it's snot
I say it's something else
You say it's cum
I say when did it arrive
You say your bed is made
I say you're talking sheet
You say your heart is torn
I say it's only love
You say it's only love
I say you're an asshole'"

Herb and I both laughed. "If that's literature," he said, "some of the love letters I wrote to my first girl friend should put me on the short list for the next Pulitzer."

"You think Jennifer Mitchell actually reads anything her editors tuck into our magazines?"

"She might check out the oily body beefcake ads in *Dynamic Look*."

I shook my head. "How does crap like this find its way into a literary magazine?"

"When the author is getting frisky with the editor. What? You didn't know?"

No. I didn't know. The indigestion I felt from swallowing that juicy morsel set the table for what was to follow.

Jimmy Nelson poked his head through the doorway. "Dan wants you to call him ASAP."

I got my boss at home. "Luis didn't do it." His voice was light with evident relief. "His lawyer just called. Luis was released this afternoon. He'll be back to work tomorrow."

"That's excellent news!" I chirped. I meant it. My admiration for Luis Alvarado, already secure, having seen him in action every morning for more than a year, had increased exponentially from having to do his job for just one day.

"It was a case of mistaken identity," Dan went on. "It was a different Luis Alvarado who skipped on the murder rap in Tampico."

"I'm not sure which is more amazing, that he was arrested so carelessly in the first place or that the Public Defender's office straightened it out so quickly."

"Public Defender? No court-appointed lawyer would have moved that fast. Luis has his own attorney."

Luis had his own lawyer? That was interesting.

"There's something else the lawyer got from Detective Imanaka, another mistaken identity. Tommy's wife was not Swiss."

"Really? But her passport . . ."

"Her passport is fake. Switzerland has never issued a passport to a Lyss Wattenwill."

"Does Tommy know that?"

"I don't know. I just told Jimmy and he didn't know. All I know for sure is Tommy got all his money from Lyss. He told me that he was broke when he met her."

I had plenty to chew on that afternoon when the Rabbit rowed me home, not even counting all the leftovers from last Sunday's splurge at the deli. For one, Detective Imanaka had not cracked the case after all. Luis was off the hook, but I was back on it. For another, it was fascinating that Lyss carried a false passport, but what did it mean? Was she in the USA illegally or was that moot after she married Tommy? If she had enough money to bankroll Tommy's investment in Liquid Avenue and, presumably, D'Amato Delicacies too, why would she need an ID as fake as the driver licenses the bouncers sold to underage kids at the club? Or had the police made another blunder, as they had done with Luis?

I was about to reach for my cedar cigar box when the phone jangled. Please let that be Rita, changing her flight plans!

"Trapp! I'm not working tonight. How about picking me up at Mel's? I've got some poop that will pickle your wiener."

Chapter Twenty-Four

When I pulled up across the street from Mel's, Deejee popped out of the doorway like a done slice of toast. She was alone.

"No Mary tonight?" I asked as she climbed into the Rabbit.

"Why? Do you dig her, you salivating dog?"

"She's pretty nice."

"Not as nice as you think. You keep your eyes on me, Buster Butt-wad. I'm all you need."

She stamped a wet kiss on my cheek, as if she were a customs agent validating my admission to her country. She wore her Chicago Bulls sweatshirt and that musky fragrance she favored. I favored it too.

Five minutes later we were sitting on my sofa. I was tubing marijuana stinkers for us "Did you hear about it?" I ventured. "Last night the police arrested Luis Alvarado for the murder of Lyss Nelson."

Deejee had got one of the stalks between her lips. "Who the fuck is Luis Alvarado?"

"Our janitor." I had forgotten. Deejee worked at night. Luis worked in the morning. She would have had no reason to meet or even hear of Luis. "They released him today. They mistook him for a guy from his hometown in Mexico with the same name."

"The cops are about as sharp as Occam's asshole. Whoever the janitor is, he didn't do it. I know who did."

I was holding a lungful of smoke. I coughed it out. "You do?"

A smug leer shaped her features. "You bet I do. I got her dead to rights. I told you I had ways of making her talk."

"Are you saying you think Elizabeth killed Lyss?"

"I know she did. Think about it. She was there that night and Tommy wasn't. She knew Lyss was doped up on codeine. She could have punched her time card and then climbed up into the storage loft without anyone noticing. If anyone found her up there, well's she's an employee—she could be getting supplies. She knew when Jimmy would close the club and go home. It all fits.

"Here's the clincher. She had a motive. Frankly, I'm surprised that you noticed. That moves you up some in my esteem."

Taking the joint from me, she leaned over and kissed my cheek again. It was nice that Deejee's esteem came with rewards.

"You were right. Strennis is baking a baby. Nobody knows about it except Tommy. And somehow you. And now me. But this is the precious part. It's not Tommy's."

"That's something worth knowing!" I was very amused. "But how does that make a motive for Elizabeth to murder Lyss?"

"That's the best part. Tommy doesn't know it's not his."

I began to see Elizabeth Strennis in a new light, an iron blue hue, much like the neon in the Liquid Avenue sign behind the bar. What a schemer! She and Tommy absolutely deserved each other.

"So," I said, knitting up stitches, "Elizabeth is twisting Tommy's prick about her pregnancy, but lying about who put her in a family way. To duck the responsibility he believes he has, Tommy reminds Elizabeth that he's married and tries to talk her into terminating the pregnancy. Since that would relinquish her hold on Tommy, Elizabeth terminates Lyss instead. You're right. It all fits."

We celebrated our cracking the case with puffs on a fresh sin cylinder. I wondered how I was going to bring these new facts to Detective Imanaka with enough proof to get her aimed in the right direction, which was anywhere but me.

"How did you manage to get Elizabeth to tell you all this? It's easy to see why she'd want to keep a lid on it."

"Female insight. Guys don't have it, so you wouldn't know. I always thought Strennis was a lonely girl. Why else would she be hanging like a Christmas tree ornament on a stiff like Tommy Nelson? Now she's in a predicament and she's got no one to talk to about it. I caught her in the women's can and got her to trust me by "confiding" that I was preggerated. I even winked out a few teardrops. She fell for it so fast I almost hollered 'timber!'

"It was pathetic. She spilled her guts to me. Now she thinks I'm her pal."

"Did she ask who knocked you up?"

"Yeah. I said you did."

"Me?" I felt dizzy. Of course, I was sucking weed.

"You're a natural for the honor. I didn't have to put much effort into it to sell it."

That was encouraging. Wasn't it? "How do we go about getting the police on to her?"

"We? That's up to you. I did my part. And you can stop bogarting that joint."

It was my turn to drag new facts into the light. "I learned something interesting today too. Lyss Nelson's passport is fake. She's not Swiss."

"Swiss. Miss. Take a piss. What difference does it make? She was a gravely peculiar chick. It was weird the way she watched Tommy and Strennis be together in the club and never said anything about it. Creepy. It's too bad she's dead, but my guess is, she won't be missed."

For the past week, I had been involuntarily involved with Lyss Nelson's death. Now I found myself curious about her life. She was not from Switzerland, as she would have people believe. She married Tommy for reasons not clear to anyone. She had money. She made no fuss when her husband openly flaunted other women in front of her. Of all the intoxicated patrons careening about in Liquid Avenue last Thursday, she had been the one taken down by a homicidal maniac like a lame gazelle that strayed too far from the herd in the heartless savannah.

Who was Lyss Nelson?

I would have liked to hear Deejee's thoughts on the subject, but she was standing, placing both her hands on my shoulders, and moving her head in as if she were about to tear into my neck with fangs. She put her generous lips on my cheek for the third time, breathing heavily.

"Listen, Buster," she whispered. "We have business in there." She indicated "there"—my bedroom—with a toss of her head in that direction. "Give me a minute to freshen up."

Well, now! Finally. Getting down to "business." Speculations about Lyss Nelson evaporated like steam from a leaky teakettle. Deejee pulled shut the plastic accordion-folding door separating my bedroom and bathroom from the rest of the apartment as she disappeared into the room.

Certainly she could have a minute to freshen up. She could have as long as she liked. In fact, she apparently needed more than a minute. After ten minutes had crawled by, I wondered how much freshening up she needed. After fifteen, I worried that something was wrong.

I put my ear to the accordion door. "Deej?" I inquired softly. "Are you fresh yet?" No answer. "Is everything okay?"

I gently slid the door open a few inches to peek. The figure in denims and sweatshirt lay sprawled on the bed. I pushed the door open a foot for a fuller view.

Deejee was snoring.

Chapter Twenty-Five

Shortly after 2:00 AM my eyes opened. I was curled on my sofa. The accordion door was still closed. I slid it open enough for my passage to the bathroom. I had to get ready for work.

Deejee was still slumbering. There was no need to wake her. I took care of my shaving and toiletries, helped myself to a quick shower, and toweled off. On leaving the bathroom, I smelled that Deejee was up. The fragrance came from the living room area where she was parked on the sofa, dragging down a reefer and sipping a Vernor's ginger ale she had liberated from my fridge.

"Good morning, Camper!" she sang merrily.

"Howdy Doody, Sleeping Beauty." I took a seat beside her.

"Care to experiment with illicit narcotics?" She waved the smoking joint at me.

"Love to, but duty calls. I need to be down to the club in about an hour."

"Christ on a stick! You do this every day?"

"With no time off for good behavior," I sighed. "I usually hit Carrow's for breakfast. Care to join me?"

If Jean was surprised to see me with company at this hour, it was impossible to tell. The heavy mascara set her facial expressions in plaster like a player in a Japanese Noh drama.

She brought me sausage and scrambled. For Deejee, she delivered a tall stack of flapjacks and six rashers of crispy bacon.

"You are welcome to stay at my place if you like, unless you'd like me to drop you off somewhere."

"Trapp, are you delirious? I want to go to the club with you. The murder was a week ago. I can't wait to see if Strennis left another stiff in the sawdust. You know how it is with these killers. As soon as they get the taste of human blood, they go on a spree."

I had no idea how it was with "these killers", but, if Elizabeth was as guilty as we thought she was, another body on the floor would flush the motive we had assigned her for killing Lyss right down the commode. We would be back to the hypothesis of a psychopath lurking in the storage loft for a random victim.

Her oversized handbag slung over her shoulder, Deejee tagged along with me for the morning drill: jangle the keys, open the office, warm up the overheads, look for messages, grab the canvas bag, proceed to the club. While I started a pot of coffee in the *cocina*, Deejee searched the premises for corpses. She was distinctly disappointed that there were none. Everything was normal.

She followed me into the walk-in cooler to watch me fuss with the safe. Seeing the contents, she cooed, "Money. Lots of money."

I didn't like the way she said it, as if the money was an object of desire rather than the lifeblood of Liquid Avenue that nourished its owners, its employees, and all the creditors that had a prior claim on it. The cold got to her, so Deejee backed out of the cooler while I loaded the collection bag. As I went out the door, a flash went off in my face, followed by the whine of the Polaroid mechanism.

"Gotcha!" She giggled. "This one will go into my Favorite Burglar collection."

Everything was normal, so it was no surprise that Carla greeted me in the parking lot when we pushed through the service door exit.

"Hi, Anthony."

"Good morning, Carla. Coffee for you?"

"Sure. Sounds good."

The three of us made an about face, re-entered the club and swung into the kitchen.

"Got enough sugar packets there, sweetheart?" Deejee remarked sourly as she watched Carla stuff the pockets of her woefully thin jacket.

"I . . . I'm sorry," Carla stammered, hanging her head. "These will be my breakfast later."

To spare Carla the embarrassment of asking, I thumbed a twenty out of my wallet and passed it to her discreetly as we went back into the parking lot.

"Thanks, Anthony. You're a prince." Carla faded back into the shadows.

"Thanks, Anthony. You're a prince." Back in the office, Deejee mocked Carla's voice. "What the fuck was that all about? If you're doing hookers, Trapp, I would expect you to do better than that."

"It's just alms-giving, Deej. One of the Five Pillars of Islam. I feel sorry for her."

"Islam? What are you, a camel fucker? I don't feel sorry for her. Whores deserve what they get. I hope to Christ you've never let her touch you. God only knows what's crawling around on her body. Ugh!"

Observing my preparations to count money she wouldn't see again until her next paycheck, Deejee quickly succumbed to boredom. "Listen, Trapp. How about giving me a ride over to Mary's?"

I glanced at the wall clock. It was 4:35 AM. "Okay. No problem. Are you sure it isn't too early?"

"Didn't I tell you Mary isn't as nice as you think?"

I delivered Darlena to gentrified Sutton Avenue, at this hour as quiet and peaceful as a graveyard. Sliding out of the Rabbit, she called back over her shoulder, "Catch up with you later, Trapp."

No sign of bittersweet separation there. I didn't even get my cheek pecked. I was relieved to have deposited Deejee safely, though, because I needed no distractions when I toted Liquid Avenue's take from the previous night. It was not until I pulled into an empty space in the public parking lot on Anacapa Street that I remembered that Deejee and I had neglected to make arrangements for the Sunday concert at the County Bowl.

In our own two-space parking lot, Luis was busy with his hose. I was happy to see him.

"¡*Buenos dias, mi amigo!*" I called out as I approached.

Luis waved. I put out my hand for a "welcome back" shake, which surprised him and made an awkward moment as he shifted the hose to his left hand and pulled the sturdy glove off his right paw so he could complete the salutation.

"*Buenos dias, Señor* Tony," the head in the Los Angeles Dodgers baseball cap nodded. In the shadow under the bill of his cap his face was indistinct, but his handshake was firm.

I wanted to tell Luis how very much more I appreciated him after having to do his job for one day, but my Spanish was not up to the task. Naturally, I knew how much he was being paid. I wanted to tell him it was not enough, but I didn't have the words for that either.

Chapter Twenty-Six

I felt no special anxiety that Sunday was just around the bend and I had booked two simultaneous dates on that day with women I wanted to keep clear of each other. Darlena Giordano was spontaneous to the nth degree. I reckoned that I could work with that. Rita was the opposite of freewheeling. I could rely on that too. When we made an arrangement together, it stayed made. She would be stepping off the plane at Santa Barbara Airport at 4:15 PM. She expected me to be there. I would be.

Throughout the day, I called Deejee three times at the number she had given for her grandmother's place, her temporary habitat. No answer. I could always catch her tonight at the club. On Fridays, all the cocktail waitresses were on duty.

To prepare for the weekend, Jimmy had placed beer and liquor orders that required most of Liquid Avenue's proceeds from Thursday night—the "lots of money" Deejee had admired so much—for cashier's checks. There was a very good reason for the inventory buildup indicated on my calendar. Tomorrow, Saturday, was October 31st, Halloween.

I had been working for Nelson, Garch and Pensacola for three months when Halloween rolled around last year on a Thursday night. I had not made an appearance at the club but I remembered how surprised and delighted I'd been to record the volume of business on the following morning. Halloween at Liquid Avenue on a Saturday night promised to be wild.

I was convinced that Elizabeth Strennis had murdered Lyss Nelson. I had no proof, so I had to allow that I might be wrong. If it wasn't Strennis, would the real killer visit the scene of the crime Saturday night when all the employees and most of the patrons would be in costumes?

Was it true that a murderer feels compulsion to revisit the scene or was that a convenient myth fostered by mystery writers? Did Sherlock Holmes have something to say about that? At some point between my locking up the office for the day and the Rabbit's delivery of me to West Valerio, I decided that I would hit the club Saturday night. I might even wear a costume.

After dinner, I felt bleary. My couch made an uncomfortable bed, so I had not had satisfactory sleep last night while Deejee was sawing logs in my bedroom. I wanted to hop down to the club to make a concrete plan with her for the Sunday concert. My eyelids kept trying to close the shutters.

I was startled awake by a soft rapping on my door. Peeking through my blinds I made out a tall dark man with a long face wearing a knee length gray coat. I didn't know him. I cracked my door.

"Yes?"

"Hi. You're Tony Trapp, right? We met at my sister's place last week. I was playing pool with your friend Darlena. My name's Pete Hardy."

"Oh, right." I pulled the door open. We shook hands. "What can I do for you?"

"It's about my other sister, Mary. No one seems to know where she is. I was hoping you might."

I invited him in, took his coat, a fine, smooth camel hair with black collar and lapels, and laid it on my bedspread, which was like resting a Picasso on a velvet portrait of Elvis.

"Could I set you up with a Vernor's?"

"You remembered! Yes, I'd be much obliged."

Pete eased himself on to the sofa. I pulled my desk chair around so we could palaver face to face.

"I'm sorry to impose," Pete began. "I just saw Darlena at the nightclub. She gave me your name, so you were easy to find. Mary spoke highly of you. I was hoping you might have seen her today."

"Mary's a doll. She likes my music library. The only times I've ever seen her she's been with Deejee, that is, Darlena. The last time I saw Mary was Monday night, when I gave her a ride home from IV. This morning Deejee had me drive her over to your sister's place on Sutton. I didn't see Mary, but it was pretty early."

"Apparently Mary and Darlena went somewhere this morning with this Lloyd character. Nobody is pushing the panic button yet, but Mary didn't show for a job interview this afternoon and, as I said, no one knows where she is. I wouldn't dream of pestering you about this if it hadn't been for that murder at your nightclub last week. It's got everybody a little tense. And, of course, Mary has her special problems."

"Problems? What sort of problems?"

Pete tapped his temple with his index finger. "The mental sort. Her behavior is mostly normal, but she gets dissociative sometimes, has trouble distinguishing the real from the imaginary. She has a tendency to lose things, to forget where she is, to wander into unfamiliar places and not know what to do, so she has to call for help." He sighed deeply and sipped his ginger ale. "Her most unnerving trait is her inability to judge people. She trusts and believes in everyone she meets. She has no mechanism to differentiate truth from lies. It's easy for unscrupulous people to take advantage of her."

Pete was staring at me as he said this. Guilt seeped into my thoughts. Had I taken advantage of Mary in some way? Had Deejee?

"This Lloyd guy gives me pause," Pete continued. "Mary likes him because he's a musician of some kind. I think he plays the trumpet. Anyway, I don't approve of him. Mary's an adult, so I can't quarantine her friends. Anne is more protective. She's the oldest of the three of us, so she's been Mary's unofficial guardian. But Anne can only guide Mary; she can't control her. She agrees with me that Lloyd is bad news, but neither of us can stop Mary from seeing him."

Or Deejee, I thought. Was she aware that Mary had "special problems"?

"I'm sorry I can't be more helpful, Pete. As I say, I only know Mary through Darlena, and I've only known Darlena for about a month."

The silence seemed to indicate that our conversation was at an end. Pete was draining his bottle of ginger ale, when something he had said registered.

"If you don't mind my asking, what kind of job was Mary going to interview for? It sounds like her problems would make it difficult for her to function in an ordinary work environment."

"True." Pete seemed pleased that I had been paying attention. "Mary couldn't possibly be a nine-to-fiver in a regular workplace. But she does have one extraordinary talent. She's a brilliant pianist. Anne set up an interview for her in Hope Ranch to tutor a gifted kid.

"Of all the things in the world Mary might do well, it would be private piano lessons. She herself was extremely talented as a child. Anne and I both had music lessons when we were youngsters, but Mary devoured music like a hungry wolf. Of the three of us, she was the brightest star, and until she was sixteen, Mary was the one who had the best prospects for a great future. She won several music competitions and she had a scholarship in the works for the Berklee College in Boston.

"In the summer after she turned sixteen, Mary attended the Interlochen Music Camp in northern Michigan. She came home changed. She was never the same again. Nobody knows what happened while she was there, but that's when the problems started."

Chapter Twenty-Seven

Pete's tale had me on the edge of my seat. I slid off the chair and encouraged my guest to continue by pulling two more bottles of Vernor's from my fridge.

"She's had professional help, of course. Psychiatrists, therapy, medications. As to the cause of her difficulties, whether they're a result of trauma or hereditary predisposition, there is only speculation. Her prognosis is cloudy. Anne is hopeful that, under the right circumstances, Mary will eventually center herself. Personally, I'm not so optimistic. I think she's getting worse. She's no danger to herself or others, not suicidal or depressive, so hospitalization is out of the question. She lives with Anne; sometimes she stays with me. It's no problem. We can afford it. My feeling is, Anne and I will be taking care of Mary for the rest of her life.

"That's why I'm here. It's kind of my job to make sure Mary doesn't drift into a dangerous situation. So, again, I apologize for imposing on you."

"What did Darlena say they were up to this morning?" There was no need to tell Pete that I was far more curious about what Deejee did during the daytime than anything Mary did.

"She said Lloyd drove them to an apartment in Isla Vista and that she left Mary there and caught a ride back to town this afternoon."

Trigo Road. That's where I had picked them up on Monday night.

"I don't know who lives there, but I believe I know exactly where that apartment is."

"Do you?" Pete leaned forward in earnest. "You know, Tony, I hate to ask you this, 'cause I've already put you out enough. Do you think you could take me to that apartment?"

Pete Hardy was the owner of the Volvo I had noticed in the driveway on Sutton Avenue, parked now in my lot. We climbed aboard and set sail for Isla Vista.

The rush hour was long past so traffic on the 101 Freeway was reasonably sparse for a Friday night. By way of conversation I asked, "Do you mind if I ask what you do for a living?"

"Not at all. I'm a lawyer. I work for the County District Attorney's Office. Anne's an attorney too and so is her husband." Pete grinned. "If you ever need a divorce lawyer, Anne is as good as they get."

I already had a divorce under my belt and a peptic ulcer to prove it. Too bad I didn't know Anne then. I hoped Pete didn't notice that I swallowed nervously and the collar on my polo neck shirt seemed to tighten. I was, as far as I knew, a principal suspect in a murder investigation and I was riding shotgun with a lawyer from the county prosecutor's team. Was this story about his sister bunkum? Was Pete really investigating me?

I ventured, "Do you happen to know Detective Imanaka of the SBPD?"

"Yes, I know Rachel. She's a first-rate detective. She's a swell person too. Some of the guys at the office have a bit of a crush on her." He favored me with another smile. "I would too if she wasn't engaged."

I pressed. "Are you involved with the Lyss Nelson investigation?"

"Good heavens, no! The police do the detective work. We prepare the cases for prosecution after indictments have been rendered by the court, based on evidence presented by the police." He laughed. "I'm not Perry Mason. This, what we're doing right now, is as close as I get to detective work. For something as serious as murder, I wouldn't know where to begin."

I relaxed. "Eliminate the obvious, I guess. Isn't that what Sherlock Holmes said?"

"The 'impossible'. That's what Sherlock Holmes said. 'When you have eliminated the impossible, whatever remains, however improbable, must be the truth'."

"Oh, yeah. That was it."

Pete was proving to be a useful resource for my own "investigation" of the murder. It would do me no damage to have a friendly face in the District Attorney's Office if Detective Imanaka decided I was the best suspect she had. I had another question for my new associate.

"Do you or the police work with a female detective named Chin?"

"You have an inquiring mind, Tony. Are you sure you're not a lawyer?" Pete smirked to assure me that he was jesting. "No. I don't know any investigators named 'Chin'. Why do you ask?"

"A waitress at Carrow's told me a woman by that name was asking about me."

"Why presume this Chin woman is a detective? Maybe she just likes the cut of your jib."

Isla Vista perches on a mesa overlooking the Santa Barbara Channel with steep cliffs pitching down to tar-laced beaches. About 70% of the population are students at the University of California. The town's twelve transverse streets end where the campus begins and melt into pathways through the long pine and redwood fence that serves as a line of demarcation.

We parked in a lot behind the apartment on Trigo Road. It was cold on this late October evening. I wore a heavy jacket. Pete had his camel hair coat. On Monday night I had watched Deejee and Mary pass through a door on the second floor of the building. Pete and I climbed a flight of pebbled concrete stairs with iron railings. I pointed to the door. Pete knocked on it.

Muffled music thundered behind the door. When no one responded to Pete's knocking with his knuckles, he made of hammer of his fist and pounded. The door cracked open, patchouli incense and deafening music floated out, and I was transported back in time to my own undergrad days when I too had an apartment in IV. Behind the fellow who opened the door I could see a tie-dyed sheet pinned to a wall.

The apartment's resident was among the 30% of the population not enrolled at UCSB. He was many semesters too old to be a student. If he was a university professor or an employee, standards had declined since my days here.

Pete came to the point. "You're Lloyd, right?"

"I know you?" The puffy, grizzled face was truculent.

"We've met. I'm looking for my sister Mary. She was here this morning."

It wasn't clear whether the door was propping up Lloyd or vice versa. "I don't know any Mary." He tried to close the door, but Pete's foot was over the threshold.

"Yes, you do. She was here today with a white girl named Darlena."

"Or Deejee," I added helpfully.

Lloyd was not in a helpful mood. "Go fuck yourself."

He tried to push the door shut again, but Pete's foot still blocked it. "All right," Pete said calmly "Let's do it this way." He reached into his coat pocket and withdrew a slim leather wallet. He let the fold drop open and displayed it for Lloyd. "We can chat here or we can go downtown. Your decision."

"You guys are cops?" Lloyd grew more alert. "The fuck didn't you say so?"

"One last time," Pete drawled. "Where's Mary?"

Chapter Twenty-Eight

"I thought you were a pimp in that coat, brother."

We stood in Lloyd's apartment. He had backed down the volume on the music. I recognized it now. Eddie Harris. *Silver Cycles*. Good one.

"I'm not your brother. I'm Mary's brother. The sooner you tell me where she is, the sooner we'll be out of this shithole."

"Okay, okay. You don't need to be a hard ass."

I was looking around Lloyd's digs. Pete's characterization was accurate. There were more tie-dyed sheets on the other walls. Flimsy cotton batiks draped over whatever it was that served as a couch. A badly lacquered telephone company cable spool served as a table, littered with empty wine bottles and pizza boxes. The place smelled like dead cigarettes and butter gone bad. A nicely framed eight by ten glossy photo of Dizzy Gillespie, with the iconic bent horn and blowfish cheeks, looked out of place leaning against a wall on the floor next to Lloyd's record player. I went to it to have a closer look.

"She left here early this afternoon." Lloyd was plainly eager to have us on our way. "Said she had an audition. I thought she was coming back, but she didn't."

"I don't suppose you know where that audition was?"

"The hell you think it was?" Lloyd pointed at one of the walls. In any other part of town his gesture would have been meaningless, but in IV it was perfectly clear. He was pointing not at the wall, but at what lay beyond the wall—the University of California at Santa Barbara.

Before we left, I had a question for Lloyd. I indicated the framed photo on the floor. "That photo is autographed with a personal greeting for you. You've met Dizzy Gillespie?"

"Hell, yes, I know Dizz. We did some sessions together in Chicago in the '60s. He gimme that when he played here at Campbell Hall."

It would have been an easy walk to the campus from Lloyd's place, but it was cold and we weren't planning on coming back, so we went in the Volvo.

"You're a cop?" I asked Pete as he tooled the car through the kiosks guarding the entrance to the University.

"No."

Pete reached into his coat and retrieved his wallet for me to examine. His mug shot sat in it along with a formal-looking card with the heading "County of Santa Barbara—Office of the District Attorney".

"That's not a badge. It's just my ID. Gets me past the bailiffs at the Court House. That was the first time I ever used it to intimidate a witness."

Something Lloyd had said had got me pushing beads on the abacus in my head. "How long has your sister been friendly with Lloyd?"

Pete considered it. "About a month now, I guess."

About the same time Deejee had been friendly with me. Two plus two equals four. "Did Lloyd just tell us he was from Chicago?"

"He said he did some sessions in Chicago in the '60s."

"Deejee is from Chicago."

"Lots of people are from Chicago. But I get your drift. You are thinking it was your friend Darlena who got Mary mixed up with Lloyd. That's interesting, but not necessarily informative. The truth is I don't care how or why Mary met Lloyd. But I'll do some background on him. For my sister's sake, I need to know if he's a dangerous character."

UCSB is a tidy campus. We could canvass it if we could get a compass heading. We began at Campbell Hall, the auditorium for large audience lectures and musical presentations.

"I get it now," Pete mused. "Mary knew she had an interview this afternoon. At some point, she got confused and believed it to be an audition or a recital. God knows, she's had enough of those in her life. This looks like a good place to start."

The auditorium was closed this evening. A glass encased bulletin board outside the building posted upcoming events in white plastic letters slotted into a black plastic frame. Nothing announced any sort of recital, audition or performance today. We marched past Storke Plaza and its carillon tower toward the UCen building, a place that housed the campus bookstore and cafeteria and fairly buzzed with students strolling about in pairs or lounging in chairs reading or scribbling in notebooks. Cork bulletin boards blazed with flyers for group meetings or other events, but nothing specifically musical.

"Maybe," Pete suggested, "we should consult one of the natives."

In a corner of the UCen foyer, a fellow was playing a guitar in Spanish classical style. He wasn't bad. We waited respectfully for him to finish.

"Very nice." Pete smiled his appreciation. "You must be a music major."

"Business Admin, dude. My dad would never pay hard bucks for me to be farting around with the arts."

"Well, you're very talented. I envy you. If you were a music major, where would you be taking your classes?"

Since I myself had been a student here, I ought to have thought of that. Retracing our steps through Storke Plaza, we found the Music and Mathematics Departments, housed in the same building they had been when I haunted this campus.

We passed along a corridor. Closed doors featured large windows with crosshatched wire buried in the glazing that made aquariums of the classrooms. Some of the rooms were dark and empty, others lit and alive with students practicing their instruments solo or in combos. One of the classrooms was much larger than the others and we could see half a dozen people standing around a piano.

"Here we go," Pete said, pulling open the door.

The tune was intimately familiar. Mary sat on a bench in front of a baby grand, entertaining her listeners with "Begin the Beguine". We took a seat among the empty desks next to a woman in a rose turtleneck cardigan who was obviously closer to my generation than any of the admirers clustered around the piano.

"This lady is incredible," she reported happily. "You should have heard her Rachmaninoff. I need the sheet in front of me to play it, but she just teased it out of her head. I was told she's been here all day, just playing for anybody who wanders in. I can't believe I've never met her before. I'm waiting to ask her if there's any chance she might be available to mentor my better students."

Pete nodded. "I think I can help you with that."

On our way back to the Volvo with Mary in tow, Pete chuckled. "I just thought of something else Sherlock Holmes said. He said, 'Life is infinitely stranger than anything which the mind of man could invent'."

Chapter Twenty-Nine

Pete Hardy had not made much of it, but I couldn't let it go. Was the disreputable Lloyd Mary's friend or Deejee's?

Suppose Deejee and Lloyd were the pals and their association went back to Chicago? There was nothing sinister about that, but it reminded me that I knew little or nothing about Darlena Giordano, about what her life had been like before we met or why she was in Santa Barbara in the first place. Could Lloyd be the reason she was here?

The best way to find out would be to ask. I had not made it to the club last night, as I had planned. The Adventure of the Missing Pianist had consumed all of my evening that I could spare. This morning I had my hands full counting Friday's night's Liquid Avenue business and doing my share to get the club ready for tonight, Halloween.

By noon, I had the money wrapped and ready for deposit. Jimmy interrupted me.

"Hey, Tony. Got a minute? I need a hand in the storage loft."

He was after the Halloween decorations—cardboard skeletons, plastic jack o' lanterns, rolls of black and orange crepe paper—packed away with the cheap Christmas and Fourth of July gear the club mustered out for holiday cheer. I clambered up the ladder, found the appropriate boxes and dropped them down to Jimmy, waiting in the hallway under the rungs.

To me there was no cheer to be found in the loft. Last week a killer had crouched here among the flimsy containers, the club junk, and the miscellaneous rubbish to plot the murder of Lyss Nelson. I pictured Elizabeth climbing the precarious ladder in her stiletto pumps and squatting down among the dust-covered cartons in her figure-hugging threads, waiting patiently and silently for everyone to leave. How did she keep all her tinkling bracelets quiet?

Why would she have needed to make a blind for herself at all? Lyss was a sleeping duck. Elizabeth, like all the other "reasons" that fetched me to the safe at unholy hours, could let herself in and out of the building any time she wanted. Why would she risk waiting in the loft when she could simply come back after Jimmy closed the club?

The police had found evidence in the loft that proved the killer had waited there. What evidence? Naturally, they had never disclosed what they had found to the public. They would be saving that for the trial as soon as they caught the murderer.

It didn't make sense that Elizabeth Strennis would coop in the storage loft. When Deejee and I had put our heads together to solve the case, we had concentrated on Elizabeth's imputed motive. It seemed damning at the time, but in the light of day, our prime suspect looked much less likely for the rap.

I was eager to discuss this with my crime-solving partner so that she could present some rationalization that had escaped me. I had other pressing matters on the tip of my tongue as well. Did she know Lloyd from her days in Chicago? Was it she who introduced Lloyd to Mary? Was she aware that Mary had mental health problems? Exactly when and where were we to meet before tomorrow's concert at the County Bowl?

I was eager enough to give Deejee a call. There was no answer.

On my return from the bank, I checked in with Jimmy to make sure he had everything he needed. The *Cocina Habana* was serving lunch. Margarito and Elena too had stocked up on supplies in anticipation of a busy night. One of their vendors had parked his truck in the lot behind the club. Luis, leaning on his push broom, was chatting with the driver.

Pursuing chat, I tried Deejee's number again. A lady with a cracked voice gave me a "Hello?"

I should not have been surprised. I knew Deejee bunked at her grandmother's place, but this was the first time I had spoken with her. "Good afternoon. May I speak with Darlena, please? This is her friend Anthony."

"Darlena?" The voice stiffened. "There's no Darlena here. You must have the wrong number."

I gave the voice the number I had dialed. She agreed that I had dialed correctly but insisted that it was a wrong number.

"Or Deejee?" I asked. "She goes by 'Deejee, too."

"There's no one here by that name either. You have the wrong number."

So now, when I succeeded in connecting with Deejee, we would have something else to chat about.

My interest in visiting Liquid Avenue on Halloween Night had moved up the need meter from curiosity to necessity. A costume would be appropriate for the occasion. Fortunately, I had one.

I have little patience for the labors involved in creating a costume and still less imagination. Years ago I had settled on a Halloween outfit that was cheap and easy. I kept it in a shoebox. I retrieved the box from my closet and dumped its contents on my bed.

I shook out the zebra-striped referee's jersey. A little ironing would straighten it. There was a whistle on a lanyard, a pair of dark sunglasses, and a telescoping white cane with a red tip. I had sneakers and black trousers. With less than ten minutes of prep and only three props, I was a blind referee.

At 8:30 PM—past my bedtime again, but it was a special occasion—the Rabbit conveyed me to the club. The public parking lot on Anancapa Street was full, so I had to hook left on East Haley and cruise all the way to Garden Street to find an available nook for the car. I could hear the music thumping within a block of the nightclub. A long line of zombies, vampires, assorted monsters, and celebrity look-alikes snaked up Anacapa, shuffling forward toward the entrance. The bouncers would not be selling any fake ID's tonight.

Naturally, I circumvented the line and went to the service door. Peanut, appropriate in the uniform of a London bobby, stood watch at the service door to prevent customers already in the club from letting their friends in through the back.

"Hey, Tony. Funny getup. I can tell it's you though. Go on in."

For tonight's special Halloween, Dan had stretched the purse to hire a name band. The disco ball spinning over the packed dance floor splashed polychromatic spots on Dread Zeppelin, a reggae ensemble fronted by an Elvis Presley impersonator that covered Led Zeppelin songs. They were excellent.

It was hopeless looking for Deejee in this mob, especially since I had no idea how she might be costumed. I made my way through the crowd and slipped in behind the bar where Jimmy Nelson was keeping an eye on everything.

"So what's Deejee wearing tonight?"

"What do you think?" Jimmy huffed. "She's dressed like a hooker, like every third chick in the place."

That description didn't much narrow the field. I doubted that Deejee would have adopted Carla the hooker's drapery. I was on the lookout for an exaggerated bosom bearing a drink tray.

She found me first. "Trapp!" Her shriek over the din pounded my eardrum. "Trust you to dress like a rules enforcer!"

"Deej! You look gorgeous. Listen. Can we talk for a minute?"

"Are you fucking delirious? No, we can't talk now. Look around. I'm working my ass off."

She grabbed the whistle lanyard around my neck and pulled my face down to hers. Full lips with peach flavored lipstick smacked my mouth.

"Meet me in front of the Bowl tomorrow at one. We'll have all day to talk."

Chapter Thirty

According to the rat-tail clock in my office, it was 12:15 PM and I was still counting the money from Liquid Avenue's booming Halloween night. I was to meet Deejee at the County Bowl in forty-five minutes. I would have to finish the tally later.

There was no need to prepare a bank deposit on Sunday. I scooped the piles of currency into my canvas collection bag, locked up, and headed for the Rabbit, parked across the street. Luis was still cleaning up our own lot. Margarito Capra was assisting him. They waved greetings at me, standing ankle deep in debris.

I rushed home, shoved the bag under my bed, visited the bathroom, grabbed a sweater and a baseball cap, and dashed off to my date with Deejee and Bob Dylan at the Bowl.

I was able to park on East Anapamu Street, step lively along the sidewalk through the cedar canopy and reach the box office by 12:50.

The concert was scheduled to begin at 1:00 PM. I hate to be late for anything, especially if I have bought tickets for it. I thought that Deejee's instruction for me to meet her "in front of the Bowl at one" was rather vague, to say nothing of shaving the time a bit too fine for a sold out event such as this. On the other hand, what was the hurry? We had reserved seats, Deejee liked to be spontaneous about things, and concerts didn't always start on the dot. As much as I enjoyed the music of Bob Dylan, the point of this exercise was to spend quality time with Deejee.

That time was going to be abbreviated anyway, because I would have to cut away by 3:30 or so to arrive on time for my other date. Rita would be strolling into the reception area at Santa Barbara Airport shortly after 4:15 PM. I had yet to devise a credible excuse to slip away from Deejee without tipping my hand about my girl friend. I would have to develop some spontaneity of my own.

There were still concert attendees milling around the box office, but the majority of the audience were already in their seats. The amphitheater itself was another quarter mile into the wooded hollow whose mouth opens at the corner where East Anapamu bends into Milpas Street. Deejee was nowhere in sight.

I had learned that punctuality was a virtue not embraced by Darlena Giordano. She came and went as she pleased. There was no reason for me to have a knot in my stomach as I peered anxiously into the faces of the people wending their way past me along the pathway that led into the forested ravine and the concrete auditorium open to the sky carved into the canyon at the end of it. Deejee would be here any minute.

By 1:30 PM I had stopped believing that. The concert had begun half an hour ago. The music was muffled but loud as it rolled out of the hills. I and a couple of security guys were the only ones still hanging around the box office. If they had found me suspicious at first, their fears had melted into amusement at the sight of me checking my watch every thirty seconds and staring into every car cruising around the bend. My situation was painfully obvious. I had been stood up.

Something was wrong. If I had possessed my ticket, I could have marched up to the amphitheater and see if Deejee was already in her seat. But she had taken the tickets. There was simply no way for me to check. I had inquired at the box office earlier before they closed. No one had had left anything there for me.

What should I do? It was not impossible that Deejee had had a very long night at the club and was still hibernating under the influence of a sleeping tablet. Or, for the same reason, she might be under the weather and unable to answer the bell.

I trudged back to the Rabbit and aimed it at Liquid Avenue.

The *cocina* was open, so I mooched a *café Cubano* from Elena and retreated to my office to ruminate. I could call her, but the number Deejee had provided had met sharp refutation yesterday. Now that I considered it, I had called that number in vain many times, but Deejee had actually answered it once, on the afternoon after the murder when I had invited her to steer clear of the club and hang out with me. Why did her grandmother—or whomever that was who had picked up the receiver—deny knowing Darlena or Deejee? What had she said exactly? "There is nobody here by that name. You have the wrong number."

She had said there was no one there *by that name*. Did she know Deejee by a different name?

I pulled Darlena Giordano's personnel file from the cabinet and laid it on my desk. It contained the minimum requisites for employment by Nelson, Garch and Pensacola: an employment application, photocopies of a driver's license issued to Deejee by the State of Illinois, her Social Security card, and the Form I-9 for the IRS that testified to her US citizenship.

There was an address on the employment app. It was the same as the Chicago address on her driver's license. Under the "In case of emergency" heading, however, there was a name, a local address, and a telephone number. The number was the one I had been calling; the address was on Arbolado Road; the name was Doris Chittle.

It was just past 2:00 PM. I knew where Arbolado Road was. I thought I might have better luck if I tried talking to Doris Chittle face-to-face.

Arbolado Road was a swell place to live. It squatted near the top of the ridge known as the Riviera that overlooks downtown

Santa Barbara, Stearn's Wharf, and the distant Mesa, and bleeds backward into Montecito. The Rabbit climbed the Alameda Padre Serra, a scenic road that winds along the spine atop the foothill. Turning right at Arbolado, the address was easy to spot. I pulled the Rabbit into a graveled parkway in front of the house.

The woman who answered my knock was younger than I expected, not yet sixty, I would judge. Her salt and pepper hair was short, topping a no-nonsense face, lined with life experience that looked hard-won. She wore a lavender pullover sweater and olive denim trousers. Two dark brown Rottweiler dogs attended her, looking calm, but alert.

She appraised me. "Let me guess," she began, looking me over from my shoes to my baseball cap. "You're here for Krystal or Diane, right?"

I had the sense that sweet-talk would only annoy her. "I'm here for Darlena."

"Are you the one who called yesterday? Didn't I tell you you had the wrong number?"

"Yes, you did. But I think what I had was the wrong name. I may be looking for Krystal or Diane."

"You a cop?"

"No. I'm just a guy who lost his date. Are you Krystal or Diane's grandmother?"

Dark brown eyes the same color as the Rottweilers' coats narrowed to a squint under thin gray eyebrows. Suddenly, she laughed, a short burst of chuckle, as if I had repeated a one-liner from a late night talk show. "Hell, no! I'm nobody's grandmother. I rent a couple of rooms in my home, that's all. I like company. The deal is, they pay the rent on time, I ask no questions. Neither of them are here right now."

"Are either of them, by any chance, from Chicago?"

I got the chuckle again. The dogs glanced up at Doris, then returned to covering me. "That would be Diane. Tell you what. When you catch up with her, tell her today's the first of the month and her rent is due."

Chapter Thirty-One

Having no other leads, I went back to the County Bowl. The concert was still in progress. The security guys were gone. With the exception of an older couple, out for a Sunday afternoon walk, I was alone.

What the hell was going on? Deejee implores me to buy us tickets for this concert, takes them from me without a murmur, and then fails to show up for the event. She tells me she's "staying" with her grandmother, and I discover that, not only is Doris Chittle not her grandmother, but Deejee is renting from her under an assumed name.

I was back in my office studying Darlena Giordano's file again. I was hungry, so I'd stopped by the *cocina* to buy a breaded chicken sandwich with a side of black beans and rice. The meal sat on my desk untouched.

I examined the photocopy of her driver's license. Could "Diane" be a middle name? No. Darlena did not have a middle name, either on her license or her social security card. The employment application held no further enlightenment, nor did the I-9. Everything seemed in order. It was unusual for an American name not to have at least three components, but by no means indicative of anything. She had listed a correct address and telephone number. She would no doubt have a reason why she had told Doris to call her "Diane".

We would some have laundry to hang on the line the next time we talked, is all. Deejee was not your garden variety pumpkin, that was certain. I guess that was one of the reasons why I found her so attractive.

While I had the drawer open, I pulled Lyss Wattenwill Nelson's file. The police had copied everything in it, but Nelson, Garch and Pensacola still had all the original documents. Lyss had not presented a driver's license. She had used her passport for identification purposes. She was—had been—married to Tommy Nelson, one of the owners, so of course there was no employment application. She had not been an American citizen, but her I-9 declared her marriage to an American, so she had the legal right to live and work in the USA. The odd thing was, her marriage was real enough, but her passport was fake. She was not Swiss. If the police had ascertained her true nationality, they had not disclosed it to me. Maybe Tommy knew.

I had taken my first bite of *pollo Cubano*, when the door opened behind me and Dan Pensacola stepped in, a fresh cup of *café Cubano* in hand. He flopped into the other chair, grinning hugely. "Did we kick ass last night, or what?"

"Oh, yeah." I agreed. "If every night was Halloween, you and Alicia would be shopping for estates among the landed gentry. We cleared over fifteen K, for sure." I took another bite of my sandwich.

"Good answer. Actually, Alicia came down here with me last night. Got her sister to sit with the kid. It was the first time she's been to the club since we got married."

"I was here too, for a minute. Sorry I missed her."

He took a swig from his cup. "Fuck me. Is that the time? I gotta run."

It was 3:45. "Oh, shit. So do I. I have to be at the airport in thirty minutes."

I dumped the rest of my plate, with considerable regret, into the very full dumpster in back, then dashed across Anacapa Street to fire up the Rabbit.

Santa Barbara Airport sprawls casually alongside the Goleta Slough. It is a small service facility for both the aerospace companies in the area and for connection flights from Los Angeles International Airport, ninety miles south. Unlike LAX, no international flights stop here; only a handful of airline companies run regular service. The terminal is small and spare, designed in the faux colonial style fashionable in these parts. There are four service counters, a few banks of telephone booths, and perhaps thirty seats in the waiting area. A Carrow's restaurant occupies the second floor.

Even at its busiest, there is never a problem with parking. I rushed north on the 101, peeled off at the Ward Memorial exit, and rolled into a vacant parking lot. I went through the terminal doors at precisely 4:12 PM. The terminal was nearly empty. At the service counter for Southwest Airlines, the connector for Rita's flight number 4849 from LAX, I studied the arrivals and departures board.

Flight 4849 had been delayed. It would not be touching down until 5:25.

Fortune was with me. This was a break I didn't even deserve. I now had over an hour to compose myself for welcoming Rita home after her three weeks in Alaska. I had not had to concoct any story to cut short my date with Deejee. I could even go upstairs and finish the lunch I had dropped in the dumpster at the club. Everything was working out splendidly.

I went upstairs. The waitress was happy to have another customer. The only other diner was an Asian woman, sipping a pot of tea and reading a newspaper. I ordered a Monte Cristo sandwich with coffee, and considered my luck. Sometime before Wednesday, when Deejee would be swinging by the office to pick up her paycheck, I would have a chance to sort out the perplexities. What was her situation at Arbolado Road? Why did she stand me up at the Dylan concert? Had she given any more thought to Elizabeth Strennis as the killer of Lyss Nelson?

In the meantime, I could relax and enjoy Rita. I was surprised to find myself rather excited to see her. After three years, I had come to feel that our relationship was more defined by its reassuring routines than by its capacity to surprise and delight. An attentive lover ought to have thought days ago to bring a token of affection for his girl friend after such a prolonged separation. I thought of that now.

There was a gift shop next to the restaurant. It sold the usual souvenirs to memorialize a departing tourist's visit to Santa Barbara, as well as current best selling paperbacks, postcards, and greeting cards—all of which were saturated with sentimental dreck. There were flowers, mostly desiccated roses wrapped in cellophane. Rita didn't care for flowers as carriages of sentiment. She was well grounded in botany, but her heart was in stones. The gift shop didn't stock rocks.

I found nothing in the gift shop that would not announce itself for what it was—an afterthought. I satisfied myself that Rita would be pleased enough to see me and undoubtedly eager to fill me in on all the happenings in Anchorage.

It was not yet 5:00 PM when I took a seat in the terminal. There were few people waiting for the next flight, only the attendants behind the counters, a janitor emptying trashcans, and the woman I had seen in the restaurant, still reading her newspaper. It was a pity I had not brought along something to read. True, I had not anticipated having time to kill in the terminal. I might have picked up one of those paperbacks in the gift shop, but I was not going to be here long enough to get involved with a novel. A newspaper would have been ideal.

I looked across the reception area at the woman reading her paper. She was looking at me. She quickly looked away, pulling her paper up to cover her face.

The only other person sharing Santa Barbara Airport with me happened to be an Asian woman? There was something I had to know.

She held her paper up in front of her, as if it were a shield to repel assaults. "I beg your pardon," I said, standing in front of her tall enough to peek over the paper. "Is your name Chin?"

She put the paper down and blushed, shrugging with that universal gesture of incomprehension.

"You are Chin, aren't you?"

"Her name is Park," said a voice behind me. "She doesn't speak English. Maybe you could tell me why you are accosting my wife?"

Chapter Thirty-Two

The confusion and embarrassment subsided in the wake of my apologies. The Parks, residents of South Korea, were waiting to board Flight 4849, on its way to San Francisco after its stopover in Santa Barbara. Mister Park had been returning their rental car.

I retreated to my seat wishing more than ever that I had a newspaper to hide behind. What had got into me that I was confronting innocent strangers with my paranoid fancies? I had best leave the detecting business to professionals.

What ought I to be doing professionally? This was a topic Rita visited with me often. She had known what she wanted to do with her life before she finished high school. I was eternally adrift.

In the physical sense, I was born disconnected. My father had been a hydraulic engineer, employed by a public utility company in San Diego. My mom was just my mom. I was their only kid.

When I was 13 years old, a few months before I started high school, my father discovered a smutty magazine in my sock drawer. It was the only time I ever saw him lose his temper.

"What if your mother had found this?" he screamed. The blood vessels in his temples were engorged with rage. Henry Allen Trapp was a man who prized his composure, voted in every election, made regular contributions to his favorite charities and generous tithes to his church. The one thing in his life that he adored absolutely was my mother. The moment he sensed that my sexual awakening presented a threat to her propriety, he made arrangements for me to have my adolescence elsewhere.

He took me to a psychiatrist, whose sober judgment was that I was afflicted with "hyper-active libido" and that it would be best for me to be in "a more structured environment."

That environment proved to be Greenlake Preparatory Academy, tucked away in Sedco Hills, California, not far from Lake Elsinore. All the students were boys. I lived there for four years.

To describe Greenlake as "structured" was an understatement. We lived in dormitories; only seniors were permitted to leave the property without a chaperone. We were awakened every morning at 5:30 AM; the lights went out in the dorms every night at 9:30 PM. On rising, we threaded our bleary way to a non-denominational chapel for a morning service, readings from Psalms or Proverbs and an uplifting hymn. We were served a nourishing breakfast, and then herded into study halls and classrooms.

Bells rang in the chapel tower to announce the time of day. When we were not in classrooms or study hall, we worked, cleaning the buildings and maintaining the grounds. There was ample time for recreation, always a form of organized sport corresponding to the season. We were encouraged to listen to any type of music we liked as long as it existed in recordings. Radios and televisions were prohibited to all but the faculty and senior students.

All of Greenlake's teachers were men. So were the head cook, the tailor, the launderer, and the handyman who repaired the lawn mowers, attended the plumbing, and so forth. Women appeared only on Visiting Day, every other Sunday. Female visitors were invariably family members of the students.

In such a cloistered community, the possibility for sexual liaisons with women was non-existent. Homosexual behavior was not tolerated, punishable by expulsion. The majority of students who enrolled at Greenlake did not stay the course due to its exceptional rigor. Eighty boys entered my class as freshman. Only nineteen of us made it to the end.

By the time I enlisted in the Navy at NTC San Diego, I was so accustomed to disciplinary structure that my wartime service years seemed relatively relaxed. The Navy too had bells and whistles to direct our activities. I was one of those seamen who welcomed these audible signals and found charm in their direct appeal to the senses.

My physical disconnection came to light after I married Susan Holson.

I was stationed at the Naval Training Center in San Diego—right where I had started—when I was discharged. Susan was a student at UC San Diego. I toppled for her like a loose mast in a hurricane. We married just before I was mustered out.

Susan wanted to transfer to UC Santa Barbara. She talked me into enrolling at UCSB to take advantage of my veteran's benefits. In 1970, my parents died in a rafting mishap on the Colorado River. I inherited their estate. We used it to buy a home in the Rocky Nook neighborhood next to Mission Creek.

Susan also wanted us to have children. After two years of fruitless coupling, we both consulted doctors. I was the impediment to our launching of the next generation.

My urologist explained that the tract had collapsed between my *vas deferens* and my *vesicula seminalis*. It is an aberration enjoyed by approximately one in every one hundred thousand male humans. Surgical procedures were available to rectify Nature's carelessness. I declined to pursue them.

Adoption was the customary alternative for couples interested in creating families by non-biological means. I was not interested in that either. My attitude became the basis for Susan's divorce.

I did not contest the divorce. The truth was that Susan and I had soured on each other. She was the most sexually uninhibited person I ever knew, before or since. Her appetite for arousal and climax served us well for the first few months of our marriage. Eventually, however, it grew painfully obvious that, outside the bedroom—and all the other places we jettisoned apparel and went after each other like chimpanzees—we had no points of contact.

When I enrolled at UCSB I was already floundering in the stream. I had no direction for my studies. I took courses that led to a degree in English because I liked to read. I had no taste at all for a postgraduate degree because that would have required buckling down and getting serious about something. If there was one characteristic about me that acquired continuity over the years it was my inability to get serious about anything.

After college, I found shelter in the reference department of the Santa Barbara Public Library for eight years. The cost of living rose while I nosed around among all the dusty books. By 1981, I had to abandon the serene corridors of printed matter for a better paying stint as an accounting clerk for the Brooks Institute of Photography.

My levity about the serious topic of gainful employment surfaced with uncomfortable regularity during my time with Doctor Barron. When I met Rita, I had been at GSP for five years. I already felt dead in the water. Rita pleaded with me to decide on a profession and pursue it. She even volunteered to pay for my schooling. After I signed on with Liquid Avenue, Rita considered my bookkeeping gig to be no better than an irritating joke, a stale anecdote endlessly repeated.

I had also failed to demonstrate measurable gravity about our relationship. The incident at GSP that cost me my job there might have broken things off between us over a year ago had Rita not been serious about me. I had to admit, after what I did, most women would have pitched me overboard without a lifeboat.

It had everything to do with Kathleen O'Keenan and my ambition to replace her as editor of *Golden Voices*. The power to make that happen lay in the hands of GSP's publisher, Jennifer Mitchell.

There had been a Fourth of July barbecue, sixteen months ago, at the Mitchell estate in Hope Ranch. Attendance was not required, but Rita had a faculty function to attend at the University and I had nothing else to do, so I went to the barbecue.

Jennifer's late husband, Gerard "Mitch" Mitchell, had done well with Golden Sunset Publications. Beginning modestly with *Otolaryngology Praxis*, inspired by his personal friendship with Harvey Hasridian, Mitch had discovered the intoxicating riches to be distilled from pharmaceutical company advertising. Later he had added *Dynamic Look*, and then *Bargain Bin*.

Golden Voices, the one GSP periodical that made no money, was a sop to Mitch Mitchell's thirst to be something other than wealthy. He had a weakness for fine art. He acquired paintings and sculptures the way Dan Pensacola collected neon signs. He was a benefactor of the Santa Barbara County Art Museum. He enjoyed the company of artists—the younger, the better—and entertained them regularly at Hope Ranch.

He had met Jennifer at one his soirees. She was an aspiring painter, about twenty years his junior. After their marriage, Jennifer traded in her passion to make pictures for a yen to buy them. Mitch had died four years after I was hired to steer *Bargain Bin*. Jennifer had inherited GSP, kit and kaboodle.

"Sen-jie laughed her ass off when I showed her that poem by Denver Lang in Kathleen's rag."

"That guy fractures me."

Herb Worthen's wife Sen-Jie was a jolly Chinese woman who had long since abandoned any of the physical reserve stereotypically attributed to Asian people, about the same time she had abandoned attention to her waist line. She held a platter of ribs in one hand and gestured with a sauce-drenched chop in the other.

"It's like, he got laid twice and he's got three books about it."

"This is what I know about barbecues," Herb observed. "After your first one, every one is an encore. They're like TV sit-coms; the same plots, the same characters, variations on the same predictable set-ups and punch lines. The only reason we go to them is because people keep having them."

"Oh, I don't know about that." Sen-Jie jibed. "I like eating now every bit as much as I did the first time I ate." She poked an elbow into Herb's ribs. "Taste buds are generous friends who never stop giving."

"I tend to agree with Herb." Our hostess had joined us. "The only reason I keep having these barbecues is because I hate dressing up."

We were standing by the swimming pool, which was what Jennifer was dressed for. Her bikini, in rust and ochre rectangles like a painting by Mondrian, made an incongruous contrast with the curvy flesh spilling out of it. Jennifer's hair was chopped short and bleached white. Sun lotion gleamed on her legs and torso. Tan lines hinted that the skin beneath the bikini was as milky as her hair.

Jennifer flashed a grin beneath a pair of bulbous sunglasses. "Anybody want to torch a couple of doobs in the pool house?"

The Worthens begged off politely, but I was always in the mood for otherness, so I headed to the pool house with the publisher. Besides, this was my chance to undermine Kathleen O'Keenan and advance my own case for stewardship of *Golden Voices*.

We had polished off the first joint before I plunged in. "With all due respect to Mitch, *Golden Voices* would not be tainted if it carried some advertising. I've been thinking about it and asking around. I'm pretty sure I could I persuade some of my contacts in the agencies to place with us. We could make *Voices* pay for itself."

"You know, Tony, you don't always have to be so buttoned up around me. Relax. Take your shirt off."

We were perched close together on a narrow divan. I was wearing pigeon gray cotton shorts and a Hawaiian shirt. Jennifer's sun block lotion had soaked dark daubs into my pant leg where she had rubbed against it. To oblige her, I unbuttoned my shirt.

"Did you know Kathleen is sleeping with one of her authors?"

"Who isn't she sleeping with? Who cares? It's not as is she's paying those monkeys. I only care about who's sleeping with the publisher."

Jennifer's hand strayed across my thigh and wandered casually upward toward the high security area. Alarms went off in my head. Her face, a brown slope topped by a snowy peak, loomed over me and we toppled over on the divan.

After some awkward preliminary fumbling and peeling, I, uh . . . plunged in.

Chapter Thirty-Three

My peccadillo might have gone unnoticed but for two unhappy circumstances.

First, my performance had been unsatisfactory. Jennifer and I had promptly pitched off the divan and squirmed around on linoleum tiles that had not been mopped lately. We were both high on pot, so our regard for each other was at best a temporary hormonal cloudburst that rained out rather quickly. The scent of Jennifer's lotion was gently innocuous at a distance, but, lying cheek-by-jowl, it smelled noxious. Jennifer's own aroma, once the Mondrian bikini slipped away, was overwhelmingly unpleasant. Like the floor we thrashed about on, she had not been mopped lately.

In short, I was not up to it. Far from acting as a man of sexual sophistication, I behaved as though I was trying to take advantage of my prom date. It didn't help that I was keenly aware that Jennifer was my boss and that all I wanted from this transaction was a promotion.

Instead, I got the sack. A week after the barbecue, I was summoned to a meeting at the offices of Fortis and Mayer, GSP's accounting firm. One of their junior accountants informed me that GSP had decided to fold *Bargain Bin*. I was given two weeks severance pay, a letter of recommendation, and a handshake. The letter was not signed by Jennifer Mitchell, the editors, or anyone who had actually worked with me. It was autographed by Leopold Mayer, CPA, one of the accounting firm's principals, a man I had never met.

Second, since my intimate encounter with Jennifer had resulted in flaccid failure, I had given her nothing more than a cheap anecdote for future gossip. She, on the other hand, had given me crabs.

My want of sexual sophistication extended to personal hygiene, so, when I became aware of the itch, I did not give much thought to its cause. The stowaways hiding in my shrubbery promptly became Rita's passengers too. Her gynecologist informed her of the nature of the unwelcome infestation and where it was most likely to have come from.

Rita's confrontation with me was memorable. She was utterly calm about it, even solicitous in recommending the antidote that cleared up my itching. She was also absolutely firm in showing me the door. She gave me a week to clear out of her Samarkand home, and even advanced me the money to pay the first month's rent and cleaning deposit for my apartment on West Valerio.

Doctor Barron kept me at arm's distance for three weeks, but eventually we reconciled with the tacit understanding that, if I fucked up again, we were finished. That was when Herb Worthen hooked me up with Robert Bellaire, a former accountant at Fortis and Mayer who had gone into business for himself. Robert persuaded Dan Pensacola to plug me into Liquid Avenue.

My excitement surprised me. I had not seen my girl friend for three weeks. Now that she was near, I began to feel clear-headed again. Rita Barron was the best thing in my life, maybe the only thing in my life that made it mean anything. Why was I so reluctant to admit it? She wanted me. She wanted us to be together. That I found her beautiful and desirable was an axiom. She was smart, focused, and steady. Best of all, she was fun. We shared a sense of humor and outlook. We understood each other. We just flat out got along.

What was I thinking that I should risk losing Rita by screwing around with an indefinite article like Deejee? Somewhere along the line, I must have lost my mind.

While I was ruminating, the airport reception area had become more populous. It was 5:20 PM. Flight 4849 was due to arrive. Passengers like the Parks, en route to San Francisco, had gathered with their carry-on luggage and greeters of debarking travelers, like me, were collecting at the terminal door to watch the plane land.

Right on time, it did. I watched the bobbing heads, maybe two dozen of them, pouring out of the Southwest Airlines 747 down the portable stairway to the concrete apron that led to the terminal. There was palpable eagerness among the onlookers I stood with and evident weariness in the faces of the passengers as they came through the runway gate into the terminal.

Rita was not among them.

When it became obvious that no other passengers were to be disgorged, I felt a twinge of panic. I shuffled quickly through the reception area, peering into faces and searching for solitary travelers. I went out the front door of the terminal to observe the porters moving luggage toward waiting taxis and small knots of people clustering along the curb. No Rita.

I rushed to the Southwest Airlines counter and explained to the clerk that I had missed a traveler expected to be on Flight 4849. He was sympathetic but unable to help. Doctor Barron was not on the passenger list. He did say, however, that another flight from LAX would be arriving at 8:45 PM. Perhaps my missing person had chosen the later flight. She was not listed on that roster either, but she might have a stand-by fare.

I returned to the reception area to scrutinize the people preparing to board Flight 4849. The Parks caught me staring at them again. Mrs. Park blushed. Mr. Park frowned. I went back to my seat to consider what to do next.

It was very unlike Rita not to be where and when she said she was going to be. I had already been stood up once today. Apparently, this was my day to miss connections.

By 6:00 PM, the terminal was empty again. The same janitor went around emptying trashcans. The same clerks stood behind the counters. I was the odd man out.

I could go back upstairs and have dinner at Carrow's, but I wasn't hungry. I could go home and come back later, the more sensible plan, although that later flight from LAX was past my bedtime. Regardless when Rita arrived, I still had to be up around 2:00 AM to get my day under way. I had Liquid Avenue's Halloween receipts to finish counting plus whatever business the club did tonight. I just sat there with my brain spinning.

I had been in the airport now for almost two hours. From time to time there had been announcements on the public address system. I had paid no attention to them. An announcement was tickling the loudspeakers now. It was hard to ignore since I was the only person waiting in the terminal. They were calling my name.

"Anthony Trapp. Please come to the Southwest Airlines reservation desk."

At the counter, the clerk pointed across the reception area to the bank of phone booths. "You have a call. You can take it on the white courtesy phone over there."

I put the receiver to my ear. "Yes?"

"Anthony! Where have you been? I've been trying to reach you all afternoon. I thought maybe you'd run off with Dolly or Mary."

Chapter Thirty-Four

"These migraines never stop! I've had 'em since I was a little kid. Every day! Feels like my head's going to explode like a keg of dynamite. You have any aspirin?"

Randy's voice reminded me of a cement mixer with too many pebbles in the barrel.

"I have Tylenol." I handed my boss the bottle I kept in my desk drawer.

Randy shook out six tablets into his palm and swooped them all into his mouth with an abrupt flourish, washing them down with a swig from an aluminum can of Pepsi Cola. "Let me know when Pops gets here. I'll be in the shitter."

Yesterday Doctor Barron had taken an earlier connecting flight from LAX. Rita explained that, having learned on her arrival from Anchorage that Flight 4849 was going to be delayed, she simply booked passage on another airline. She had landed in Santa Barbara at 2:30 PM; about the time I was at Arbolado Road meeting Doris Chittle and her Rottweilers. Rita had tried to call me from LA and from her home, but I had been chasing my tail around the County Bowl and licking my wounds at the office. If I had had an answering machine either at home or at the office, I would have known.

We did not see each other last night. Rita was exhausted from travel and I had sleeping to do before my early bell.

We were to meet for lunch at La Fiesta, our favorite Mexican restaurant, near the corner of Anacapa and De La Guerra Streets.

Sunday night's take was light, but the final reckoning for Saturday's Halloween bonanza consumed much of the morning. All tolled, I carted eighteen thousand dollars to the bank at noon. I felt good about that. Now there was enough in the account to cover Liquid Avenue's payroll, inventory and obligations for at least a week.

The bank was close to the corner of Anacapa and De La Guerra, so I left the Rabbit where I'd parked it and walked to the appointed meeting place. As I approached the corner, I spotted Rita coming up the street. Perfect timing. That was a good example of how we were as a couple. Our missed connection at the airport was an aberration. Typically, we had a seemingly innate sense of location and timing with each other, as if we were salmon swimming from hundreds of miles distant to spawn at precisely the right time and place.

I was on the La Fiesta side of the street, so I waited as Rita crossed at the intersection. She looked exactly as she had looked three weeks ago when I had driven her to LAX for her departure to Alaska. She wore Levis and sturdy hiking boots with a red and gray sweater. A dark blue denim jacket surrounded her shoulders. I knew well the gentle curves of small breasts, proportioned hips and articulated calf and thigh muscles that lived beneath the chilly weather threads. She waved at me with a compact tick-tock motion of her right arm. I smiled broadly. It was exciting to see her. It was homecoming.

"Doctor Barron, I presume." My little joke was tiresome since I had used it so many times, but it enjoyed the virtue of intimate familiarity.

"Anthony," she sighed.

We embraced. I wrapped my arms around her upper torso and squeezed hard. Her arms went around my waist.

Something was wrong.

Rita was not a tall person. Her head tucked comfortably under my chin. I couldn't see her expression. Her arms did not tug me close as they customarily did. Our bodies met, but there was space between us.

"It feels like I've been away for a hundred years."

Rita had ordered a plate of beef enchiladas. I was waiting for my chicken flauta. We munched chips and salsa.

"How I've missed this! There's Mexican food in Anchorage, but it tastes like it traveled five thousand miles to get there."

Rita's oval face was cherubic with full cheeks and widely spaced eyes. Baked tortilla chips crackled in her mouth; a dollop of salsa sat on her lower lip. My desire for her heated me to the melting point.

"Remember the first time we came here?" I stirred sugar into my coffee cup. "The night after the Wall came down? We promised ourselves we would celebrate European unity every November with Meso-American grease."

"I remember that you were totally stoned and I was two beers past insanity. Our promises to each other always had a tendency to dry up as soon as we exposed them to the light."

We gazed at each other over the red and white checked tablecloth.

"Anthony," Rita's smile faded. "I don't know how to tell you this. I've met someone."

It was strange that my immediate reaction to this declaration was relief. I was right. Something was wrong. It would have been small of me to pretend I did not know what she meant.

"You mean you're sleeping with someone." I smiled encouragingly. "Tell me about him."

She cocked her head. "Really? Okay. His name is Richard. He's a geologist. No surprise, right? He works for Exxon. Actually, I met him years ago at a seminar. We had read each other's papers on shale strata. I never knew what a great guy he was until we worked together. We, well, we're in love."

My smile was frozen. I wanted my face to make a more complicated expression, but it wouldn't.

"You know, Anthony, you are taking this really well. I thought you'd be upset."

"No, I'm not upset." How could I be? I had asked for this. "I'm on your side, Doc. I want you to be happy."

Rita did not look happy. Our waitress appeared with our food, so we had an excuse to stop talking for a moment and poke our plates with forks. My relief did not last long. I began to feel numb and empty. My flauta was as tasteless as wet newspaper.

A tight smile nudged its way into Rita's lips. "Since you're being such a good sport about this, I might as well push my luck and admit that I lied to you yesterday. About that flight from LAX? I came home earlier because I couldn't face you at the airport. I'm sorry I wasn't able to catch you before you went to meet me. But, after all the travel, I absolutely dreaded that we would have some emotional scene and say a lot of awful things to each other."

I laughed. It was good to have something to laugh about. "I don't blame you. I would have lied to me too under the circumstances."

As our mood lightened, the food started to taste better.

"What's going on with that murder in your nightclub? They catch the guy yet?"

"No. As far as I know, the police still think I'm the guy."

"That's heavy. You have any ideas of your own about it?"

This might have been an excellent time to mention that I was discussing this very question with my new friend, Darlena Giordano. I sensed that I held all the sympathy to be conjured in this conversation. My confession that I too had "met someone" would squander my advantage pointlessly.

"I thought I did, but I was wrong. I should leave the crime-solving to the police."

"We can't all be Sherlock Holmes, can we?"

The delicious flavor had returned to my flauta. I added a few dabs of sour cream. "I guess you'll have some catching up to do at work since you've been away so long. When do you think we could get together?"

"Get together?"

The levity that had seasoned our meal now dissipated, swept aside in a sudden gust of approaching change.

"Richard is staying with me until the weekend. I'm afraid I won't have any time to meet with you."

"Richard is here?"

"Yes. He lives in Newport Beach, but he's on vacation this week, so I invited him to stay with me. Maybe the three of us could get together for lunch later this week?"

I left La Fiesta with no sympathy at all in my pocket and a plate of wet newspaper in a puddle of sour cream cooling at my table.

Chapter Thirty-Five

I was in no mood to go back to the office, but I had no choice. I had to give Jimmy Nelson the cashier's checks I had bought from the bank for today's deliveries. I trudged up Anacapa Street to retrieve the Rabbit.

Should I take this business with Rita and Richard seriously? She said they were "in love", but what did that mean? We had been together nearly three years. In fact, our third anniversary, November 9th, was one week from today. On our first date we had watched on television as triumphant East and West Germans ripped apart the Berlin Wall with hammers, crowbars and bare hands. It was quite a moment, unforgettable in itself and auspicious for us, even if the event—far too politically and geographically distant to have a direct affect on our lives—was more symbolic for us than consequential, as it was for Europeans.

Rita and I celebrated the Fall of the Wall every year. I took it for granted we would be celebrating it this year too. Unless this Richard guy was a monkey wrench rattling around in my relationship. I could see why any man would consider Doctor Barron a wonderful catch. He might very well believe himself to be "in love". I just couldn't see Rita up and leave me after all this time. She didn't make important decisions like that in a couple of heartbeats. It was so unlike her.

It was unlike her to lie to me too. She had been so afraid of an emotional storm with me that she had taken pains to avoid it and then withheld the truth about it. That was something I might do. It just showed how very alike we were. There was no way she was "in love" with Richard. She was just having an affair. No big deal.

I wanted to have an affair too. Was my involvement with Deejee a big deal? Was I "in love" with her? I didn't know yet. We had some talking to do. In any case, did I not now have license to run at Deejee without guilt? What's good for the goose and so forth?

Outside my office, my prime suspect for the murder of Lyss Nelson was waiting.

"Tony! Thank God you're here!"

"Elizabeth. What can I do for you?"

"My car won't start. It's over there in the lot." The bracelets jingled as she waved her arm at Anacapa Street. "Must be a dead battery or something. I was going to call Triple A. I need to get back to work."

As a damsel in distress, Elizabeth would stimulate any man's fantasy. Today she wore a white cotton dress with pink splashes hemmed above the knees and red leather pumps with three-inch heels. A brown wool sweater with crimson buttons fell from her shoulders to her thighs. I peeked at her midriff to see whether I could detect the child she was carrying.

My keys jangled as I pulled the retractable chain on my belt. "Sure. I can help you with that. I have jumper cables in my car if you want to see if we can get it going before you call Triple A."

"I was supposed to meet Tommy here, but he didn't show." Elizabeth mapped her circumstances while we crossed the street. "I was about to go into the club and look for Jimmy or see if the restaurant people would let me use their phone."

"Tommy's missing again? Maybe he's at The Addison."

"Yeah, maybe. I haven't seen him since Halloween night. Everyone seems to think I always know where he is, but half the time I don't."

As a knight in shining armor, I was not Elizabeth's first choice, but in this instance, I had the right steed. She laughed out loud when she saw the Rabbit. "Oh, my God, Tony. We have the same car!"

Elizabeth's 1982 Volkswagen was three years newer than mine and far prettier, but it was indeed a Rabbit. I maneuvered my beast into place beside hers, hooked up the battery cables, and managed to put fire into her engine.

"Good job, Tony! Thank you." Her Rabbit purred sweetly. She left it running and stepped out of it to reward me with a fat wet kiss on my mouth. Her lipstick tasted like cherry cough drops.

"You saved my ass, Tony. You're a real sweetie pie. I'm sorry I yelled at you last week. I was just upset that the cops came to see me at the bank."

"Well, as you said, 'No harm; no foul.' Last week was very upsetting."

Elizabeth climbed back aboard her Rabbit. She rolled down her window. "I'm really glad you showed up, Tony. I wasn't looking forward to asking Jimmy for help. He's been really mean to me lately. Anyway, you're a sweetie. Thank you! See you on pay day."

Elizabeth glad to see me? That was a first. I was going to have to erase her from my list of murder suspects, however. If she couldn't cope with a failed car battery on a sunny afternoon, how could she manage a murder with her own hands in a dark nightclub? Apparently, she was telling the truth last week when she claimed that she didn't know where Tommy was when Lyss was killed. She had lost track of him again. If Tommy was not the baker of that bun in her oven, who was? And what did she mean about Jimmy's being "mean" to her lately?

I needed to have that talk with Deejee. Much had happened since Halloween Night.

Jimmy was not in the club when I went in to hand over the cashier's checks for today's deliveries. I would have liked to ask him if there was anything about Elizabeth that he felt like sharing with me, but Jimmy and I never talked about anything other than club business, so he was hardly likely to start burbling to me about personal matters. I went back to the office to leave the checks where he could find them.

A black and white vehicle belonging to the Santa Barbara Police Department idled in the parking lot. Two patrolmen sat in it. What were they doing here on a Monday afternoon? I was about to advise them that delivery trucks might be pulling in here shortly when the two officers emerged from the squad car and approached.

"Anthony Solomon Trapp?" One of them had stepped forward while the other hung back.

I acknowledged that I owned that name.

"We would like you to come down to the station with us."

"Am I, um, under arrest?"

"Not yet. We've been instructed to invite you."

"And if this is not a convenient time for me?"

"Well, then it would be an arrest."

Chapter Thirty-Six

From East Figueroa Street, the patrol car pulled into the driveway next to the police station and parked in the rear of the building. The three of us went through a back entrance, marched down a corridor past empty holding cells, and turned into a booking area.

As a uniformed sergeant took all ten of my fingerprints, I asked one of the men who had escorted me, "I thought you said I was not under arrest."

"You're not. If you were, you'd be charged and in handcuffs."

"Why am I being booked?"

"That's not for me to say. You can ask the detective in your interview."

Good enough. I felt comfortable with asking Rachel why I was still under suspicion. For a downtown police station in a modest metropolitan area on a Monday afternoon, the place was not terribly busy. I was the only customer. The sergeant took my mug shot, and my two escorts led me to an interview room.

I was left alone in the same room as my earlier interrogation last week by Detective Imanaka. The same rectangular windows set high on the wall, the same beige paint, the same table with the microphone and the ashtrays, the same metal chairs with baize plastic seats and backs.

When the door opened, however, it was not the same detective. A small man in a worsted plaid sports coat and gray trousers came into the room briskly with a folder under his arm. He dropped the folder on the table with a sharp slap and removed his coat, hanging it neatly on the back of his chair. He wore suspenders over a pink shirt with a gray knit tie.

"I'm Detective Mike Dimes," he announced. "I need to ask you a few follow-up questions. I'd like you to clear up a couple of points for me."

Detective Dimes had opened the file folder and peered into it as he made his terse introduction. Now he fixed me with light blue eyes over a straight nose and a close-cropped mustache.

"Where is Detective Imanaka?" I demanded.

"Yours is not the only case Detective Imanaka has to investigate, Mister Trapp. This process will go much more smoothly if you let me ask the questions."

I ignored this. "Why have I been booked if I am not under arrest? When are you going to read me my rights?"

Detective Dimes sighed. "Mister Trapp, please. You have not been 'booked'. You have been finger-printed and photographed to assist us in our investigation of a murder." He looked at the open folder. "As to your Miranda rights, according to your statement here, Detective Imanaka advised you of them last week and you said that you understood. Is that not true?"

"Yes, that's true. She did."

"Would you prefer to have an attorney present for this interview?"

The only lawyer I knew happened to work for the prosecutor's office. Pete Hardy would not likely be allowed to sit in on this.

"No. I don't mind answering questions as long as I'm not under arrest."

"Okay, then. Thank you. Let's see if we can proceed without antagonism, shall we?"

I nodded my assent, but I offered no guarantees about the antagonism. The Santa Barbara Police Department had not picked a good day to put me under the lights.

"Tell me about your relationship with Lyss Wattenwill Nelson."

"Relationship? Who says I had a 'relationship' with Lyss Nelson?"

The detective consulted his folder. "James Nelson did. He's your club manager, right?"

"And Lyss Nelson's brother-in-law. Look. I have no idea why Jimmy—James—would make such a statement. The only time I ever saw Lyss was when she came to my office looking for Tommy—Thomas—her husband."

"So your relationship with Lyss was just telling her where to find her husband?"

"I never knew where her husband was. Apart from that, I handed her a paycheck once a week. That's all."

"Did you happen to know her nationality?"

"According to the passport in her file, she was Swiss. A few days ago, Dan Pensacola, one of Liquid Avenue's owners, told me she wasn't."

"So you would have had no way of knowing that she was not really Swiss, that her Swiss passport was fraudulent?"

"Lyss was married to one of the owners. She was already on the payroll when I started working for them. I don't recall that I ever looked into her personnel file until your investigation into her death."

"How long have you been working for . . ." Detective Dimes shuffled papers in his folder, "Nelson, Garch and Pensacola?"

"Since August 1991."

"What did you do before that?"

"I was a magazine editor for Golden Sunset Publications, over on East Canon Perdido Street."

"Was there any particular reason why you left that job?"

"The company decided to stop publishing the magazine I edited. My services were no longer required."

"It had nothing to do with your relationship with Jennifer Mitchell?"

"Who says I had a 'relationship' with Jennifer Mitchell?"

The detective went to his notes again. "One of your former colleagues. Do you know a Kathleen O'Keenan?"

"Of course I do. We were not on very friendly terms. Did Jennifer Mitchell tell you I had a 'relationship' with her?"

"I don't see that in my notes."

"I was dismissed because they stopped publishing my magazine. I have a letter of reference from Fortis and Mayer that explains all this. I can produce it for you if you like."

"That won't be necessary. I'll take your word for it for now."

The detective consulted the notes in his file folder, announcing my other ports of call as if he were a tour guide. "Prep school, Navy, college, Public Library, Brooks Institute."

Dimes closed his folder. "I only have one more question for you, Mister Trapp." He paused dramatically, making sure I was looking directly at him. "When you first saw Lyss Nelson's body in the nightclub on or about 3:30 AM on the morning of October 23rd, you believed she was asleep. Is that correct?"

"Yes. That's exactly what I believed."

"Well, sir. According to your background, you're not a degenerate. You've had schooling, refinements. You're a Navy man. As one man to another, why didn't you cover Lyss Nelson with something? Wouldn't that have been the decent thing to do?"

It was my turn to sigh. "Detective Dimes. I don't frequent nightclubs. I don't drink. I don't like deafening music. If I didn't work there, I would never set foot in a place like Liquid Avenue. After more than a year of being in this business, I've got used to seeing people get drunk and behave in appalling ways. Lyss Nelson got drunk and passed out in the club at least once a month. Her husband was aware of it. Her brother-in-law, the club manager, was aware of it. They felt Lyss was safe enough lying there until she came around. I felt it would have been inappropriate for me to disturb her."

When the detective released me, no one offered me a ride back to my car. It was only eight blocks away, so I took it on the hoof. On my way out of the station, I stopped by the front desk to essay a query of my own.

"Do you have a woman working here by the name of Chin?"

"Not on my duty roster." The desk officer turned pages on a clipboard. "Nope. No Chin at this precinct."

Walking down the wide concrete steps to the sidewalk in front of the station, Detective Dimes' last question plagued me. He was right. It would have been "decent" of me to drape some sort of cover over unconscious Lyss Nelson and my attempt to excuse myself on the grounds that it was someone else's responsibility was unworthy of me.

What was it Dan Pensacola said? "There can always be decency." What was wrong with me lately? Had I become one of them, the nightclub crowd, the noisy, jostling, puking mob, tone deaf to every consideration other than my own intoxication? Why were the police hounding me? Was there really some mysterious woman named Chin sniffing my trail? Why was I goofing around with a dopey girl like Deejee? Was Rita actually "in love" with someone else? How did I get myself into this mess?

And, by the way, who killed Lyss Nelson?

Chapter Thirty-Seven

"Anthony."

"Good morning, Carla."

I had not noticed the figure shivering in the shadows until she hailed me.

"I could really use a cup of coffee."

She looked like she could. Her thin shabby coat barely covered her hips. Carla's protection from the cold weather ended at the tatters of her cut-off jeans. She didn't even have socks for her sneakers. We went into the *cocina*, where she stuffed her pockets with sugar packets and half-filled her coffee cup with cream.

I wasn't sure if it would be much help, but I gave her three twenties this morning. Then I had a notion.

"I wonder if you would be interested in doing me a favor. Naturally, I'll be glad to pay you for it."

"For you, Anthony, anything."

"Remember that fellow you located for me last week, one of the club owners? His name is Tommy Nelson. Could you find out for me whether he's staying at The Addison again? Maybe you could meet me here tomorrow morning if that's convenient for you and let me know if he's there?"

Carla grinned. Her teeth were awful. "You want me to do a little spying for you?"

"I'd be grateful."

"Say, whatever happened with that murder here? Did the police catch the killer yet?"

"No. They must not be making much progress because they still think it's me."

"It's not you. Trust me. You're not the type."

I had no basis for an investment of trust in Carla, but she had been right about Tommy last week and she was right about me. Maybe I had lost my sense of decency, but I was not a killer.

It never took long to count Monday night's receipts. I had the deposit ready before the bank was open. Yesterday I wanted to have a few choice words with Jimmy about his report to the police that I had a "relationship" with Lyss, but he was busy receiving a beer delivery when I reached the club, and I was fed up with Monday, so I put off that conversation until today. Jimmy wouldn't be at work until 11:00 at the earliest.

It was as good a time as any to get started on the payroll. I pushed open the "Employees Only" door to collect the time cards. Camped on one folding chair with her legs propped on one another, cigarette smoldering in her fingers, my partner in crime solving, Darlena Giordano, took me in with a scowl.

"Deej! Am I glad to see you!"

"Really? But not glad enough to show up for our date on Sunday. Where the fuck was your gladness when you kept me standing around for an hour in front of the County Bowl?"

"What? You were there and you didn't see me? I know I cut the timing a little fine, but I was there at least ten minutes before one o'clock."

Absurdly, I looked at my watch as I said this. Deejee snorted.

"One o'clock? What's the matter with you? Are your ears painted on? I told you to meet me at 'noon'. The concert was supposed to start at one. Why the hell would I have you wait until the last minute to meet me?"

I had wondered about that. I was pretty sure she said "one." But I might have been mistaken. It had been intensely loud at the club on Halloween night and, apparently, I was not myself lately.

There was nothing to gain in disputing her. "Deejee. I'm so sorry! I guess I fucked that up. What can I do to make it right for you?"

"You could start by buying me breakfast."

I had already been to Carrow's, so I took Deejee to the Jolly Tiger, another of my favorite local eateries. While she attacked a tall stack of pancakes, I got started on the questions.

"How did you get into the club this morning? Did I forget to close the service door?"

"I was there all night. Jimmy let me sleep in the loft."

"You slept in the storage loft? Nobody would give you a lift home last night?"

"I'm between homes. I got tossed out yesterday because I couldn't come up with the rent."

"Doris evicted you?"

Deejee's head snapped up. She stopped chewing. "How do you know about Doris?"

"On Sunday, after I, ah, messed things up, I went looking for you. Your address is in my files."

She put her fork on her plate, wiped her mouth with a napkin, and spoke with emphasis. "Listen to me, Trapp. I'm going to let you off easy this time because it's your first offense. But let's get this straight. I don't put up with spying on me or stalking. If we're going to mean anything to each other, you need to respect me and give me space. Don't ever go prying into my life. I will tell you everything you need to know."

"All right. I understand. I apologize. I panicked when I missed you at the Bowl. Do you mind my asking what was the situation at Arbolado Road? Doris seemed to think your name was Diane or Krystal."

"Doris is a dyke-and-a-half. All she wants is some extra dough for taking in tenants, as if she needed any more money. She didn't ask for any details about me, so I didn't give her any. Krystal's name isn't Krystal either."

"So you are out of there. Do you have any plans for a place to stay?"

"I'm working on it. I've got some leads."

"Would you like to pitch your tent at my place for a while? Until one of your leads materializes?"

I flew that idea out there quickly, but I had already given it some thought before I put air under its wings. Rita was back in town, but she had made it clear that she was occupied, at least until this weekend. I could put a roof over Deejee for the time being without incurring either guilt or Rita's ill will. After all, what was good for the goose, and so forth. Besides, unless my ears were painted on, Deejee had just intimated that we were going to mean something to each other. It was about time we got started on that.

"Okay, sure. Thanks, Trapp. I like your place. It's white of you to offer."

I suspended my questions for the time being. This evening would be soon enough to recap recent developments in the murder case we wanted to solve, or any other developments that might arise along other lines. Deejee finished her flapjacks. I settled our bill.

Darlena Giordano traveled light. Apart from her commodious shoulder bag with the Polaroid camera and God only knew what else, she had only one suitcase for clothing and a vanity case for cosmetics. I had her installed at West Valerio in minutes.

"Make yourself at home," I invited. "I should be off work by about 3:00."

Deejee knew where to find the fridge. She knew where I kept my cannabis too, so I was confident she would be comfortable in my absence.

On my way out the door, I paused. "I forgot to ask. How did you like the Dylan concert?"

"I scalped the tickets. While I was waiting by the box office, I overheard a couple of fossils hoping to score some tickets blathering about seeing Dylan in Greenwich Village thirty years ago. I got a hundred bucks apiece from them. Too bad it wasn't enough to pay my rent."

Chapter Thirty-Eight

The *Cocina Habana* was open for business by the time I returned to the club. I stopped by to pick up a *café Cubano* and say *hola* to Elena and Margarito. I went down the hall to the employee break room to pick up the time cards and bumped into a man I didn't usually have much to say to. Today I was feeling more talkative.

"Mornin', Jimmy."

"How's it going, Tony? How'd we do last night?"

"Just under sixteen hundred. The usual Monday night."

"I pinched a hundred out of the bag under your desk. Gotta buy some supplies this morning."

"Okay." The smell of mentholated cigarettes reminded me that Liquid Avenue had sheltered an overnight guest. "Deejee was here when I came in this morning."

"Oh, yeah. I told her she could park in the loft for a night or two, but not to make a habit of it." He shook his head. "Women. Some of them are so flakey you want to handle them with tongs."

"Did you happen to notice the squad car in the lot yesterday?"

"No. The cops were here again? What did they want this time?"

"They took me over to East Figueroa to talk with a detective named Dimes about my 'relationship' with your late sister-in-law."

"You had a relationship with Lyss?"

"Of course not. Dimes said you told them I did."

Jimmy frowned. Puzzlement pretzeled his face. "No. That's not what I said. I remember it now. That Asian detective asked me if Lyss was friendly with anyone here in the club. I told her that you had a 'good relationship' with Lyss. Hell, Tony. You were the only one she ever talked to. Lyss was as quiet as a falling feather. Everyone else around here thought she was a weirdo. It didn't help when Tommy started bringing Elizabeth in here. I told him he was acting like a chowderhead, but Tommy never listens to me."

Jimmy's explanation squared the corners for me. It was easy to see how the police misplaced a modifier somewhere along the line and misinterpreted Jimmy's remark. It only cost me a couple of hours of anxiety and an extra tablespoon of acid on my peptic ulcer.

"Speaking of Elizabeth," he continued. "I think I should fire her. She's got nothing to do when Tommy's not in the club. It bothers everybody who's actually working that she gets a paycheck for doing nothing."

Did Jimmy know Elizabeth was pregnant? More to the point, did he know that Tommy was not the seed planter? What the Nelson brothers knew or didn't know had never been my concern before, but now I couldn't seem to take a step without tripping over their fraternal affairs. Tommy had virtually confided to me that he wanted Elizabeth to terminate her pregnancy and that Jimmy was zealously opposed to that as a matter of religious principle. So he must know. And now he was talking about terminating Elizabeth.

I felt sorry for Strennis. As I ploughed through the payroll calculations, a chill walked up my spine unrelated to the November climate. Liquid Avenue was not a happy workplace. Nasty things went down here. I was not at all sure I wanted to be a part of this. What alternative did I have? For the present, none. I was an office worker. I kept my head down and worked.

After I wrapped things up for the day, I pulled on my coat and walked across the street to retrieve the Rabbit. The door handle on my car was cold. It was chilly today and damp. The marine layer usually burned off in the afternoon sun, but it had settled in, as if it were here to stay. I was glad I had a coat.

I took my hand off the door and looked across the parking lot at the rear ends of the shops and restaurants that sat shoulder to shoulder on State Street. I walked over to the back entrance of a thrift store called Second Chance.

I examined a long rack of coats among the women's apparel, selected one in good condition that seemed about the right size, bought it, and went back to the Rabbit. I dropped my parcel behind the passenger seat, feeling just a little bit warmer.

I let myself into my apartment quietly. "Deejee?" I called softly. She was not in the living room or kitchen. The accordion door shielding my bedroom was partly closed. Snoring bubbled from the fully dressed figure sprawled on my bed. I pulled the door shut.

She had not bothered to put my cedar cigar box back on the shelf, so I noticed immediately that my marijuana supply had diminished to crumbs. Before I even scraped together a brain apostle for myself, I put in a call to Bogo. I didn't catch him home, so I left a message on his machine. So useful, these answering machines.

Deejee had found her way into the pantry and the refrigerator. Boxes of cookies and crackers were empty of contents and lay crumpled on the counter next to the sink. Drained cans of soda stood next to them. So did my last two bottles of Heineken beer, two green pillars surrounded by trash like an abandoned temple on an island in the Aegean Sea.

There was enough in my cigar box to roll up a thin fumigator. I slouched on the sofa, puffing and ruminating.

Who killed Lyss Nelson? We were no closer to knowing that than we were the morning I found the body. Who had daddied Elizabeth's kid-in-the-works? That would be something worth knowing, wouldn't it? Tommy had disappeared again. Did that have any significance? Did Deejee know about Mary Hardy's mental health problems? Did she know Lloyd from her days in Chicago or was that just a coincidence?

Was Rita serious about Richard? Was this a good time for me to be entertaining overnight guests? What exactly was good for the gander?

I awoke flat on my back on the sofa, with a feeling of tremendous pressure on my chest. The flash produced a painful brilliance that dissolved into red spots as the whine of the Polaroid mechanism reported that I had been shot.

Deejee stood, giggling. "Jesus, Trapp. You were out like a squashed possum."

The pressure lifted. My guest had been kneeling on my chest. As my eyes cleared I could make out the Chicago Bulls logo on her sweatshirt. "What time is it?" I coughed.

"It's after 7:00. Time for you to get me some beer."

Chapter Thirty-Nine

It was easy enough to fetch Deejee's beer. By 8:00, she had sloshed her way through the best part of a six pack. I didn't drink beer and I had nothing left to smoke, so I satisfied myself with watching my guest make herself at home.

We were not viewing television or listening to music. We finally had that talk I had been angling for since Saturday.

"I don't think Strennis is our killer."

Deejee had pulled her Bulls sweatshirt up over her head and dropped it on the floor. She wore a gray sports bra under it. She had traded her jeans for a pair of shiny purple gym shorts. She swirled a Heineken bottle.

"There's no way she would have climbed that ladder and waited in the storage loft until the wee hours like the police say. The only way Elizabeth kills Lyss is if she let herself back into the club later. If it was premeditated, that would have been extremely risky. If it wasn't, if she just happened to come back into the club for some other reason and took advantage of the situation, then we are back to motive. Why would she murder Lyss if Tommy believed she was carrying his child? And, by the way, Tommy is missing again. I'm not convinced he is entirely off the hook just because the clerk at The Addison gave him an alibi. They could have cooked up something between the two of them. Of course, that would make Kent an accomplice, which would really make things complicated. I just wish I knew who was the father of Elizabeth's kid. I have a feeling this whole business is wrapped up in that. I don't suppose there's any way she would tell you that?"

"What?" Deejee stared at her Heineken bottle, her eyes no more in focus than a family home movie of the kids unwrapping presents under the Christmas tree.

"I said I wish I knew Elizabeth's kid's father. I think Lyss Nelson's murder has something to do with it."

"I wasn't listening. Who cares about Elizabeth? I've got problems of my own. How long do you think I could stay here?"

That was indeed a problem. Rita may or may not be in love with someone else, but I did not intend for her to find out that I was harboring another woman. I had invited Deejee, but the invitation was not open-ended. After all, this wasn't The Addison.

"You can stay until the weekend. Saturday, maybe?"

Deejee was moving. The beer bottle fell to the floor. She swept one of her legs up over mine and slid into my lap, her face inches from mine.

"Saturday? I just arrived and you're already throwing me out?"

"That's not set in stone, Deej. I just grabbed a day out of the air. You said you had some leads?"

"Yeah, I do. It'd be easier to follow them up if I had wheels. It's pretty comfy here though."

Her face edged closer. "You're all right, Trapp. You're a bit of a daffodil, but you've got potential."

Now her cheek rested on mine. She whispered in my ear. "We could make a go of it, starting right here, right now. This is what I need to know. What would you be willing to do for me?"

Right here, right now, I was willing to do a lot for her. My hands found their way to the strap on Deejee's back hugging her bra to her thick body. I started to tug on it. She put her hands on my shoulders and leaned on me with all her weight.

She was still whispering. "Would you be willing to buy a car for me?"

I was not expecting a concrete wish. I thought we were going to feed each other romantic pabulum for a while, and then translate the heavy breathing into athletic sweating. It was easier to have a real object to demonstrate the extent of my willingness. I was a bookkeeper. The question was simple, involving numbers and calculations.

"Sure," I whispered back. "I could do something like that."

It grew quiet in the apartment. The only sounds were the ever present rush of traffic out on the 101 Freeway, my breath, getting a little labored with Deejee using me as a living mattress, and her moist exhalations, fragrant with Dutch beer.

"Would you be willing to die for me?"

That was more like it. A silly question; a declaration of eternal devotion kind of question. I don't recall any of my lovers having posed it before, but I was ready to fall in with the spirit of the moment.

"I would cheerfully suffer martyrdom for you, darling. I wouldn't even ask for a blindfold and a cigarette."

She had taken my earlobe in her teeth. She nibbled gently. Her voice rasped in my ear. "Would you be willing to kill for me?"

Did I just hear that? Were my ears painted on? What kind of question was that? In the spirit of the moment, I started babbling.

"Well, yeah. I suppose. If it was a case of protecting you from some dire situation. It's hard to imagine the circumstances that would call for it, but, yeah. I think we've all got it in us if need be—the will to take a life to protect someone we, uh, someone we care for. I don't own a gun, you know—just so you know. Randy said I should be armed, carrying all that money to the bank every day. But that's Randy for you. Me, guns make me nervous. And this wouldn't be the best time to apply for a permit anyway, since the police believe I'm a murder suspect.

Oh, that reminds me. Did I tell you that they had me down to the station again yesterday? Some new detective named . . ."

The dead weight of Deejee's body bore down on me. Dribbles of saliva pooled in my ear. My audience was asleep.

Chapter Forty

I was feeling rusty after another night of sleeping on the sofa, as if my joints needed oil. Deejee had decided to accompany me to Carrow's for breakfast.

"Hey, waitress," she hailed Jean. "This coffee come from the Arctic Circle? We need refills over here. And maybe this time it could be warm?"

Jean swung by our table with her coffee beaker and topped our cups. "Will that be all, ma'am?" She was not smiling, but then, she never was.

"I'll let you know." Deejee shook a cigarette out of her pack. When Jean moved off, she lit it, stirred her coffee, and stared after her. "I wonder how long that lady's been dead," she muttered. "She looks embalmed. Can you imagine waking up in bed next to her every day?"

I was trying to remember what it was like to wake up in bed at all. A headache was trying to sneak in at the base of my skull. So far, I had thwarted it with Tylenol, but the battle wasn't over yet.

"Did you mean what you said about buying me a car?"

We had each ordered French toast, but neither of us had made much progress with it. I worried the corner of a slice amply drowned in imitation maple syrup with my fork. "I think I could manage that." I tried to look cheerful. "It couldn't be anything truly sweet, but we could find some solid transportation for you."

If she needed a car to track down those housing leads, I was in favor of it. As a houseguest, Deejee had not proved to be ideal. I wondered how Rita was doing with her houseguest. What was his name? Robert? I sincerely hoped their breakfast this morning would be as glum as this one.

"As long as it's better than that piece of crap you're driving, it will do." Deejee stabbed her cigarette in an ashtray. "I'll look at ads today; see if I can find something decent."

I planned to take her back to West Valerio, but it was too early for Deejee to start following her "leads" and I was out of marijuana, so she went to the club with me. She dogged my steps as I executed the usual drill. I punched my time card, made a pot of coffee in the *cocina*, and carried my collection bag to the safe.

Tuesday night's receipts were not much more than Monday's. Nevertheless, Deejee cooed, "Money. Lots of money." It no doubt seemed so to someone who was penniless. Good thing for Deej today was payday.

Carla was waiting for me outside my office.

"Hi, Anthony." She glanced at Deejee. "Uh, hi."

"Good morning, Carla. I'm pleased to see you. I've got something for you."

"I have something for you too."

Deejee sniffed, "If you two are going to hump each other, I'll thank you to take it to the break room. The storage loft is comfy too, if you don't mind roaches and rat shit."

I opened my office door and handed Deejee my canvas bag. "I'll be right back."

Carla and I walked across Anacapa Street. It was so damp this morning that dew was already collecting on the Rabbit, even though it had been at rest for only half an hour. I reached behind the passenger seat, drew the parcel I'd picked up at Second Chance and handed it over.

"What's this, early Christmas?" Carla smiled. Her teeth were not so distracting when the light was dim. "Good heavens, Anthony! For me? It's beautiful!"

Carla brushed the coat against her face, as pleased as a kid with a new bike. She shrugged off the jacket she was wearing and let it fall to the asphalt. I held the coat for her as she slid into it. "Oh, Anthony. It's so lovely!" She pinched one of the sleeves. "And sturdy! This is fantastic. How could I possibly thank you enough?"

She moved forward and clapped her arms around me. The coat retained the strong dry cleaning odor that came along with every article of clothing I'd ever purchased at a thrift store. It masked the nauseating smell of Carla's hair.

"Your man is at The Addison, alright."

We paced back across Anacapa Street. Carla clutched her new used coat around her waist, as if she were afraid it might fly away on its own recognizance.

"He checked in Sunday morning at 2:00 AM. According to Kent, he hasn't been out of his room since. He's ordered pizza twice and take-away Chinese once. Do you want me to keep an eye on him?"

"No. That won't be necessary. Thanks, Carla." From my wallet I extracted three twenties. "You're the best spy I've ever had on my payroll."

"So. You fucked her in the back seat of your piece of crap? I admire your flexibility. When are you going to spend some on me?"

My houseguest was in a better mood. After my restless night on the sofa, flexibility was the last asset at my disposal. Still, it was nice to know Deejee was still interested. "We have time now. You made the loft sound pretty sexy."

I took a step toward her. A smirk rippled on her generous lips. "Slow down, cowpoke. We'll do the bucking bronco later at your corral." She poked my chest with a fingertip. "Be sure to bring your lasso."

"Okay. All right, then." I had a few things to tick off the To Do list before that could happen. "I should get cracking. Today's payday. Plus I have to drop off a check at the State Board in Ventura this afternoon."

"Pay sounds sexy to me. Can I have my check?"

"Dan hasn't signed the checks yet. I'll have to call him to see whether he's coming in or I'm going out to his place."

"Overdose of formality, I think. Let me see my check."

I riffled through the checks, prepared yesterday. I gave Deejee the one made over to her. She sat down, pulled a pen from her bag, and signed the check with Dan Pensacola's name.

"There you go." She waved the forgery at me. "Not bad, huh?"

It was always bad to sign your boss's name on a check. I gulped, at a loss to formulate my horror in words.

"Come on, Daffodil. Lighten up. He'll never know the difference."

I drove Deejee back to West Valerio, keen to have her out of the office before any more pranks occurred to her. We were out of beer again, so I stopped at a liquor store.

"This is dumb." Deejee pointed out. "There was beaucoup beer in the walk-in cooler at the club."

"Jimmy knows exactly how much beer he has on hand. He counts it every day."

"Between you and Jimmy, there's so much counting going on in the club it's a wonder anyone can get a murder committed there without getting it on the scorecard." Deejee spoke to the clerk behind the counter. "You have any of those magazines with all the cars for sale?"

"Right there." The clerk waved at a stack of magazines piled on a newspaper rack. "Help yourself. They're free."

In the Rabbit, I flicked on the overhead lamp. "May I see that magazine for a second?"

It was called *Bargain Shopper*. The format was very familiar. It should be. The masthead informed me that the publisher was

Golden Sunset Publications. When I had edited this rag, it was called *Bargain Bin*.

"Son of a bitch!" I bleated. "They never stopped publishing this. They just changed the name."

This was no time to back fill the story for Deejee. At West Valerio, I loaned her a spare apartment key, wished her luck on the car shopping, and promised I would be home after I returned from Ventura.

Back in the office, I intercepted the headache trying to crawl under my skullcap with two more Tylenols. I dragged the collection bag from under my desk and began to sort its contents.

Someone had put her hand in the cookie jar. At a glance I estimated that seven to eight hundred dollars had disappeared. I reached for the Tylenol jar again.

Chapter Forty-One

I had given the key to my apartment to a thief. Was there anything at West Valerio she might help herself to? Sadly, there was not. Deejee certainly had no interest in my books or cassettes. My television and stereo were as old as the fossils in the cliffs at Point Arguello. Nothing in my wardrobe would be of value to her—I owned no sweatshirts bearing the logo of any Chicago sports franchise.

It was not much of a chore to count what was left of the money. I decided, about the time my headache subsided, that I would keep Deejee's performance this morning under my hat. A loyal and decent employee of Nelson, Garch and Pensacola would have told the owners they had a lemon on the payroll that needed to be pruned. I kept my jaw wired shut.

What bothered me was not my empowerment of an untrustworthy companion, but that I had installed her in my apartment where she might be discovered by Doctor Barron.

What were the chances that Rita might swing by my place unannounced? On past form, none at all. It would have been extremely un-Rita to be so spontaneous. On the other hand, she had been doing un-Rita things lately, like lying to me about her connecting flight from LAX and falling in love with some other guy. Suppose she had a disappointment with Robert, or

Randall, or whatever the hell his name was, and she showed up at my place in tears, looking for reconciliation?

She would call first. That's what Rita would do. She was as courteous and correct as a lady-in-waiting at Buckingham Palace. That personal steadiness and consideration for the feelings of others was one of the things I valued about her, not that I had remembered to compliment her for it lately.

The phone went off.

"I'll be in to sign the paychecks in about twenty minutes." Dan sounded a bit stressed. I could tell because he never sounded stressed. He was one of the most easygoing men I had ever worked for. In the background, a baby was wailing. "How'd we do last night?"

"We've had better Tuesday nights."

"I was trying out a new band last night—The Vicious Fishes. I guess they don't have much of a following yet."

The parade of pay seekers began with a bright jingling. "Hi, Tony," Elizabeth purred.

"Good morning, Elizabeth. Dan's on his way in to sign the checks. Shouldn't be long. Have a seat."

She did. Her pumps were royal blue. The denim slacks complemented them nicely. An aquamarine blouse swooped low enough at the neck to call attention to glitter sparkling on her chest. Chocolate brown lipstick made it seem as though her mouth had been fashioned in a candy factory.

"It was awfully sweet of you to give me the jump start yesterday."

"My pleasure. That battery give you any more trouble?"

"I had it replaced last night."

"Are you okay?"

I tried not to look directly at her stomach, bulging imperceptibly beneath her brown wool sweater with the crimson buttons.

Elizabeth was puzzled. "Sure, I'm okay. Why do you ask?"

"Yesterday you mentioned that Tommy was missing and Jimmy was being mean to you."

She tossed her head and giggled. "Oh, that. I think I was just feeling a little dramatic, what with the dead battery and everything. Everything's fine. It's nice of you to ask."

"Tommy is at The Addison. Apparently, he's been there since Halloween night."

Elizabeth blushed. "Is he? I'm not surprised." She looked at the floor, bending over slightly. For a moment, I thought she was about to be sick, but she straightened up again, the ruby flush on her complexion fading to pallor. "I know he likes to joyse the smack, but it's just a vacation for him. He gets overwhelmed with things sometimes. He's really a good guy. He treats me nice."

Dan Pensacola eased himself through the office door. "I'll bet you're waiting for me."

"Can I have Tommy's check, while you're at it?"

Dan executed the two checks for her and Elizabeth went out the door tinkling.

"Was that Tommy she was talking about? It's been a while since I heard anyone call him a 'really good guy.'"

"Jimmy said he's thinking about letting her go."

"Really? I think I'll let the brothers work that one out. I've got my own crisis."

Dan slumped in the chair, scratching his name on the rest of the paychecks. He sighed. "My wife wants me to sell the club. I still have a chance to go in with my friend in Canoga Park on his restaurant/bar proposal. Alicia's been pressuring me to go for it every day since Saturday night."

He finished his signing, gathered the checks together and made a deck of them by tapping their edges against the desktop. "It was a mistake to bring her here on Halloween. It reminded her how squalid her life used to be when she worked here. I can't argue with her. No matter what I say about Liquid Avenue, she trumps it with, 'We have a child now.'"

Dan had no reason to linger, so he shoved off, leaving me to greet the pilgrims eager for their paychecks. By 1:00 PM I had been to the bank for the deposit and cashier's checks. I reckoned it was time for the Rabbit and I to head for our weekly date with Judy Crenshaw in Ventura.

The phone summoned me as I was locking up. I came back in to acknowledge it, hoping it was Rita, ready to call a halt to her temporary insanity.

"Tony? It's Pete Hardy. Remember me from the other night?"

"As a matter of fact, I thought about you the other day when Detective Dimes had me over to East Figueroa for another interview."

"Mike Dimes? He's okay. He's not as sharp as Rachel Imanaka, but who is? I hope you have a lawyer with you when you're talking to those folks at the precinct house."

"Is there anyone you could recommend?"

"Certainly. I'll make some calls for you. I owe you one for helping me out with Mary. By the way, that woman we met at the campus? She's already got Mary tutoring two of her students. That worked out really well.

"The reason I'm calling is, I thought you might want to know, I did some background on Lloyd. He was telling us the truth. His name is Lloyd Demont Thurlist. He really is, or was, a horn player in Chicago. I couldn't confirm whether he worked with Dizzy Gillespie, but he was a dues paying member of the musician's union and he has two album credits.

"So Lloyd checks out. I hope he has sense enough to stay away from my sister, but he doesn't seem like a dangerous cat. The interesting thing is, there was no record of your friend Darlena. There were four Darlena Giordanos listed on the real estate rolls in Cook County over the past ten years. None of them conform to your Darlena's age or physical description. She had no bank accounts anywhere in Chicago, and no credit cards. If she owned a vehicle, it must have been registered in a different state. The State of Illinois has never issued her a driver's license."

There was nothing I could contribute to make the silence at my end of the line meaningful. Pete added the cautionary advice for me.

"Let me make some calls. I think you need a lawyer."

Chapter Forty-Two

There are always surfers at Rincon. No matter the weather, the time of day, or the season of the year, the promontory that pokes into the sea at Rincon Beach makes a natural harbor that focuses the swells and pumps incessant waves at the shoreline. On this November afternoon, the gray sky made the ocean look surly and the gently bobbing black wet suits potential victims of any pent-up anger Mother Nature might have in store.

If a monster tsunami suddenly reared in the Channel and roared in to sweep all the traffic off the 101 into the sea, it would not add much to my misery. Dan was talking about pulling out of Nelson, Garch and Pensacola. That would shred the partnership like taco lettuce. There wouldn't be enough left of Liquid Avenue for Luis to haul to the dumpster. I would be out of a job.

I was now complicit in a crime. The criminal was holing up in my apartment. Almost everything she had told me about herself was a lie. The reason there was no middle name on the documents she had presented for employment at Liquid Avenue was because they were fakes. I still thought of her as "Deejee", but it was unlikely that her name was really Darlena Giordano.

What was that business she had been drooling on about last night? Would I be willing to "die" for her? Would I be willing to "kill"? Suddenly, what had seemed merely disconcerting was now downright scary. She had spent Monday night in the storage loft at the club. Was that the only time she had camped there? Had she been there the night Lyss Nelson was strangled? Was the killer Detective Imanaka was trailing lifting Heinekens on my living room sofa?

I had considered going straight home to confront her with the absence of background Pete Hardy had discovered about her. At the Jolly Tiger, Deejee had given me a grave admonition about probing into her past. I wanted to get back the money she had taken, but what would I do if she denied it? She had forged the boss's name on a company check right in front of me. What more proof of villainy did I need to request that she find somewhere else to stay?

That was the part that was scraping my ulcer. Never mind that Deejee had just ripped off a sizeable chunk of change and forged a signature under my nose or that she might be the strangler who had ended Lyss Nelson's life. What had become the giant pea under the mattress was my fear that Rita would find some crazy accidental way of learning that there was a woman in my apartment. If she was undecided in her affections between me and Robert or Randall, that would tear things up right there. I was long since out of second chances with Rita Barron.

I didn't go home first. I was zipping down the highway now because I had a 1:30 PM appointment with Judy Crenshaw. In the fourteen months since she had struck the deal between the State Board of Equalization and my reckless employers, I had never missed an appointment. I didn't want to miss one now.

I announced myself at the reception desk in the State Board building. Ordinarily, I marched up to the third floor as soon as I had checked in at reception. Today I was asked to wait in the lobby.

"Right on time! As always."

Judy swirled into the lobby looking like a bridesmaid fresh from the wedding. Her canary yellow dress billowed at the hemline just below her knees and hugged her waist and torso like stripes on a hornet. Her brown leather heels clicked on the tiles in the lobby, open at the toes and secured by ankle straps. Her brunette mop was long and straight, with a braid on one side dangling among the tresses.

Judy Crenshaw arrested the eyes in a way that made Elizabeth Strennis look like she was trying too hard. I was never going to see Judy's footwear on either Rita or Deejee. I stood as she entered, took the hand she held out to me in greeting.

"This way," she smiled, gripping my hand firmly. "I hope you don't mind. I wanted to have a private word with you. I'm sorry to keep you waiting. I was on a conference call with Brad Sherman and Matt Fong about yesterday's election."

We went through a door on the ground floor that let us into a conference room. We took cushioned seats at one end of a long burnished walnut table. I completed the business I had come for by sliding the cashier's check across the table. Judy took it without looking at it, pouring her gaze on me as if I were the most valuable object in the room, although the table alone was worth ten of me.

"I examined your file this morning, Tony. You haven't missed or been late for a single payment. I want you to know that I appreciate it. I only wish my own staff was so diligent."

I kept my gaze steady on her, in case this was a job interview. I had already checked her left hand for a wedding ring in the event that this was something more. If Judy was spoken for, she was not advertising it with jewelry.

"There's one thing I have always wanted to ask you. That's why I steered us into this private room where we won't be disturbed." Judy's voice had grown soft.

"You strike me as an honest man, Tony. You're a man whose word means something; you have principles. I think you're a bit deeper than some of the people I see every day." She swung her head around emphatically to indicate that she was referring to everyone in this building and perhaps beyond, in the world at large. Her braid swung behind her head and back again, dropping over her ear.

"This is my question for you, the only question that matters. Have you accepted the Lord Jesus Christ as your personal Savior?"

I was wrong about Judy's jewelry. She was in fact advertising her ardor, not on her ring finger, but around her neck. She wore a thin gold necklace with a plain gold cross. Judy was spoken for alright. In my blinding fascination with her come-fuck-me shoes, I had not noticed her perfectly evident marriage to a Higher Power.

There are moments for which there are no parallels in one's life experience and therefore no template to guide action or utterance. I responded to Judy's question as a man carved in granite. I said nothing.

Our private interview quickly dissolved into polite dismissal. Piloting the Rabbit north on the 101, the sky was darker by several shades. The surfers still bobbed in the waves at Rincon, but I was prepared to swear that they were all looking anxiously over their shoulders at the unforgiving horizon.

As if my guilt quotient was inexhaustible, I had found another raven to peck at my conscience. I had neglected to vote in yesterday's national and state elections. Until Judy mentioned it, I had forgotten. I customarily went to the polls with Rita, another of our familiar routines. In Doctor Barron's absence, I was already shirking my civic duty.

Was I ever looking forward to going home less than I was now? I had no other play than to face off with Deejee and cancel her stay at West Valerio. She wasn't going to like it and she wasn't going to like me for showing her the door. What else could I do? It was time to start cleaning up my mess. There was no better place to start than at home.

"Deejee?"

The apartment was dark and quiet. I got lights up and looked around. Deejee was gone. There was a note and a magazine on the sofa. The note read:

"Trapp. One of my leads worked out! I got a place to stay. Look at the car I picked out! You should move on it fast before someone else grabs it. See you at the club! D.G."

The copy of *Bargain Shopper* lay folded open to a specific page. She had circled one of the ads with the pen she'd used to write the note. There was a grainy picture of a sports car. Underneath it the caption stated:

"1983 Porsche 944. $5,000. Call (805) 969-2156. Serious buyers only!"

Deejee wanted me to buy her a Porsche? Was she serious?

I guess she was. She still had the key to my apartment.

Chapter Forty-Three

I was brooding. I had switched on some music to brood by, the Beatles's *Magical Mystery Tour*.

I wished I had a sparkler. Deejee had cleaned me out of cannabis. The refrigerator was similarly ransacked. She had left me only two bottles of Vernor's ginger ale. I was sipping one of them. I had not begun to solve any of my problems, but I was damned glad Deejee was gone.

Halfway through *Fool on the Hill* someone put knuckles on my door. I peeked through the blinds. The sun had just slipped down below the Mesa, but there was light enough to see the blue pea coat and rainbow knit cap. I swung open the door.

"How's it going, Tony?"

"Hiya, Gene. Care for a ginger ale?"

Bogo took a seat on the sofa. "The Beatles," he nodded in approval. "I just heard *Paperback Writer* on the way over here. It's funny how, after all this time, their music still sounds fresh."

"The benefit of relentless originality."

"Sorry I didn't call ahead. I'm afraid my news isn't all that good. These virgin martyrs were all I could find." He let three joints roll out of the palm of his hand on to the seat cushion between us, retrieved one and stuck it between his lips. "I'll keep looking."

He put ignition on the herb straw, inhaled, and handed it over. He exhaled an aromatic fog. "Oh, by the way. Natalya left me."

"Left you? Your wife called it quits?"

"Probably. She went back to Novosibirsk. Said she was homesick. I doubt I'll ever see her again." He sucked the puffer. "I admit I rushed into the marriage. But I'm all out of things to say about women."

"That's too bad," I exhaled my own exhaust fumes. "Half of men's conversations are about women."

"And half of women's conversations are about themselves. I'll tell you this, though, Tony. The dumbest woman ever born knows more about life than the smartest man who ever lived." He patted his stomach. "It's all about this."

"It's all about hunger?"

"Reproduction, fool." Bogo laughed. "Hormones. Chemistry. Psychological aptitude. Philosophical predisposition. Life stuff. We guys, we don't stand a chance. We think we know things, but we're just cogitating, just making shit up.

"Take the male black widow. He's one-tenth the size of his mate and copulation is his kamikaze mission. The female eats him immediately. You could almost feel sorry for the little bastard, except his sole purpose in life is to make more black widows."

Susan Holson had calmly demonstrated how right Bogo was on that point. When she divorced me, I had let her take our house near Rocky Nook Park. Eight years later, she had sold it for five times the price I had paid for it from my parents' estate. She then left town, taking my good fortune with her, like Mission Creek stealing flecks of gold and silver from their mountain lodes to carry off to the sea, leaving me only my peptic ulcer to commemorate our marriage.

We lapsed into quiet, content to let the very original Beatles do our thinking for us. They had just started *Hello, Goodbye* as Bogo reached for the second joint.

"Breakups." The lighter was busy again. "The Beatles broke up before *Abbey Road* was in the can."

"1969." I agreed. "The year of the pop band breakups. Cream. The Hollies."

"The Byrds, the Buffalo Springfield," he chimed. "Traffic."

"Some of those band dissolutions were just re-shuffling the deck, though. Think of all the excellent albums from that year. Crosby, Stills and Nash. Neil Young."

"Blind Faith. James Taylor."

"Jack Bruce. *Songs For a Tailor.*"

"Jackie Lomax. *Is This What You Want?*"

Our snickers subsided. We smoked in respectful silence as the Fab Four worked their way through *All You Need Is Love.* When the record concluded, the traffic on the 101 Freeway resumed the duty of entertaining us.

Bogo summed it up. "Boy, that's really loud."

"That's why I keep the door and windows closed all the time. I try not to think about all the steel tonnage flinging its way at this building on rubber wheels in slippery weather."

Bogo nodded. "And I try not to think of the earth as a shooting gallery for asteroids."

We contemplated the sonic waves of California Interstate Symphony Number 101 in C Major.

"There's rhythm in it though, when you listen." Bogo observed. "It's like a river out there, sometimes rushing by, sometimes flowing smoothly. It's hypnotic. It's comforting."

Bogo left, promising to keep his ear to the ground for cannabis acquisitions, leaving me to enjoy the cadences rising and falling in the traffic racing by outside to unknown destinations near and far. I caught that cork-in-a-stream feeling, vulnerable flotsam helplessly surrendered to forces beyond my control.

It was hypnotic. It was comforting. I slept.

Chapter Forty-Four

I nestled the Rabbit into a convenient spot in the public lot near the bank. Wednesday night had been surprisingly busy. Apart from the general guidelines regarding weekends and holidays, there was no was no scientific method to gauge how much business the club would see on any given night. Much depended on the class and exam cycles of the local colleges. The relative popularity of the band *du soir* affected the head count, but only marginally. Other than that, predictive accounting for Liquid Avenue was all astrology.

The unanticipated bulk of last night's proceeds ameliorated my guilt about the missing money from Tuesday's take. I was the only one who had noticed Deejee's pilferage. There would be no repercussions from the victimized parties Nelson, Garch and Pensacola. The logical implication was that the repercussions would have to come from me.

Santa Barbara is not a major metropolis. It never surprises me when I run into somebody I know. So why did it surprise me when I ran into Rita?

They were parking in the public lot as I returned to the Rabbit from the bank. Rita's green BMW roadster was unremarkable—I saw a dozen just like it every day. Rita herself was unmistakable. She emerged from the driver's side of her car wearing a familiar knit wool cap much like Bogo's but in the same shade of green as her Beamer. That meant the fellow climbing out of the passenger side must be . . .

"Anthony! What a surprise to see you. May I introduce you?" She hooked her arm through his. "This is Richard. Richard, this is Anthony."

Richard, Rita's new lover, was unremarkable in much the same way that Rita's BMW roadster was. He was not flashy; he was not over-dressed; he did not come on like a four-alarm fire. I could tell, though, that he was fine-tuned and could accelerate and hold the road through the turns. I had no doubt that his interior was handsome and durable.

"Hello, Anthony! The pleasure's all mine. Rita tells me you've read every book since the invention of the printing press."

Richard was not as tall as I. His handshake was firm and friendly. He wore his smile comfortably, as though it was no stranger to his face. He was outfitted in a heavy overcoat, something that must have been useful in Anchorage.

"I've probably read all the trashy books, but Rita actually *remembers* what she reads."

"We're headed to Las Pampas for lunch. I've been salivating for Argentine beef." Rita tugged playfully on Richard's arm.

"I'm a card-carrying carnivore." Richard added. "Rita said the *empanadas* here are a religious experience."

"She's not wrong," I confirmed. The last time we spoke, Rita had mentioned the possibility of the three of us breaking bread together. It would have been awkward for me to invite myself to their lunch and painful to be a witness to their religious experience. I hefted my empty canvas collection bag. "I'd better get back to the office. If you have an appetite for bovine flesh, I recommend the *bistek* sandwich at *Cocina Habana*."

Three days ago, when we had met for lunch, I sensed something wrong in Rita's greeting hug. The contact felt incomplete; no current flowed between us. Seeing the geologists move off together arm-in-arm, it was obvious what was wrong between Rita and I. Richard had moved into the space between us.

In my apartment that afternoon, I went back to the brooding. I was annoyed that I was out of weed. Bogo would dig up some joy for me sooner or later, but just now I could really use something to loosen my screws.

Was it possible that I had lost Rita? Wasn't it only two weeks ago that she had invited me to join her in Anchorage? And now she was sporting about town with a new lover? My fear that she might catch me with Deejee at West Valerio now seemed as silly as a dread of hobgoblins under the bed.

The ringing phone scattered my thoughts. I picked it up.

"Trapp. Jimmy doesn't want me working the floor tonight. Please come and get me. I'm at your office."

Deejee didn't sound right. To my knowledge, Jimmy had never sent her home on a regularly scheduled work night. Did they have an argument? Did Jimmy give her the heave ho? Did someone find out about the stolen money? And when did Darlena Giordano ever say "please"?

Since I was just picking up a passenger, I sailed the Rabbit into the parking space next to the dumpster behind the club. Deejee was waiting outside the service door. She slid into the passenger's seat.

"Jesus Christ, Deej! What happened? Are you okay?"

"Not very okay. Just drive."

"I'm driving you to the hospital. You should have that looked at."

Deejee's left cheek was swollen from the side of her mouth to her eyeliner. It looked as though someone had tried to make raspberry Danish on her oatmeal sallow face. In an hour or two she was going to have a deep dark shiner.

"Trapp. Listen to me. I'm not going to the fucking hospital. I'm fine."

Tears leaked through her bravado. Sluices darkened with eye shadow coursed toward her chin. She yanked tissues from her Goliath bag and dabbed at her eyes.

"Okay, sweetie. Whatever you say. Am I taking you to your new digs?"

"No. Let's go to your place."

She was disappointed that I had no marijuana to share. It didn't seem to be the right time to mention that she herself had cleaned me out. "My man Bogo is on the case. He might even find something for us by tonight."

"Your man Bogo? What is he, a clown? Listen, Trapp. You have any painkillers? Morphine? Codeine? I was counting on scoring something at work tonight, but fucking Jimmy sent me home. He thought *this*," she pointed at the mushy melon growing on her face, "would be bad for business. Asshole."

The only time I ever had painkillers was when the dentist rolled up his sleeves for session work on my choppers. I didn't have any now, but I thought I knew who might be of assistance.

"I've got an idea. Let me go back to the club. You relax here. Please pick up the phone if it rings. It could be Bogo—by the way, his name is Gene. I shouldn't be gone more than an hour."

Deejee held open the door to my refrigerator. "When you come back, don't forget to bring some Kools and beer."

Chapter Forty-Five

It was an hour after sunset when I left the Rabbit in the public lot and crossed Anacapa Street. There was a short line at the entrance to the club. I strolled past it slowly, went left around the corner on East Haley, left again at the driveway next to the building, and left again at the tiny parking lot, completing my circumnavigation of Liquid Avenue.

I had never seen Carla in the daylight. The dark was gaining now, but I didn't really know where to look for her. The club was not her only business venue. My plan was to cruise East Haley and the alleys behind the clubs on State Street on the lookout for her. I was hoping to get lucky. The only times I'd asked for her assistance, Carla had been surprisingly helpful.

There was no sign of Carla. I did see another sign, however, that led to another idea. The marquee above the entrance to The Addison was brightly lit. So was the lobby, which did little to glamorize the three dusty armchairs, occupied as usual.

The front desk clerk wore no nameplate, but he was friendlier than Kent, his daytime colleague. The Clerk-With-No-Name admitted that he had a guest named Tommy Nelson and even volunteered to ring his room for me.

"Tell him it's Tony Trapp." I advised. "Tell him Jimmy sent me."

The clerk had a brief conversation at a switchboard out of earshot. He replaced the headset and returned to the front desk.

"Go on up. Room 216."

Tommy answered my knock. "S'open. C'mon in."

What is must? I will have to look it up. I may not know what it is, but I know what it smells like. Must smells like Tommy's room at The Addison.

There was also a faint aroma of pizza, carpet cleaning solution, sanitary deodorant blocks, and a metallic tang I could not identify. The furniture was spare, only a double bed, a bedside stand with a reading light, an overstuffed armchair, a table with a captain's chair, and a dresser with a television bolted to its top. A tall lamp stood in one corner; a small lamp sat on the table. Behind the table, drapes were drawn over the room's only window, which, without the window treatment, would have overlooked East Haley and Liquid Avenue across the street.

Tommy reclined in the bed against a pile of pillows. "Tony! Glad you came by. Maybe you could do me a favor."

Elizabeth had said Tommy was on "vacation". He was dressed like a tourist. He was barelegged in a pair of Bermuda shorts. An extra-large long-sleeved tee shirt hung on his skinny frame silk-screened with the image of a marijuana plant and the words "Life is a garden. Dig it!"

What he had been doing since Halloween night was obvious. His setup was on the table: syringe, hypodermic needles, rubber tie-off tube, blackened tablespoon, and portable Bunsen burner attached to a small propane cylinder. All the paraphernalia was gathered on an antique serving platter that, with a bit of silver polish, would probably be the shiniest thing in the room. This was not Tommy's first "vacation".

"Jimmy said he didn't have time to deal with it. I need someone to get over to the Ticketron office and get me two seats for tomorrow night's Lakers game at the Forum. They're opening the season against the Clippers."

"I could make that happen." I had recent ticket-buying experience. "Any preference on the seating?"

"Yeah. I want to sit next to Jack Nicholson. But I'll take any two seats I can get."

"For you and Elizabeth?"

Any angler who has ever tossed a baited line into a promising stream knows the exultant feeling. The result of my casually innocent cast was an abrupt and immediate strike.

"I'm done with Elizabeth."

The silence that closed around this remark invited Tommy to elaborate.

"I was never in love with Lyss. For the fact that she was just strange. Foreigner. Didn't have much to say. She had money. I don't know where from. She said the municipalities hassled her because she had so much of it. As soon as we got married, they left her alone.

"She was okay in bed. Just not very interested in sex. It was bizarre that she never said anything about me and Elizabeth. She almost encouraged it. She didn't know Elizabeth was with child."

Deejee was right. Strennis was gestating.

"The icing on the spaghetti is Jimmy. He wants to marry her. She's not interested. He says he's in love with her, but I don't know about that. He's being such a jackass about that kid. No abortion! Is that a loving attitude? Now that Lyss is gone, Elizabeth wants to marry me. No way! I told her I'd help her shut down that pregnancy, but she doesn't want to do that either. She's dangling it over Jimmy's head. He probably wants me to fire her—if she keeps twisting my prick about pushing me to the altar I will. It might have been a mistake for me to put her on the payroll. I was just trying to be nice to her."

I was lost. "How is Elizabeth dangling her pregnancy over Jimmy's head?"

Tommy's gaze had been wandering like a lost pigeon. Now it roosted over the tarnished tray on the table. "Did you miss a stitch?" He stirred, swinging his bare legs over the edge of the bed. "It's Jimmy's kid."

Tommy slouched over to the table, easing himself into the captain's chair. I had better get a line on what I was looking for before he resumed his "vacation".

"I'll get those Forum tickets for you tomorrow morning. Maybe there's a favor you could do for me in exchange. You happen to know where I can get my mitts on some painkillers?"

Tommy bent over the tray, intently tapping white powder from a glass vial into his blackened tablespoon. "See that bedstand? Open the drawer. There's a couple of bottles of codeine in there. Take one."

In the bed stand drawer an array of plastic prescription bottles in various sizes crowded together like soldiers hiding in a foxhole. The first one I picked contained codeine tablets. I slipped it into my pocket.

"How about I come by the office to pick up those tickets tomorrow at noon?" Tommy concentrated on squeezing water from an eyedropper into the tablespoon. "Just take the money to buy them out of the safe and charge it to me. I'll leave it up to you to figure out the accounting sorcery."

I would add that to the growing list of things left up to me to figure out.

Chapter Forty-Six

"Well, well." Deejee shook out the codeine tablets, took four and swallowed them with a swig of Heineken beer. She counted the rest as she dropped them back into the bottle. "Twenty-six." She read the label. "Long's drugstore on State Street. Courtesy of Emily Van Vliet. I wonder how many hands this bottle passed through on its way to Tommy's hotel room?" Twisting to one side to place the bottle on a library shelf, she winced and grunted. She re-opened the bottle, took two more pills and washed them down.

"Make that twenty-four. Good work, Trapp. I knew you had potential."

"Glad I could help. Mind if I ask what happened?"

"Just a misunderstanding. I owe a guy some money. He thought I was going to pay him back today. He got impatient when I couldn't."

"So he beat you up?"

"He got in a couple of good shots, that's all. No big deal."

"Are you kidding me? Some guy laid his hands on you in anger? Where is he? Let's get the cops on his ass."

"Trapp, your chivalry is showing. The guy had a right to be pissed off. We're not calling any fucking cops, okay? My business is my business. I've had beatings before. This was nothing."

I knew better than to ask questions about Darlena Giordano's "business". That was a pity because my unanswered questions about the lady sitting on my sofa were lining up like customers waiting to buy concert tickets. The beer and the six codeine tabs went to work for me.

"I learned to hustle pool when I was a street kid in Chicago. My mentor was a junkie called Samuel. He'd been a math teacher before he got into the powder. Sam taught me geometry—in my opinion, the only science worth knowing. I've had a weakness ever since for guys who are good with numbers.

"Every once in a while I would clip some dude with no sense of humor and he would settle up with his fists. I had to stay on the move. I changed my name five times before I was fifteen years old.

"My name really is Darlena, by the way, but not 'Giordano'. Don't ask me what my birth name was. I don't even remember. None of the foster families I lived with ever thought it was worth mentioning. It doesn't matter anyway. Who cares?"

"Was it Lloyd?" Deejee was taking her beating better than I was. I was angry and I wanted someone to know that smacking Deejee around was going to have consequences, serious consequences.

She snorted. "Lloyd? If that old poop ever put a finger on me, I'd bury a Bowie knife in his chest. He's just a burn-out from the Sixties, a pathetic drug dealer." Deejee took a pull from her Heineken bottle. "Don't press, Trapp. Let it go. Some of the people I've run with—you don't want to know. I get tired sometimes, let my guard down." She poked me in the ribs with a finger. "Maybe like I'm doing now.

"The thing of it is, I'm too old for this. I'd like to get into harness with somebody, somebody I can trust, someone to back my plays. This life I've lived? There's not been a lot of sweetness in it. It's always been a scramble from one thing to the next. Some of my dance partners have been savages, no sense at all about the lines the law draws between good people and bad people."

Deejee's bottle was empty. She dropped it on the floor. "Here's your moral universe in a nutshell, Trapp. Where do good people go when they die? They go to the cemetery, same as the bad people."

She reached for the bottle of painkillers, twisted off the cap, and let two more codeine tablets roll into her palm. "Make that twenty-two. Thank you, Emily. I could use another beer."

I went to the fridge to oblige her. I could use a joint. "Did my man Gene call while I was out?"

"Bogo the Clown? No."

That was disappointing. It meant that supply in the pot market had fallen behind demand, always a temporary condition but ever a nuisance. Eventually, economics would prevail, but for the time being there was a marijuana drought.

"But your bossy sister called."

My bossy sister? "Who?"

"Rita. Your sister. Remember?" Deejee smiled broadly. "She said something about an anniversary dinner. She said you should call her tomorrow."

Shit! All week I am practically waiting by the phone and Rita finally calls when only Deejee is here to answer. Did things fall apart between her and Richard?

"Right." I answered slowly. "Our parents' anniversary. Coming up next week. I forgot."

Deejee laughed like a barking seal. "You and your sister in Alaska celebrate your parents' wedding anniversary? What, your lives were scripted by Hallmark greeting cards? Trapp, you are truly a hoot and a half."

Deejee was feeling better. That was good, I suppose. She grinned slyly.

"She's not your sister, is she?" She poked me in the ribs again. "You've got a squeeze on the side you've been keeping from me?" She laughed again. "Christ-on-a-stick, Trapp. You've got a dark side. Maybe there's hope for you yet. With a little work I could help you improve your bullshitting skills. We could be a good team."

By the time Deejee passed out on my sofa, the benefice of Emily Van Vliet had been reduced to eighteen pills. I struggled to heft my unconscious guest so that I could transfer her dead weight to my bed. I removed her sneakers, folded a blanket over her, and returned to my sofa to listen to her snore.

There was no reason for Deejee to arise at my ungodly hour and accompany me to work, but she was already up and tapping into the pill bottle when I awoke.

"I'm thinking pancakes. How about you?" She kissed my cheek.

We went to the Jolly Tiger for breakfast. Jean would be working at Carrow's this morning. The next time I sat Deejee down in her station someone was going to get food adulterated by loogies or worse. On the other hand, she might have noticed Deejee's black eye with appreciation and credited it to my account.

I wondered what Rita would be having for breakfast this morning and with whom. I had becalmed myself about her telephone contact with Deejee. The cat had slipped the bag for sure. But now I had license to entertain female guests, didn't I? What was good for the goose?

The truth was, I had no interest in the balancing of scales or any kind of sexual arithmetic. Rita's reference to an "anniversary" was our own, on November 9th, next Monday, the third anniversary of the Fall of the Berlin Wall and of our own falling in love. The fact that Rita still wanted to observe the occasion told me everything I needed to know. I wanted Rita back. I wanted Deejee to hit the road.

"Did you have a chance to check out that car I want?" Deejee munched a rasher of bacon.

Shit. I had forgotten about that too. "Uh, no. Not yet. You want a used Porsche? It would be awesome—you'd look great in it—but wouldn't it be a standing invitation to costly maintenance and exorbitant insurance?"

"Remember what I said about 'sweetness'? I want some sweetness in my life, Trapp. And I want it now."

Chapter Forty-Seven

With the aid of the coffee I brewed in the *cocina*, Deejee took the codeine count down to twelve. She had enough opiates in her system to numb a rhinoceros. It was not enough, though, to coax her into the walk-in cooler with me to retrieve the money from the safe. I couldn't blame her for that. I went in alone, teased the safe open, and transferred its contents to my canvas bag.

Something was different about the club when I emerged from the cooler with my gratifyingly bulging collection bag. I stopped and eye-swept the long dark room with its shadowy shapes and incidental reflections. What was it?

It was dark; that was it. Darker than usual. When I realized why, my breath caught in my chest and my heart began to gallop. There was no steady blue glow from the neon cluster on the wall behind the bar.

The Liquid Avenue sign was gone.

Hadn't it been there only a few minutes earlier, when Deejee and I had come into the club? It must have been there. I would have noticed its absence immediately, as I was doing now. As I was now noticing Deejee's absence also.

I scampered for the service door, crashed though, and peered into the chilly gloom behind the club. If she was toting a three-foot by four-foot construct of glass tubes and metal framework, she couldn't have got far. When I went out to Anacapa I spotted her in the parking lot across the street heading for my car.

She had reached the Rabbit when I caught up with her. The sign rested against the back bumper. Deejee was trying to lift the hatch on the Rabbit's back.

"Deejee! What are you doing?"

"Damn. This thing is locked. Open it, will you?"

"We're not taking the sign. Are you kidding? Dan would be devastated. You're going too far. This is crazy."

"This is worth a couple of thousand bucks. I already have a buyer. Stop whining and open the damned hatch before somebody sees us."

"No. We have to put it back up where it belongs."

"It's a little late for that. I had to tear it off the wall." She showed me the rear of the sign where brackets were still attached. "I was surprised it was so easy. What do they make those walls out of?"

She had a point. To re-hang the sign behind the bar was going to require carpenter skills and tools I did not possess. I doubted that Deejee would be much help with that, even if I could persuade her it had to be done. We were already running out of time. Luis would be at the club in less than an hour.

I studied the sign as paralysis froze my decision-making faculties. Was there any way I could just put the thing on the floor behind the bar and claim that's how I found it, fallen, but not damaged? No. Jimmy would know the sign was intact when he closed the club. If the sign had fallen from the wall, it would not only have shattered, it would have smashed some of the liquor bottles and glasses stored underneath it.

We could not return the sign without raising more awkward questions than would be asked if it were simply missing and presumed stolen. As it was, I was going to be subject to a grilling over this. Too bad I had not yet taken the bullshitting lessons Deejee had prescribed for me. Detective Imanaka had already proved I was a bad liar.

Deejee had cut off other options. The safest course was to carry out the theft.

"Trapp! Watch the birdie."

The flash went off as I turned, followed by the Polaroid whine. In the pre-dawn dimness, I was momentarily blinded. When my sight re-booted itself, Deejee was shaking the snapshot to give it air. She slid it into her voluminous bag.

"If you've got any hair on your popsicles, you'll get that hatch open so we can get this beauty back to your apartment before sunrise."

I opened the Rabbit's rear end hatch, still not fully committed to this plan. Deejee took one end of the sign and started lifting. "For God's sake, Fairy Princess. Give me a hand."

The Rabbit had room enough to accommodate the twelve square feet of tubes and frame, but negotiating its passage through the hatch was more tricky than it looked. It was cold and wet in the parking lot. In the few minutes I'd been arguing with my partner, dew had begun to collect on the sign. Deejee had her end balanced in the hatchway. I lifted my end, twisted it to clear the hatch door and its sliders, and lost my grip on it. The sign slipped out of my grasp and, tearing itself from Deejee's clutch, dropped sharply to the pavement with a smothered pop and a metallic rattle.

We stared at the gazillion glass shards that had spelled "Liquid Avenue". Their spelling days were behind them. I had an incongruous thought. Dan Pensacola had mentioned that neon was one of the "noble" gases. I would have thought a smashed neon tube would smell noxious, but there was no smell at all that I could detect. All that was left of the nightclub's noble identity and *raison d'etre* was a bent metal frame and uncountable fragments of guilt scattered on the asphalt.

"There goes the down payment on my Porsche," Deejee noted sourly.

My brain stirred. "We have to clean this up." I didn't know exactly how any of this could be traced back to us, but why take unnecessary risks? "Here. Let's get this thing in the car."

We lifted the sign's frame, shook off attached bits of glass, and shoved it through the hatch. I ran back to the club for cleaning supplies. I located a push broom, a dustpan and a plastic trash bag. As I sprinted back across Anacapa Street, it occurred to me to wonder where I had left my canvas collection bag.

I had left it with Deejee. It sat where I had dropped it, next to the Rabbit. Deejee worked the push broom; I moved the dustpan around. In about ten minutes we had as much of the glass debris bagged as we could see. Whatever glittering bits might become visible in the daylight, they would not be enough to be incriminating. I tossed the trash into the Rabbit. Leaving Deejee in the passenger seat, I grabbed the money and rushed back to the club to return the broom and the dustpan. I opened my office to stash the collection bag. It was still dark when I got the Rabbit in motion.

Deejee had not said much while we were busy erasing the mess. She was quiet as we cruised the empty streets. I needed a dumpster, but it was certainly not going to be the one at West Valerio. There were trash bins next to the Safeway market on De La Vina Street. I rolled through their parking lot. The store was not open yet, but the lights were on—too much illumination for safe dumping. Adjacent to the Safeway there was a parking lot for the venerable Arlington Theater. No lights disturbed the dumpster behind the building. I caught a break. There was no padlock on the dumpster.

With the Volkswagen's engine running, we tossed the frame and the trash bag into the bin and made our getaway clean. I was by no means out of the woods in this caper, but I felt light-headed with relief. As long as I denied knowing anything, I didn't see any way my hand in it could be detected.

I still had time to get back to the club before Luis arrived and discovered that the sign was missing. When that happened, I felt it would be prudent to be in my usual place at my usual time.

I still had a passenger. "Would you like to go back to my place or is there somewhere I can drop you?"

"Yeah. Take me down to Stearn's Wharf." Deejee was subdued, but she did not seem to be glum.

"What's at Stearn's Wharf?"

"Business."

The harbor was only five blocks from the club. That was convenient. I knew better than to ask what "business" Deejee was conducting at Santa Barbara Harbor at 4:30 in the morning.

"There." She pointed to The Catch, an all-night coffee shop on Cabrillo Boulevard directly across from the pier.

I pulled into a parking slot. The Catch had customers, even at this time of the morning. Apparently Deejee was not the only one who liked to do "business" in the small hours. She reached up to the Rabbit's roof and snapped on the interior light.

"You're going to get after that car for me today, right?" She was digging in her Goliath bag. She found what she was looking for and pulled it out, holding it under the light for my view.

It was the Polaroid snapshot, a nicely composed frame that neatly showed me standing next to the Liquid Avenue sign leaning against the Rabbit. Having given me a few seconds to register its significance, Deejee slipped it carefully back into her bag. She spoke calmly.

"If your commitment to buy me that car wavers or if you decide your squeeze Rita needs more attention than I do, remember that I have this photo and think about all the people you don't want to see it." She smiled. "I play for keeps, Trapp. In case you hadn't noticed."

Chapter Forty-Eight

At ten minutes past five, the knock I was waiting for rapped my office door.

"¡*Señor* Tony!" Luis stood in the lot, his Los Angeles Dodgers cap tipped up on his brow. "*En la sala. ¡Por favor!*"

I followed him into the club. Standing in front the *Cocina Habana*'s service counter, Luis pointed across the long dark room to the black hole behind the bar where the sign had been. "*¡Mira!*"

"*Yo sabo*, Luis. I saw it earlier." I shook my head, as if in disbelief. "*Yo sabo* it was not you." I tapped my chest. "I will tell Jimmy and Dan. Okay?"

I would of course verify that the sign was missing before Luis arrived. Telling Jimmy was not going to be a problem. Telling Dan was another matter. I had rehearsed my story. I planned to stick to it, hell or high water. If Dan suspected I had anything to do with the disappearance of Liquid Avenue's holy totem, this would be my last day on the job.

I suppose there must be a moment for every drowning man when, in flailing panic, he realizes there is nothing to hold on to and he accepts that these desperate horrific minutes will be the last of his life.

I had not quite reached that point, but I was drowning all the same.

My crime-solving partner had become my crime-committing accomplice. It was impossible to know how much money Deejee had lifted from the collection bag while I was scrambling to cover our tracks. Thursday night had been very busy. In fact, every night since the murder of Lyss Nelson had been more busy than usual. Was it coincidence or was there some ineluctable fascination with murder that drew the customers in so they could tell their friends, "I got drunk and puked in the Death Club." We could probably sell silk-screened tee shirts with that declaration on the front and the Liquid Avenue sign on the back.

There was a considerable amount of money to count and I had got a late start. No one would ever know that Deejee had pinched about two thousand dollars from the collection bag. There was the down payment on her Porsche right there.

Deejee had made it very clear that blackmail was one of her specialties. It was going to cost me about five thousand bucks to get that Polaroid back. I wasn't sure where that money was going to come from, but between my bank account and credit cards I was confident I could scrape it together. Whatever it would take to get this succubus out of my life, I was willing to do it. I had a copy of the *Bargain Shopper* with the Porsche owner's phone number. I would call as soon as the hour was decent.

I also had to get over to the Ticketron office and buy Tommy his tickets for tonight's basketball game in LA. He said he would be coming into the office around noon. There was a Ticketron at The Wherehouse music store in San Roque Plaza off upper State Street. They would open at 10:00 AM.

There was something else I was supposed to do today. I frowned, trying to recall what it was. It was a mere tickle of a chore, understandably swamped by the crime wave rushing through my workplace this morning—theft, destruction of property, embezzlement, extortion. What did I expect? Liquid Avenue was already a murder site. Whatever my chore was, it would come to me.

At 9:00 AM, I rang the number in the *Bargain Shopper*. I made contact with a fellow who called himself Doug. He acknowledged the Porsche was still in his driveway. I assured him I was a "serious" buyer and made an appointment to see and test-drive the wheels Sunday afternoon.

The only way to deal with dread is to face it squarely. My next call was to Dan Pensacola. All I had a chance to say was, "The Liquid Avenue sign is missing." He instructed me to stay put. He would be right in.

Dan and I stood in front of the bar, gazing up at four ragged punctures in the sheetrock, bleeding bits of paint and plaster into a very empty space.

"Incredible." A scowl that might scare away a hungry shark embedded itself along Dan's jaw line. "Have you talked to Jimmy yet?"

"Not yet."

"And this is exactly how you found it when you came in this morning?"

"I haven't touched a thing. Neither has Luis."

"Incredible." There was enough light in the club to see that Dan's face was stone white. "Alicia was right. This motherfucking nightclub is more trouble than it's worth."

Dan took it upon himself to summon Jimmy to the club. I told him Tommy had promised to come in around noon.

I locked the office in mid-tally and took a break to run over to Ticketron. Why Tommy had waited until the last minute to purchase tickets for the popular Lakers' season home opener against their cross-town rival Clippers was baffling. The event was certain to be sold out.

Tommy had trusted his luck. His optimism was rewarded. I managed to get him two adjacent seats up near the Forum rafters. I would deduct the cost from his next paycheck.

Dan was on the phone with the police when Jimmy arrived. I went into the club with him. When he saw the empty space above the bar he snorted, tucking his laugh into his sinus cavity.

"I always hated that fucking sign. Don't tell Dan I said so, but I hope the cops never find it."

Since my chat with his brother last night, I saw Jimmy Nelson from a different angle. He did not seem such a cipher now that I knew he was in love with Elizabeth, had got her in a family way, and wanted to do the right thing by her. It must have been as much a pain in his ass to watch Elizabeth in the club with Tommy as it would have been for Lyss.

I saw his point of view about firing Strennis too. On the surface, it seemed a heartless attitude, since he knew she was pregnant with his child. She had another job at her bank, but, deprived of her effortless income from Liquid Avenue, she might find his matrimonial intentions for her more welcome. As long as love had nothing to do with it.

If I understood Tommy, Elizabeth did not want to terminate her pregnancy. She wanted to have the kid with Tommy at her side. Jimmy's inflexible opinion about abortion may have contributed to her turning against the putative father.

From a moral point of view, Jimmy was in a tough spot. His Catholic principles were not entirely irrational, although they were as sickeningly paternalistic as everything else about his religion. I didn't share his attitude, but I sympathized with his dilemma.

Tommy was punctual. True, he didn't have far to walk. He trundled across the street from The Addison at 12:00 PM.

"Get me some tickets? What's with the police again?"

"I did. The cops are in the club with Dan. There's been an incident."

"Great! Where are the seats?"

I handed over the two Forum passes for tonight's game. "Nosebleed section. Best I could do."

"S'okay. Thanks." He looked them over. "Any issues with the sorcery?"

"I'm taking the expense out of your next paycheck."

"Excellent. If anybody wants me, I'll be in LA." He glanced out the door at the patrol car in the parking lot. "Someone else get killed last night?"

"In a way, yes. Before you hit the highway, you might want to have a pow-wow with Dan."

Chapter Forty-Nine

It had been a long day. Pensacola stuck with the police patrolmen while they interviewed Jimmy, Luis, and me. Jimmy said the sign was in place when he locked the building at 1:30 AM. I told them I had noticed the sign was missing when I punched in at 3:30 AM, an hour and a half before Luis arrived.

The theft of a sign was not on the same order of magnitude as a murder—although Dan was more visibly upset about it than he had been about the killing of Lyss. There were only the two uniformed investigators, no forensic team, and no yellow tape. One of the investigators, however, had been on board in the earlier crime scene and he remembered that the killer had waited in the storage loft, so they rummaged around up there for while before they came up empty.

"Your thief probably waited up there," an officer named Blixten pointed out. "Maybe he read about the murder in the newspaper and he wanted to have a copycat thrill. One thing for sure. You guys should consider more security for this building; an alarm at least."

I didn't finish counting Thursday night's proceeds until after 2:00. By the time I had taken the deposit to the bank, obtained the cashier's checks for today's deliveries, and bought myself a *pollo* sandwich at the *cocina*, it was nearly 3:30.

I was sitting in my apartment, wishing I had enough pot to roll a puffer, and listening to the traffic assert itself out on the 101. There really was a rhythm in it when you listened, as Bogo had observed. The big rigs carried the bass line, hammering eighteen-wheel arpeggios on the asphalt, while the sedans ran tenor, holding the curves in the road with mid-range pitches, and the sports cars plucked pizzacato timbres, whizzing through gear changes on squealing tires.

Where was Deejee at this moment? Where was that Polaroid? Early anthropologists recorded that modern tribal people feel superstitious apprehension when seeing themselves in photographs. They believe the camera captures their souls.

In the snapshot, I am busted: caught in villainy, my true self unmasked, my shabby soul captured by a cheap camera operated by a conniving witch. How was that superstitious?

Deejee was going to be at work tonight, black eye notwithstanding. Couldn't I just go down to the club, let myself into the employee break room, dig Deejee's carryall shoulder bag out of those gym lockers, and ransack it?

No. Deejee was reckless, not stupid. By now that photo would be somewhere I could never find. It was her passport. I was going to have to buy it back and Deejee was setting the price.

I let the traffic soothe me. It was close to Friday evening's rush hour. I fancied I could detect rubato in the wheels, the subtle speeding up and slowing down that expressed the individual melodic interpretations of the artists in the driver's seats. Tommy Nelson was out there somewhere, snaking his way through stop-and-go LA traffic on his way to the Great Western Forum in Inglewood. Tommy had me buy two tickets for this event. Elizabeth was not going to be his date. Who was?

Rita! I was supposed to call Rita today. That was the chore that had escaped my attention. She had called about our anniversary date. What could be more important than that?

"There you are!" Rita's voice was sunshine. "I was going to try you at your office, but I figured you must be busy."

"It was busy. Since that murder two weeks ago, Liquid Avenue has been a more popular attraction than the Mission. It's been ridiculous busy. How are you doing?"

"Richard and I are behaving like tourists who just got off the Greyhound from Des Moines. As a matter of fact, we were at the Mission yesterday. I thought about you when the tour guide at Saint Anthony's Seminary told us that musicians come from all over the world to record in their Christ The King chapel because it has unique acoustic properties."

"That's pretty cool. I didn't know that."

"Was that your new girl friend I spoke to?"

"I don't have a new girl friend, sweetheart. That was Darlena. From work. She came by to toke some weed."

"Dolly. Mary. Darlena. Your social circle is expanding, Anthony. Do you think you might be able to fit me in for dinner Monday night?"

"Well, I don't know, Doctor Barron. I'll have to check with the maitre'd to see if we've had any cancellations, but we might be able to squeeze you into a table in the back. Will that reservation be for two or three?"

She laughed softly. "Just you and me. Richard is going home Sunday afternoon."

I liked the sound of that. If I could have some time alone with Rita, maybe I could restore the magic, rekindle the romance. These last three or four weeks, when I thought about it, were simply aberrant. Rita's protracted field trip to Alaska, the murder at Liquid Avenue, my absurd infatuation with Darlena Giordano—all of these things were weather phenomena, temporary congeries of heat, wind and water. The fundamental climate of our relationship was temperate, warm and steady. There was a reason why we had been together three years, why Rita still wanted to celebrate our anniversary. We still loved each other. Everything was going to be fine.

"La Fiesta?"

"Pick me up at six."

Tradition. These formulaic step dances we perform with each other are comforting in their repetitive routine, their invariant ceremony, their reassurance that, regardless of vicissitudes in the weather, everything was going to be fine.

Chapter Fifty

"Hi, Anthony."

"Good morning, Carla. How are you?"

My favorite apparition and most resourceful associate wore her thrift store coat with evident pride. "I'm warm for a change. Thanks to you. How about you? Everything okay?"

Everything was going to be fine. At the moment, however, I still had concerns. My normally unflappable boss Dan Pensacola had his back up like a cornered scorpion. My girl friend Rita Barron was still arm-in-arm with another man. My nemesis Darlena Giordano was out there somewhere with a poison dart in her shoulder bag that was only going to cost me a five thousand dollar Porsche to disinfect. And the Santa Barbara Police Department suspected me for a crime I didn't commit and didn't suspect me for one I did.

"Okay, I guess. Thanks for asking. How about some coffee?"

"I saw the police were here again yesterday. Are they still investigating that murder?"

"I hope so. Yesterday they had other business here. Let me show you."

In the club, standing in front of the *Cocina Habana's* counter, where Luis and I had stood yesterday morning, I pointed, as Luis had done, at the empty space behind the bar at the far end of the room.

"That's where the Liquid Avenue sign used to be. Somebody took it. My boss Dan had the police in to investigate. It belonged to him personally. He said it's rather valuable. He's taking it pretty hard."

We went into the kitchen. Carla began to fill her pockets with sugar packets. She grinned at me, an ugly, turn-your-head-away grimace that advertised the rude want of amenities on the cold streets inhabited by the less fortunate. "There's a lot more room in this coat! I can keep enough sugar in here for a three-course meal."

In the parking lot, I gave her four double sawbucks. I was starting to think of Carla as my employee. She deserved compensation.

"You're such a nice guy, Anthony. I hate to impose on you, but I wonder if I could ask for a favor. I have an opportunity to, uh, 'cater' a party at the college out in Goleta this evening. Is there any chance I could catch a ride with you?"

Why not? Rita was occupied. I wanted to steer clear of Deejee. Bogo had not turned up anything yet to re-stock my cedar cigar box. I had no pressing engagements. A run out to UCSB would be a good opportunity to hear about my new employee's background.

Whatever Deejee had taken from the collection bag would never be missed. Friday night had produced another windfall. There was so much money to tally, I had to set some of it aside to count later so I could make my bank deposit and buy cashier's checks for today's deliveries before the bank closed at 1:00 PM.

I was back in the office when Carla returned at 3:00 for her ride to Goleta.

"Are you hungry? Can I treat you to lunch?"

"Good heavens, Anthony. That's so nice of you! I don't remember the last time a gentleman offered to buy me lunch."

The poor thing. I had never seen her figure above her legs and I couldn't see it now under her winter coat, but I imagined she resembled four toothpicks stuck in a prune. If she survived on sugar packets and God-only-knew what else, she probably couldn't muster much appetite.

"Since this is a rare occasion, you should have the pleasure of picking the cuisine. You fancy anything special?"

"Really? You're so thoughtful. You know what I haven't had lately? Chinese! Do you think we could order some Chinese take away? That would be wonderful."

I felt my employee warranted better than takeout, so I piloted her to one of my favorites, the Lotus Blossom, where we went on in and took a table. Carla sipped green tea and studied the menu for ten minutes. I didn't rush her. She settled on Mongolian beef with shrimp egg roll appetizers. I was mistaken about her appetite. She had brought one. It was a pleasure to watch her eat. She was unexpectedly mannered and demure, chewing small bites thoroughly with obvious relish. She left with a small sack of almond cookies under her arm and a grateful smile surrounding her atrocious teeth.

I thought she might need to freshen up before "catering" the college party I was delivering her to. We went to West Valerio, where I invited her to take as much time in the bathroom as she needed to be ready for her close-up.

We were on the 101 in light traffic on course for Goleta by 4:30. Neither of us had said much. Carla was gracious enough to enjoy her ride and meal with a minimum of superficial chatter, which suited me because I was preoccupied.

"Are you sure you're okay, Anthony? I don't want to pry, but you seem to have something on your mind. It's none of my business, but, if talking is your thing, I'm a good listener."

Talking was not my thing. On this rare occasion, however, I felt like sharing with my new employee. What could be the harm in it?

I began with a sigh. "I'm not the nice guy you credit me for, Carla. I've got myself in hot water." I shook my head, eyes fixed on the highway ahead. "That missing sign in the nightclub? That was my fault. Remember that woman who came into the club with me a few days ago? Her name is Darlena. She tried to steal the sign. I didn't try to stop her. Then we broke it."

I glanced at Carla for evidence of her disapproval. Her lips were pursed; her eyes scanned the broken white lines that separated the traffic lanes zipping under us. She nodded. "I saw that. I was in the parking lot."

"No kidding?" My eyebrows went up. "Did you see her taking a picture of me holding the sign next to my car?"

"I wondered what that flash was. For a second I thought she might have shot you."

My head swiveled to assess her seriousness.

"After all, you had a murder in your club two weeks ago."

"She might as well have shot me. That photo is a cannonball. If my boss ever sees it, he might shoot me too."

"So this Darlena person, she wants to use that picture to get something from you?"

"She will trade it for a Porsche she expects me to buy for her."

"That sounds expensive. Are you gonna do it?"

"I can't think of any other way to get that photo back. I loaned her a spare key to my apartment. I need to get that back too."

"If you get the picture back, how can you be sure she didn't make copies?"

I hadn't thought of that. I presumed, since the snapshot was a Polaroid, there would be no negative. But, by now, Deejee could already have made a dozen full-color duplicates at any copy shop in town. My situation was much worse than I imagined.

"There's more. Darlena has been stealing money right under my nose; she forged my boss's signature on a company check; the identity documents she gave me when she was hired are false. I don't even know her real name. I put her up in my apartment because she got her ass kicked by some bully boy; my girl friend found out about that, and she's probably going to leave me."

"Your girl friend would leave you for that?"

"No. Not just that. Rita and I have been together for three years. She's a geology teacher at the university. She's given me every chance. Now she's met some fellow that's serious about her. I think . . ." I searched for the proper cliche, "her heart is torn. Like I said, I'm not the nice guy you take me to be.

"It might not be too late to patch things up with Rita. We have an anniversary coming up on Monday, and she still wants to observe it. I'm pinning my hopes on that."

Carla indicated the Ward Memorial ramp for our freeway egress, the utility highway that ran out toward the ocean, the Goleta slough, the airport, and the south side of the university. Short of the campus, she pointed to Sandspit Road, an exit that spilled into Goleta Beach County Park.

"This is good, right here." A strip of parkway with lavatories and a playground with kids' equipment ran contiguous with the beach and its volleyball courts. "There's the party host." A Volkswagen camper, distant elder cousin to my own Rabbit, with peace symbols painted on its sides, would convey Carla for the remainder of her trek. "You can drop me off on the macadam here."

I did not like the look of that camper. It was the vehicle of choice for every Hollywood movie serial killer cruising for shapely hitchhikers to snuff. By the look of her, Carla was a lady who had been around the block enough times to know the difference between an innocent John and a psychotic slasher. My employee could take care of herself.

I was fond of Carla. Something about her suggested that her life would be worth hearing about. Besides, who uses words like "macadam"?

Chapter Fifty-One

I stirred brown sugar into a bowl of oatmeal at Carrow's. Last night I had eaten lightly at the Lotus Blossom with Carla. My appetite was still absent without leave. I munched buttered sourdough toast without enthusiasm, looking over the morning newspaper without interest.

"Top that off for you?" Jean poured from her coffee carafe. "Remember that Asian woman I told you about? The lady named Chin? She was in here again yesterday morning."

"She was?" My head swung up. "Did she ask any more questions about me?"

"No, she didn't. I asked her if she was a friend of yours. She said, 'Not yet.'"

"Did she have a business card or something? Maybe I could call her and see what she wants."

"She didn't leave one."

I had too much percolating under my skullcap for this. I was weary of mystery. If this Chin woman knew where I ate, she undoubtedly knew where I worked, and, probably, where I lived. Why all the cloak and dagger?

If I was tired of mystery, I was absolutely sick of counting money. American dollars literally spilled out of the safe and tumbled to the frozen buckboards that floored the walk-in cooler. I'd filled the collection bag and still had handfuls of currency to scoop into a plastic trash bag. There was no pressure to prepare a bank deposit on a Sunday, but there was so much dough that I had to bear down on it if I wanted to finish the count before my afternoon appointment.

Including the money I had not had time to deposit Saturday, I had packed over fifteen thousand dollars into the collection bag when I walked it out to the Rabbit shortly before 2:00 PM.

Doug lived on Butterfly Lane in Montecito among the preserves of the elite. The Porsche 944 sunned itself in his driveway. I had to admit it. It was a lovely machine.

Personally, I care less for sports cars. The qualifying adjective "performance", applied to automobile engines, is a synonym for "maintenance." I could admire it as an art object. It was cherry red with black trim and tan leather interior. It was as specific an expression of testosterone as a Marine tattoo. It was as self-consciously sexy as a men's magazine centerfold. It was not my type, so I would never love it. But I could confess to lust.

Doug greeted me at his front door. "You're late."

"I'm sorry, Doug. I'm working today."

"That's no excuse. You should never keep anyone waiting."

I agreed with him on that. I looked at my Movado. It was two minutes past the time we had set for our test drive.

"All right, then." I didn't want to make an ordeal of this. "Maybe we should get started on the test drive."

"Hold on a second. There's some formalities."

We passed through a sizeable foyer lined with travertine tiles. Directly in front of the entranceway, a pair of enormous statues of medieval knights hacked out of limestone guarded Doug's castle. We went into a den that was twice as large as my apartment. In the den, two brushed leather couches attended a polished coffee table of burled oak. A glass-enclosed case on one wall caught the eye immediately, as it was meant to. It displayed six hunting rifles and six pistols of various caliber and manufacture, all shined impeccably, silently marking the days until their next safari. On three walls, the mounted heads of game animals—a lion, a tiger, a boar, an assortment of elk and gazelle crania—stared implacably into space. A rearing, full blown California brown bear and, for some reason, a yak, were attached to pedestals to ensure their stability.

There was a file folder on the coffee table. Doug took one of the couches and I parked myself on the other. He wore a short-sleeved, collared white shirt with a green logo that said "Pebble Beach Golf Links." He sipped from a bottle of Pellegrino that he placed fastidiously on an onyx coaster.

"You have to realize that I've had a lot of offers on my car. Everyone wants the Porsche mystique. Not everyone deserves it. I turned down a couple of buyers who offered me more than I was asking. They were not Porsche caliber people."

I was distracted by all the dead marble eyes peering blindly and intently into the forever they could not have anticipated. I was not a hunter. Nevertheless, hunting trophies always made me feel guilty, as if it was up to me to apologize for the merciless savagery of my species.

"Did you shoot all those animals?"

"My father took down the prey from Asia and Africa. The North and Central American kills are mine."

"Your dad shot a yak?"

"You sound like one of those whiny, neutered liberals who go into convulsions when someone steps on a potato bug. Real men are not afraid of killing. We've been killing animals for millions of years. Hunting is a sport. People who can't accept that should just shut up and go back to their fruits and nuts."

"Hunting will be a sport when the animals have rifles too. Until then, it's just a pastime."

Where was my diplomacy? I needed to schmooze this white hunter so I could buy his car and get Darlena Giordano off my back. Insulting him was not likely to buy me the Porsche "mystique". Maybe I was fed up with people not taking death seriously.

I expected Doug to show me the door. Apparently, his contempt was trumped by his desire to bag a customer. "You want to buy my car or not?"

"That's what I came for."

He opened his file folder and withdrew a preprinted form. "Then I'll need you to sign this waiver and give me the two hundred dollar deposit."

"What? Why would I give you a deposit before I decide to buy the car?"

"You weren't listening to me. Lots of people want to buy my Porsche. I need a demonstration of your sincerity. This waiver indemnifies me if you damage my car during the test drive. You get the deposit back when you buy the car. If you didn't want to buy it, you wouldn't be here wasting my time."

I had enough cash on hand in the Rabbit to buy his car three times. I was tempted to forego the test drive and show this troglodyte how real men hunt for automobiles by plopping my canvas bag on Doug's coffee tale and counting out his five thousand bucks in singles in exchange for the Porsche's pink slip.

It was just a formality, a ceremony I had to observe to satisfy an insecure man's need to stay in the driver's seat while he was selling his car. To speed things along, I signed Doug's waiver, gave him his two hundred in twenties, and took the test drive with him sitting nervously in the passenger seat.

The flaming chariot looked like something Phaeton himself would proudly employ to pull the sun across the sky, but it handled like a tugboat. I knew this wasn't the model that took all those trophies at Le Mans, but still . . . I didn't expect a Porsche to corner like a fishing barge.

It didn't matter. The test drive, like the insurance waiver and the deposit, was a formality. I had to endure this comedy and buy this bucket of bolts to escape Deejee's clutches.

"I'll buy it for five thousand." I informed Doug, returning his ignition key. "I can pay you tomorrow."

"Okay. Agreed." Doug said, trying not to look relieved. "But tomorrow's not convenient for me. Have the money here Tuesday at noon. Cash or money order. And don't be late."

"I'll take my two hundred back, if you don't mind."

"You weren't listening. I said the deposit will be deducted from the purchase price. It's non-refundable. Read the waiver you just signed."

I dispensed with formality. "Have it your way. I'll be back Tuesday at noon."

We didn't shake on it.

I was not expecting company, but Bogo was waiting for me in the parking lot at West Valerio. His 1989 Dodge Colt sat next to the empty space where I stabled the Rabbit.

"Hey, Gene! You stumble into some joy?"

"Not this time. I kind of stubbed my toe though."

In my apartment, we sat on my gray sofa, nursing Vernor's bottles.

"Sorry I've got no sparklers on hand. I'm out."

"Might not do much for me anyway." Bogo's rainbow wool cap slumped on his bowed head. "I got divorce papers from Natalya. She not only called it quits; she wants half my assets. Jesus fucking Christ. We were only together a few months. You happen to know a good divorce lawyer?"

"As a matter of fact, I do. Her name is Anne. She lives over on Sutton Avenue. I'll put her in touch with you."

"I was asking for it with a mail order bride. What was I thinking? I'm going to get eviscerated by a saber-tooth tiger."

"You're being threatened by an extinct predator? I just met Homo Erectus in Montecito. The guy has more dead animals in his cave than the La Brea tar pits. He talked about killing as if was the whole point of human evolution."

"He's wrong. Reproduction is the whole point of human evolution. Even with all the killing, we will probably have seven billion people shoving each other around on this planet within twenty years."

"Present company excepted."

The rainbow cap popped up; a grimace zippered Bogo's mouth. "Then there's you. Nature's one-eyed jack. Everyone else is Johnny Appleseed, but you can plow any field you like and never have a harvest. You're a lucky man, Tony."

Bogo, who knew better than to wager on horses, had gambled on a romance with long odds and lost. "Life is infinitely stranger than anything which the mind of man can invent."

How about that? I remembered a quote from Sherlock Holmes.

Chapter Fifty-Two

I thought Deejee would call Sunday afternoon to see how I did with the Porsche, but she didn't. All things taken into consideration, including the bag with fifteen thousand dollars under my bed, I slept reasonably well.

I was hoping to run into my new employee in the parking lot, but Carla did not emerge from the shadows.

As usual, Sunday night's receipts were modest. I was grateful for that. I had withdrawn two hundred dollars from my ATM to repay the money I had borrowed from the collection bag. By 9:30, I had my bank business ready.

It was always a satisfying moment for me when the money was safely deposited. As a point of pride taken from one's occupation, it wasn't much to put in the headlines—not equivalent to transplanting a kidney or negotiating a corporate buyout—but we bank our pride when we've earned it, even in small deposits.

The rumble from the voice box preceded the salutation. "Mornin', Tony."

Randy took the other chair, his cold Pepsi gripped in his fist. "Pops been here yet?"

"Not yet."

"I had a bad night. I've got these neck pains. No matter how I turn my head, agony. Feels like I've been crucified. Say, I didn't see you at the funeral."

"What funeral?"

"On Saturday morning. At Sacred Eucharist Church. They buried Lyss."

I stopped fussing with the money and faced him. "Nobody mentioned it to me. I would have liked to say *adios*."

"It was no big deal. A lot of muttering in Catholic. Tommy didn't show either. Jimmy and Dan were there. Dan's really pissed about the sign."

The silver Rolls Royce purred in the parking lot and came to rest. "Oh, good. Here he is." Randy went out the door.

It took them long enough to get around to laying Lyss to rest. I suppose police forensic needs had everything to do with that. Poor Lyss. Even her husband had not bothered to turn out for her interment.

I was still expecting a call from Deejee. Did she want me to buy that car or not? I had calculated that, by squeezing cash advances out of my credit cards and sucking my bank account dry, I could get the forty-eight hundred dollars lined up to get Doug's autograph on the Porsche's pink slip. I wanted Deejee's confirmation and her company when I went back to Butterfly Lane on Tuesday to complete all the "formalities".

I took care of the banking, visited the *Cocina Habana* for a *café Cubano*, and went back to the bookkeeping. My phone rang. Finally!

It was not Darlena. It was somebody much better. "Anthony! I'm sorry to bother you at work. Something's come up. I wanted to get your opinion."

"Of course, Doc. Everything okay?"

"Oh, sure. Better than okay. Richard went back to Newport Beach yesterday. Then he called to let me know he'd got home safely. He's so considerate. Anyway, the reason I called is because I seem to have won a prize in some sort of random drawing. Instead of going to La Fiesta tonight, we're going to have a gourmet dinner catered at my place. I hope that's okay with you. I know we have our traditional observance for the occasion, but this is out of the ordinary and it sounded very exciting and it's all free.

"Would you like to come by my place at 5:30? I asked the caterers to start setting up at 6:00."

"I'll be delighted. I'm intrigued."

"Too good to be true, right? And the timing? Anyway, I hoped you could come early. In case it's hinky in some way."

That was charming. Rita had agreed to have people over to serve us a gourmet meal, but she wanted me to be there when they arrived in case there was a catch. Good thinking on Doctor Barron's part. It was unlike her to be impromptu about our anniversary dinner, but I agreed with her. It sounded very exciting.

There was no special reason why I should have been invited to Lyss Nelson's funeral. It was spiteful of me to feel resentment just because I was the one who seemed to be most upset about her death, I was the one the police still suspected had strangled her, and I was the one who was trying hardest to crack the case.

I could scarcely claim my investigation had contributed much to finding the killer. In turning over the rocks to see what lay beneath them, I was restricted to speculations about motive. If the murder was a random act of psychosis or another notch in the belt of a serial killer, my speculations were pointless. I would never know the motive. If it was somebody I knew, there had to be a reason. The Tommy-Jimmy-Elizabeth triangle looked promising because an unborn child was involved and hard feelings can arise in such situations. Try as I may, I could not see anything in the Strennis pregnancy that might lead to murdering Lyss. It was Jimmy who wanted to marry her, not Tommy. The death of Tommy's wife had actually put him off Elizabeth.

Did Darlena Giordano do it? She had asked me if I would kill for her. Would she kill for herself? Now knowing what I did about her—and very much aware of what I did *not* know about her—she seemed as capable of murder as anyone I could name. She certainly had the opportunity.

I was back to motive. What quarrel could possibly have arisen between Lyss and Deejee that would end with a corpse lying in the sawdust?

I threw in the towel. I was no more a crime solver than I was a Formula One auto racer. I might as well suspect Trigger and Peanut. Or Chin.

It was time to make myself presentable for my most important date in three years. Tonight I would reclaim Rita. I never thought of people as possessions in any sense, but I wanted to think of Rita as mine. In the romantic sense. In the have and hold sense. In the matrimonial sense.

It was time for me to do the right thing for my girlfriend.

Chapter Fifty-Three

Rita's place was in the Samarkand neighborhood, an appealing section of town folded into the low hills between the Riviera and the Mesa. She owned a three-bedroom, three-bath home with a curving driveway. Old-fashioned brick facia ran halfway up the exterior walls, topped by tan stucco and chocolate brown trim. It was even prettier on the inside. I used to live here.

I had parked in this driveway so often I could have let the Rabbit find its familiar old spot on it own. Rita met me at the door.

"Hi, Anthony."

When she hugged me, the invisible space between us seemed as solid as either of our bodies. I aimed to close that gap.

It had been only six weeks since my last visit, so I did not expect anything to have changed. Nothing had. The same smells, the same furniture, the same objects on the walls, the same layout—everything was as it had been since I was a resident.

One funny thing about Doctor Barron and I—another inexorable proof that we belonged together—was that we were both collectors. I possessed, and continually added to, a substantial collection of books and music. Rita had rocks.

One entire wall of her living room was a mineral museum. Doctor Barron's collection of geological specimens was spectacular. One hardly needed to be a rock hound to be dazzled by the brilliant array of quartz crystals: adamite, limonite, manganite, vanadinite, vesuvianite, carnelian, wood opal. These crystals wrenched from the earth's crust could well have passed for visitors from Jupiter's moons, they were so unearthly. Rita assured me that, although the original molecules had come from the Kuiper Belt, the Oort Cloud, and stellar neighbors long deceased, these beautiful formations were entirely terrestrial. I volunteered to make labels for them, mostly for my own benefit. Rita, who could explain clearly exactly what these objects were, what they were made of, how they were formed and where, pooh-poohed my librarian's approach.

Standing in front of her eye-grabbing geodes, I remembered that Rita would know why I had smelled nothing when Deejee and I broke the Liquid Avenue sign. "Why is neon a 'noble' gas?"

"Because it doesn't mix with anything. In Lavoisier's day, when gases were first being separated and identified according to their properties, aristocrats didn't mix with commoners. Neon, helium, argon, krypton, xenon, and radon: colorless, odorless, tasteless, inert. 'Noble' gases don't make smellable chemical compounds."

On her television, there was a recent photograph of Rita's daughter Lillian. She had lived here too for a few months before she transferred from UCSB to UC Santa Cruz. Lillian was brisk and unfriendly to me at first, but eventually her attitude warmed because we were both English majors. I helped her write a couple of term papers. After I introduced her to the work of Italo Calvino and Robertson Davies, we had inexhaustible topics of mutual fascination and we got along splendidly.

Rita had not married Lillian's father. They had only stayed together a year or so after Lillian's birth and then went their separate ways. Rita rarely mentioned him, but when she did, there was no bitterness. She'd gone on to complete her education, including the doctorate, and raised her daughter by herself.

"You won a prize in a drawing?"

We camped in the living room, waiting for the employees of Your Xanadu to arrive and set up our epicurean feast.

"Weird, huh? This lady came to my office yesterday and said they had picked my name to receive a free dinner for two as a promotional gimmick to get their new business off the ground."

"Let me guess," I interrupted. "It was an Asian woman named Chin, right?"

"No." She frowned. "It was an English lady. Here's her business card."

The plain white card read:

Your Xanadu
Virginia Washington
Proprietor

"And your name was selected at random?"

"From among a list of 'ideal clients', as Virginia described it. The idea is, they are starting their business by giving away free dinners for a month to generate word-of-mouth buzz. They decided to approach professional people first, those most likely to use their service in the future. So their hope is, they'll get people like me—like you and I—to fall in love with them and tell everybody their catering is incredible."

"Interesting. What sort of food are we having?"

"Virginia showed me their catalog of international cuisines. It's amazing really. All varieties of mouth-watering ethnic stuff: Japanese, Korean, Thai, Vietnamese, Indian, Persian, Egyptian, North, Central and South American, all the Euro specialties. For tonight, I kept it simple. We're going Italian."

"I have no problem with that."

We had no problems with Your Xanadu. It was not a scam. It was not a hoax. It was not a bizarre plot to invade Rita's home and kidnap her. At 6:00 PM on the dot a small panel truck pulled into the driveway. Two girls in starched, immaculate white uniforms with matching caps went to work in Rita's kitchen, transporting trays, covered bowls, ice chests, and an electric heating apparatus. They wore white nameplates with bold, black letters that identified them as "Kimiko" and "Nancy".

For the next three hours, Kimiko and Nancy went back and forth between Rita's kitchen and dining room serving us courses. They didn't say much, limiting themselves to polite queries as to our exact preferences. They had brought a boom box and played Italian music. They supplied wine that I did not drink but that Rita reported was superb.

Around 9:00 PM, Kimiko and Nancy cleaned up, packed up, and departed with best wishes and the hope that if we were pleased, we'd tell others.

We were sated to the point of belt unbuckling and Rita was a little drunk. "What did you think?"

"I thought it was marvelous. You're the one who's been to Italy. What did you think?"

Rita giggled. "I think our meal never got within five miles of a genuine Italian. I ain't complaining. It was delicious. The price was right." She giggled again.

"If they can afford to do that for enough people, it's a great promotion. They probably ought to put the company name on the uniforms and the truck. That might help people remember them."

"They're a new business. They might be holding back on that until they're off the ground."

There's nothing like a boatload of bread and pasta, and in Rita's case, alcohol, to slow things down. The lassitude settled in as soon as our Xanadu attendants puttered away. We were too engorged even to switch on the television.

"Shouldn't we make a toast to German reunification or something?"

Reunification was what I was here for. I hoisted my bottle of mineral water. "I'll drink to that."

Unlike many, Rita was a sweet drunk. She never raged, never got belligerent, never lapsed into harsh antagonism or sobbing self-pity. She tended to giggle, burble, and fall asleep well before any of the nasty effects of alcohol took effect. Best of all, she tended to be amorous.

Before I had set my bottle on her coffee table, Rita rolled across my body, planted her face in mine and stuck her tongue in my mouth. From there, nature and three years of habit took the reins.

We found our way to Rita's bedroom, let textile impediments tumble to the floor, and fell on each other. In the comfortable, easy way she took me inside her, it was as if I had never been away. She was slightly asthmatic, so Rita's deep breathing carried a gentle rasp that never failed to excite me. We fell asleep in each other's arms. I was home again.

I awoke early, as always. Rita was already up; I could smell the coffee simmering in the kitchen.

She sat at her breakfast table. "I didn't want to wake you." She smiled. "Please, have a seat."

Rita knew how I like my coffee. She poured, stirred, and set a mug in front of me, returning to her seat. I tried to formulate a phrase that would appropriately launch this glorious new beginning for us.

"Anthony, I have something to tell you. I'm leaving."

"Leaving?" That concept was not in the phrase I was cooking in my mind. My words were going have something to do with love, commitment, putting the past behind, and so forth.

"Richard and I are getting married. I'm moving to his place this weekend. I'm putting the house up for sale. By this time next week, I'll be living in Newport Beach."

Chapter Fifty-Four

I was not in a state of surprise, but I was certainly in shock. I gave breakfast a pass. After a brief stop at West Valerio, I went straight to work.

I shuffled through the sawdust numb, my collection bag hanging limply in one paw. I noticed the formless shadowy pile under one of the tables, but gave it no mind. Monday night's club proceeds were light. I would tally them in no time. Then I could start on the payroll or anything else to keep my mind occupied.

Rita was leaving. This week. It was over. How did I not see it coming?

I refused to ask myself who was to blame. I wasn't going to like the answer. It stared at me accusingly every time I looked in a mirror.

Shortly after 5:00 AM Luis knocked on my door. "¡Señor Tony!"

I followed him into the club. He pointed at the shape under the table. "¡Mira!"

By 5:30, Liquid Avenue was a crime scene again. The yellow police tape was everywhere. The SBPD forensic van was parked by the dumpster and the team was combing the club for clues. I was under arrest.

I had admitted to the first officer on the scene that I knew the victim. The name I had for her in my personnel file was Darlena Giordano.

I was sitting in the familiar interrogation room on East Figueroa Street with Detective Imanaka. We were waiting for my lawyer.

"You are aware of your rights, Anthony. Is there anything you'd like to tell me off the record? You know perfectly well that the more cooperative you are with us, the smoother things will go here."

I shook my head. I had been escorted through the back entrance in handcuffs. I was no longer cuffed as we waited for an attorney from the Public Defender's office.

"How about some coffee? You know, Anthony, I took your advice. I took my fiancée to dinner at the *Cocina Habana* last week. It was great! Their *pollo* melts in your mouth while it blisters your palette with cayenne and paprika."

I manufactured politeness. "I'm a big fan of their *pollo Cubano* sandwich. Coffee sounds nice, thanks."

"The handcuffs were excessive, I'll give you that. Officer Cepeda was a bit more aggressive than he needed to be. You have to understand, Anthony. My team has been working very hard on this case. Now that we have a second murder on our hands, we are all taking it personally. It's a good idea to wait for your legal representative, but if there's anyone who can verify where you were last night, you could be out of here in an hour."

I hated to involve Rita in this. Three hours after her final kiss off, I had to ask her to come to the police station to vouch for me. She convinced Detective Imanaka that I had been in her company from 5:30 last evening until 4:00 this morning. It was a fantastic break for me that, of all nights, my last night with Rita exonerated me of killing Deejee. Rachel released me, patting me on the back with friendly advice, "If you have to leave town for any reason, please let me know."

On the wide concrete steps leading to East Figueroa, Rita shook my hand. It was hard to believe that, twelve hours previous, she'd had her tongue in my mouth. She had no smile for me.

"Hear that, Anthony?" She cocked her head, as if she were listening. "That's the fog horn going off in your head. You're lost. Find yourself a direction. Stop scraping your ass on the rocks."

I walked back to work.

I ignored the investigation still in full swing at the club. Tomorrow was payday. People were still going to need their pay, regardless what else was going on in their workplace, their city, their world. It was my job to make sure they got it. I did my job.

In a state of mind a zombie would appreciate, I went to the bank to make my deposit and came back to the club to finish the payroll. I had not eaten since last night, when my manicotti came courtesy of Your Xanadu. I wondered if I would ever feel hunger again.

Deejee was dead at the hands of the serial killer we and the police had failed to track down. The odious fact was that, whoever the killer was, he had solved a serious problem for me. If either the incriminating photo of me with the Liquid Avenue sign or the key to my apartment had been in Deejee's bag, I would still be in police custody. Where could they be? As long as they were floating around out there, I was on thin ice.

I had been skating all morning. Had it been necessary to talk to either Detective Imanaka or the Public Defender's lawyer, I would have been obliged to say more about my dealings with Deejee than I had any inclination to disclose.

The victim had not been identified for Rita or she might have recalled that Darlena had picked up the phone in my apartment last Thursday night and was, therefore, a member of my "expanding social circle."

According to the employee time cards, Elizabeth had not worked in the club last night. If luck continued to ride with me, the police might not interview her and Strennis might not tell them that Deejee had informed her that I had put her in a pregnant way. Deejee, as it happened, was not pregnant and even if she was, I was incapable of fatherment, a medical fact I could easily prove. Nonetheless, I would much prefer that my association with Deejee, such as it was, be laid to rest with her.

When my phone barged in on my reverie, I looked at it for a long moment before answering.

"Tony? Pete Hardy. Naturally, our office was notified that there's been another killing. I have information that might interest you. Can we meet somewhere? I should tell you that I know Rachel had you in for questioning this morning. I'm not calling in any official capacity. Our conversation will be confidential between you and me."

"How about Stearn's Wharf?"

Twenty minutes later, I was strolling towards the sea end of the pier with the District Attorney's lawyer. It was quite cold; heavy clouds gathered over the Channel; a gray choppy ocean bristled with whiteheads. I wore my purple parka. Pete swept along in a black wool coat that flapped slightly in the breeze. We had our hands in our pockets.

We had to speak up to be heard over the elements, the creaking of timbers, and the crack of sails as boats left their slips and headed into the Channel. We could have shouted if we needed to. We were not going to be overheard.

"It was a strangulation, same as last time. The victim was doped with opiates and killed sometime between 1:00 AM and 3:00 AM. The similarity to the earlier murder strongly suggests serial killer to the police.

"Now that we have fingerprints to go on, we have identified the person known as Darlena Giordano. Name: Darlena Widmer. Born: Fremont, Ohio, December 1946. When she lived in Chicago, she was known as Dana Gordon. That's why we didn't find a driver's license from the State of Illinois. It was under a different name. She never did time, but she was wanted by Cook County authorities in connection with an extortion case that led to the suicide of an automobile dealer in Berwyn, Illinois.

"We don't speak ill of the dead, Tony, but I think we can count ourselves lucky. Darlena was not a nice person. Eventually, she would have dumped all her troubles on our doorstep."

Eventually? My dalliance with Darlena Giordano had already cost me Rita; if my true connection with her could be established, the police would have me in cuffs again; if that Polaroid surfaced and fell into the wrong hands, Dan Pensacola would disembowel me. Deejee had already dumped enough troubles on my doorstep to have my apartment quarantined for toxicity.

"Here's the thing. This is why we're talking. I don't want to know what you and Darlena Widmer were up to. My concern is to keep Mary out of this. The only ones who know my sister was friendly with Widmer are you and Lloyd Thurlist. I'm not at all sure whether Mary even remembers you two or Darlena. I'm keeping my eye on Lloyd. I'm willing to roll the dice on you. Can I trust you to keep quiet about Mary and Darlena?"

It was easy to give Pete that assurance. It was very much in my best interest to pretend that my connection to Darlena Giordano Widmer was tenuous, casual, and short-lived. She was stretched out on a slab in the morgue and I was already bleaching her from my past as if she were no more than an unsightly stain.

There was something I was supposed to do today. I had made no reminder notes for myself, so it must have been something I would be sure to remember. For any of my chores that went unattended today, I granted me absolution.

The payroll was ready for signature by 3:00 PM. I rang Dan Pensacola to arrange for his signing of the checks. He invited me to bring them to Virginia Road.

We met in Dan's neon showroom office. The signs were not lit today. The only illumination flowed from the lamp on his desk. Shadows moved around on Dan's face as he busied himself with his pen.

"You are among the first to know, Tony. I sold the club. This will be Liquid Avenue's last payroll."

I sat on my sofa at West Valerio, listening to the traffic on the 101. It sounded wet out on the road; the rush and roar punctuated by slippery splashes. The high-pitched whine of a sports car squeaked by. I remembered what it was I was supposed to do today.

I got him after three rings. "Hello, Doug. It's Anthony Trapp."

"You have your nerve, jackass. I waited for you here until 12:30. Where the hell were you? I don't think I want to sell you my Porsche. And I'm keeping your two hundred dollars for my trouble."

"Really? I will try to live with my heartbreak. In the meantime, I have some 'mystique' for you. Go fuck yourself."

Chapter Fifty-Five

The club was closed Tuesday night. There was no money to count. Today would be everyone's last Liquid Avenue payday.

I took an extra hour of sleep. It was almost daylight before I unlocked my office. Luis was at work, methodically mopping the hallway behind his "Slippery When Wet" sign. Maybe nobody had told him it was all over.

Dan Pensacola called at 8:30 AM. "Here's the deal. The new buyers cashed out Tommy and Randy last night. Everybody gets paid through Monday night. I'll pay you and Jimmy and Luis for yesterday and today.

"The new owners are going to have a salsa nightclub. They may interview some of our bar tenders and cocktail waitresses, but they have their own administrative people in place. Margarito and Elena are going to extend their lease and keep *Cocina Habana* open.

"The new folks want to get started on remodeling the building as soon as possible, so we are quitting the premises today. I'll be in this afternoon to collect your keys. I need you to meet with Robert Bellaire and bring him up to speed on the books, so he can close everything down for tax filing purposes."

The first Liquid Avenue employee to arrive for his last paycheck was Tommy Nelson.

"Tony! I guess you heard. The club got sold. What's the bottom of the line?"

"Do you mean how much profit or loss resulted from the sale? That would be a question for Robert Bellaire. I don't have numbers on the sale of the club."

"Hey, did you watch the game Friday night? The Lakers won in overtime."

What I wanted to ask him was not who won the game but who sat next to him at the Forum. Before I got the query past my lips, Brandilyn Archiver came through the door and slipped her arm through Tommy's.

I located their two checks, passed them over and they went out the door arm-in-arm. The redhead paused in the doorway.

"Bye," she said.

Most of the other employees came and went. Some were aware that their next stop would be the Employment Development Department to sign up for unemployment benefits. Others seemed to believe they would be working tonight as usual. None offered fond farewells.

Jimmy folded his check and slid it into his shirt pocket. "If anybody needs me, I'll be in there taking the last inventory."

At 11:30, Elizabeth Strennis walked in. My back was to the door. I didn't hear her enter.

"Oh, Tony! Can you believe it?"

Her volcanic mass of hair was dark and damp, snarled into clingy tangles. I had not heard her entrance because a bright blue raincoat draped from her shoulders to her kneecaps, and long sleeves muffled her bracelets. Her big green eyes were wet.

"Can I have a hug?"

I stood and embraced her. Her arms pulled me tight. She shivered and started to cry. I lightened my hold on her to give her chest room to swell with sobs. Her fragrance was sweet and fruity, something like apricot or peach.

"Tommy dropped me. He wouldn't say why. He just said he sold the club and he's moving." Intermittent sobbing rudely interrupted her words. "What am I going to do?"

I released her so I could reach for the box of tissues in my desk drawer. Brown mascara forced its way down her cheeks in muddy rivulets. I dabbed at the mess carefully. Elizabeth's eyelashes stuck to each other. She blinked.

"Tony," she sighed. "You've always been so nice to me." She pulled me close again, the hard polished nails on her fingertips digging into my back. "What do you think? Maybe if things were different. Do you think you could ever be interested in someone like me?"

The problem was that I would always be interested in someone like Elizabeth. I would never be interested in the child rounding into shape in her womb. If I had the connecting pipes to make progeny, I would have fathered children years ago.

"Sweetie, you are impossibly beautiful. The list of men who could be interested in you would be longer than a Tokyo telephone book. The name at the top of that list happens to be in there"—I indicated the club with my thumb—"counting liquor bottles. Why don't you go on in and have a chat with him?"

Three men trooped into the office together. The short one with the cement mixer voice asked, "Has Tommy been in yet this morning?"

"You just missed him."

"Son of a bitch! He's supposed to meet me here today about my thirty thousand clams. If that fucker thinks he can duck me, I'll pull off his nuts and feed them to a faggot. Is Jimmy here?"

Lawrence and David, known to their admirers as Trigger and Peanut, smirked and said nothing. I handed off paychecks. Trigger went out the door. Peanut opened his arms.

"Gimme a squeeze, bro." We embraced with brief, manful, mutual thumps on the back. "Good luck, Tony. See you around."

Randy was back. "Jimmy's talking to Elizabeth. Hello! Look who's here."

The silver Rolls Royce, sliding in as smooth and noiseless as a submarine, claimed a space in the parking lot. Randy walked out to greet it.

He was back almost immediately. It had begun to rain. Cold heavy drops splashed in the parking lot, pounding the dumpster and the Rolls' roof in steady meter like symphonic tympani.

Randy wiped his dripping freckled forehead with his open palm. His rusty eyebrows went up slightly. "Pops wants to talk to you."

Chapter Fifty-Six

I turned up my collar and shuffled out into the rain. The rear door on the passenger side of the car swung open. I climbed aboard. It would be pointless for me to describe how it feels to occupy the backbench of a Rolls Royce. I have no vocabulary adequate to the task.

A panel of opaque polymers separated the front section from the back. An Asian man in a seersucker suit and a powder blue silk shirt open at the neck shared the deep cushions with me. He was no taller than a parking meter and not much wider. His face was round, brown, lined, and spotted with dabs that might have been melted Milk Duds. His eyes were almonds in beds of cream. He was somewhere between 50 and 150 years old.

"The time is propitious for us to meet, Mister Trapp. May I call you Anthony?"

"Sure."

"I am Yee."

And you are me and we are all together. What could this coddled fossil possibly want with me?

"Think of me as your *deus ex machina*. I have three gifts for you, Anthony. This is the least precious of them."

He handed me a japanned box in black lacquer with yellow floral designs. I had seen these, or something like them, at every

Pier One emporium I had ever shopped in. As I lifted the lid, the aroma stormed out and assaulted my olfactory receptors. The box contained about an ounce of delicate cannabis buds of rich Kelly green shot through with gold veins. They did not sell these at Pier One. This was the most potent-looking ganja I had ever seen.

"Wow. Thank you, Mister Yee." He had got my attention. I could hardly wait for the other two gifts.

Yee studied me thoughtfully, as if he were trying to decide whether I was worth anything more precious than he had already given.

He spoke. "Who do you think will inherit the earth, Anthony?"

What? Was this some kind of Bible study test? Was this old coot going to pitch me soul-saving Christianity like Judy Crenshaw?

"The meek, I suppose."

"A poll parrot answer, Anthony. Matthew, Chapter Five, Verse Five. Not surprising for someone drenched from childhood in your culture. You are an educated man, but you have never given the question much thought, have you?"

"I'm not what you would call a religious guy, Mister Yee."

"It is not a religious question, Anthony. It's an historical one. It was considered and answered by someone from my culture five centuries before your tradition of Matthew was cast in writing. Confucius wrote that it is the "enduring" who will triumph in the end.

"I would ask you this. Who has been more enduring than we Chinese? We have been culturally cohesive for nearly four thousand years. Our various political systems have washed over us like waves in roiling waters, but these are ephemera, mere shapes and forms. The water itself endures. Invaders that have tried to overwhelm us have found themselves absorbed. In the 1800s we were known as the Yellow Peril. In this century, we have been identified as the Red Menace. In the next, we will be the White Light."

To my mind, China was the Purple Haze. Enormous. Ancient. Enigmatic. They had ideographs instead of an alphabet. Their language sounded like my singing in the shower. My shoeboxes of tape cassettes contained not a single note of Chinese music. When I was in elementary school, there were always two little boxes in the classrooms we were supposed to drop pennies into—one was for the redemption of "pagan babies"; the other was vaguely for "China Relief". When my Mom wanted me to eat every morsel on my dinner plate, she would always say, "People in China are starving." If the bottom of that plate was stamped "Made in China", it was the cheapest dinnerware you could buy—you didn't use it to serve your guests.

My host was still speaking.

"At this moment, one person in every five on our planet is Chinese. Within one hundred years, that ratio will be one in three. In the century following that, every person on earth will be Chinese."

Yee paused. His eyes bore into mine. Was he waiting for me to respond? The atmosphere in the Rolls had become heavy, permeated with solemnity. Or was that just the cannabis and sandalwood fragrance drifting up from the box in my lap?

The creases in Yee's face made a smile. "Have no fear, Anthony. I am not speaking of world domination of the jackboot variety. I am speaking of inevitability. We Chinese will prevail because we are best suited for it. We neither know nor care about the human physiognomy of the future. Racial characteristics are also ephemera, as irrelevant as the specific creeds of antipathetic religions, the doctrines of competing political systems, or the arbitrary boundaries of nations drawn on maps.

"I said that I have three gifts for you. The second, infinitely more valuable than the contents of that box you hold, is Knowledge. Tell me, Anthony. What is your definition of Knowledge?"

I was beginning to get the sense of this back seat tête-à-tête. Apparently, Yee just wanted someone to talk to. No doubt Randy was a disappointing conversationalist.

"Knowledge is an accumulation of factual truths," I ventured, "tested by experience over the course of time and verified by correspondence to reality."

I thought that was a fairly serviceable definition off-the-cuff. Yee shook his head.

"Another burp of the parrot. You repeat received wisdom. You have not troubled to hold your ideas up to the light for examination. You associate "fact" and "truth" carelessly, then position them against a backdrop of "reality", as if you were a photographer trying to find the most complimentary angle to reveal your subjects.

"Facts are not islands, isolated and complete in themselves. They are more like landings on an infinite stairway, temporary rest stops for momentary perspective. I will cite an example:

"For the best part of twenty-four hundred years, the 'atom' posited by Leucippus and Democritus was held to be the ultimate indivisible unit of physical matter. Physicists and chemists therefore searched for and indeed found this hypothetical entity. At the end of the 19th century, it was received wisdom that the atom conformed both to the gravitational mechanics of Newton and the electromagnetic calibrations of Maxwell. By the beginning of the 20th century, physicists believed that, as soon as the dualistic nature of light as both particle and wave was resolved, there would be nothing left for physicists to discover. In the 1920s, however, the theoretical work of Planck, Einstein, Bohr, Schroedinger, Pauli, and Heisenberg demonstrated that the notion of an "indivisible unit of matter" was merely a convenient model—a fact—that summarized what had been assumed up to that time. The closer physicists were able to peer into the atom, the less actual matter was there for them to observe. Furthermore, the act of observing itself changed the character of the phenomena under observation. The limits of observation suggest that uncertainty will always be the stairway that surrounds our temporary landings of 'fact'.

"As to 'truth', the notion has no meaning in itself. What is true merely stands in opposition to what is false. Truth in any ultimate sense is a delusion. Those who claim to possess it are fools.

"What we perceive as 'reality' is pure invention. Our minds construct it for us so that we may survive from moment to moment among endless waves of otherwise chaotic sensation. We do not have the capacity to comprehend what is truly real. Consider this. Many of the earth's organisms can 'see' the moon. Their perception of this celestial object guides their cycles of feeding, migration or reproduction. How many creatures can grasp what this object actually is, how it stands in relation to our planet, of what material it is composed, or whether other such objects exist in the universe? How many creatures possess the cognitive processes to frame such questions?

"In our century, physicists have discovered that space and time—two concepts that are crucial to our apprehension of the universe we inhabit—are twin aspects the same phenomenon. Space was previously understood to be synonymous with emptiness and time with irreversible temporal motion. Both space and time conform to geometries inaccessible to our senses. We are inescapably imbedded in the framework that contains them.

"In our apprehension of 'reality' we are in the same position as that of apes beholding the boundless sea. It serves us well that we ask questions, that we hunger for understanding, that we form models of 'reality' to satisfy our appetite to know who and why we are.

"It is a mistake to imagine that our questions will ever lead to final answers. The best we can ever hope is that our appetite will not be sated, that we will continue in our compulsion to pose questions. It is perilous for us to know. In the unwise and the unwary, knowing becomes Knowledge and Knowledge hardens into belief.

"Belief is the death of knowing and the tombstone of Knowledge."

Chapter Fifty-Seven

Yee was staring at me again. I was speechless. His philosophical disquisition certainly made me feel like an ape. Where were we sailing on this boundless sea? Hadn't he just said that his second gift for me was Knowledge?

"I have explained all this for a purpose, Anthony, as you will see. I have a few more things to say, but before I continue, would you care for a liquid refreshment?"

As a matter of fact—a temporary rest stop for momentary perspective—my throat did feel a little dry. "Sure, Mister Yee. That sounds good. What do you have?"

Yee turned to his side of the Rolls and slid open a panel in the leather siding. I could not see past his matchstick torso, but I heard ice crackling followed by the sound of consecutive pops, bottles being opened. He turned my way and damned if he didn't hand me a Vernor's ginger ale. He had one for himself. He sipped it. I was about to ask him, "how did you know?", but our subject was Knowledge and I realized that this was his way of showing me there was no end to what he knew.

"Thank you."

"You're welcome." Yee's smile moved the creases in his cheeks again. "The beverage of choice for discerning gentlemen. Wouldn't you agree?"

"Completely."

"I promised that I would make you a gift of Knowledge, Anthony. Would you like to know who killed Lyss Nelson and Darlena Giordano?"

I was so startled I nearly choked on my swig of Vernor's. Yee knew the identity of the serial killer? Did he himself have a hand in the murders? Were these horrifying crimes part of his loony Fu Manchu plot for Chinese mastery of the world?

"Of course I'd like to know, Mister Yee. So would the police. They still think I did it. If you have any information, shouldn't you be telling them about it?"

Yee held up the palm that was not holding his ginger ale. "Your concern is understandable, Anthony. Have no fear about the police. Detective Imanaka no longer suspects you. These are crimes she will never solve, however, because the murderer is a professional who has taken pains to mask their purpose. The police are transfixed by their beliefs, by what they take to be the "facts" of the case—the evidence that supports their supposition that the killer is psychopathic, vicious and irrational.

"My second gift to you is this: the killer was Carla."

And the Walrus was Paul. Carla? The pathetic street lady?

"Carla? I'm sorry. Mister Yee. How could that be? And even if it's true—I mean, not false—why would she do it? How do you know any of this? And why have you not told the police?"

Yee nodded approvingly. "At last you are asking questions, Anthony. I see that my confidence in you was not misplaced."

Yee had confidence in me? After knowing me for fifteen minutes? Was that good?

Yee took a long pull on his Vernor's, lubricating his throat for storytelling.

"Carla is not what she seems. She is a professional assassin, an agent of the British Secret Intelligence Service. She assumed the protective coloration of a homeless prostitute to deflect attention, to defuse curiosity, to have a vantage point to stalk her prey, access to an ideal location to accomplish her assignment, and, most importantly, to disguise the whole affair so that it would never be traced to its source.

"That was the delicate aspect of her mission. It was an act of post-facto espionage, Anthony—an overdue redress for a past injury. But the assassin could not simply strike her target and leave behind any speculation that the killing had a political motive. The American government could not permit operatives of foreign intelligence services to conduct such business on American soil, particularly agents of American allies. Such a scandal would have diplomatic repercussions and might lead to economic sanctions. It was imperative that the police be misled.

"The police are already aware that Lyss Nelson was not what she seemed either. They have got no further than the discovery that Lyss Wattenwill carried a fraudulent passport, that she had never been a citizen of Switzerland. What they do not know, and will likely never know, is that Wattenwill had been an agent of the Stasi, the East German Secret Intelligence bureau.

"After the destruction of the Berlin Wall and the reunification of East and West Germany, the Stasi disbanded and scattered to the winds to escape retribution for their excesses. Some went east and found shelter in the Soviet Union and employment with the KBG. Obviously, they are now out of work. Others were able to acquire new identities and the resources to relocate in the west—customarily expropriated from the unfortunate victims of their iron-fisted suasion.

"Wattenwill—her identity in East Germany was Brunhilde Koenig, probably itself an assumed name—reneged on an arrangement she had made with MI6 to defect to the West in 1986. In negotiating her defection, she had provided British Intelligence with a list of names of her own contacts, English citizens in East Germany who provided the Stasi valuable information in exchange for commercial advantages. Koenig subsequently had these people killed to prevent their arrest by London and any public trials that might jeopardize Koenig's operations. Two of those English citizens happened to be double agents, working for MI6.

"The arm of the British SIS is long and their memory is ineradicable. Koenig's treachery could not be tolerated if they hoped to maintain esprit within their ranks. They were willing to undertake risk to, let us say, close Koenig's account."

I really was an ape. My head was spinning. All this Cold War spy stuff—it was like a Le Carre novel or an episode of *The Sandbaggers*. Only it was happening in my backyard.

"You were aware of all this and you just let it happen?"

"When I identified myself as your *deus,* Anthony, I did not mean to imply that I am omnipotent. Carla had been briefed to communicate her plans to me. If I had not been made aware of her mission, I might well have unwittingly jeopardized it. In the short term, there is nothing I can do to alter the behavior of well-trained people determined to effect their ends, regardless of their moral ambiguity. I am Chinese. My interests lie in the long view."

"But what about Darlena Giordano? Was she a spy too? How did Deejee get involved in all this?"

Yee drained his ginger ale and turned to the sliding panel next to him. I heard the crackling ice and the soft pop of a cap coming off a fresh bottle. My fingers were still wrapped around mine, untouched since Yee had embarked on his spellbinding tale of foreign intrigue and familiar faces struck dead on my doorstep.

"That's where you come in, Anthony." Yee's voice was gentle, sympathetic. "Your involvement with Giordano gave Carla exactly what she needed to cover her tracks."

"Hold on, Mister Yee!" I was holding a cold Vernor's in my hand, but I was getting a little hot under my collar. "What do I have to do with any of this? This is just unreal!"

"Once again you invoke reality as if it were a yardstick for your perceptions, when precisely the opposite is the case.

"It was necessary for Carla to make the police believe a serial killer was at work in their domain. That was why she did not disappear immediately after she had dispatched Koenig. Another murder had to be staged with the same *modus operandi* as the first. It was not necessary, but proved to be doubly convenient that it could be committed in the same place.

"Carla's choice of a second victim provoked scruples, not as to its justification, but as to its selection. It had to be a woman, but not just any woman. The victim had to be someone unlikely to provoke sustained outrage from family members or to generate extraordinary pressure on the police from local residents. It had to be someone without deep ties to the community."

"Someone who would not be missed," I blurted bitterly. "Except by me."

"You will miss Rita Barron, Anthony." Yee spoke sharply. "You will not miss Darlena Giordano."

Yee knew about Rita? I had to stop being surprised by what he knew.

"Did Giordano try to extort anything from you?"

He had me there. I ought to have felt shock about Yee's inexhaustible supply of knowledge about my personal life, but I was hanging my head, stung by what he had said about Rita.

"She wanted me to buy her a car. Her hold on me was an embarrassing photo that implicated me in a theft."

Yee slipped two fingers into a pale blue shirt pocket, withdrawing two objects. "Would this be the embarrassing photograph?"

He placed the Polaroid in my lap on top of the lacquered box. I examined it. I looked as guilty as a white guy in a pith helmet with his foot on the carcass of a dead elephant.

The other object was the dull brass key that fit the lock on my apartment door.

"How on earth did you get these?"

Yee was sympathetic again. "Carla lifted them from Giordano's belongings. She was ruthless, Anthony, not heartless. Before she killed Koenig, she arranged an alibi for

Tommy Nelson by providing him a substantial supply of heroin. And before she murdered Giordano, she set up the alibi for you with the dog and pony show called Your Xanadu."

My head snapped up. I stared at Yee. "How could she know about my anniversary date? Are you saying Carla was working with Rita?"

"No, Anthony. She was working with *you*. Do you recall any occasion when you might have told her about your situation with Giordano?"

Sweet fucking Jesus. That ride I had given her to Isla Vista. I had emptied my lunch pail in her lap just because she was there. She had opened me up like a box of Cheerios. I had thought it was interesting that she had called the asphalt road "macadam". Who would use that word? An English person, that's who.

"Carla liked you, Anthony. In killing Giordano, she was looking out for your interests as well as her own."

Chapter Fifty-Eight

I was sorely upset by all these revelations that entangled me with murder and tugged away the wool that blinded my eyes. I didn't like it that Yee knew so much about Darlena and me. I liked it even less that he knew so much about Rita.

I had lost the woman of my life. I deserved it. Worse, I had lost her for no reason. Rita loved me. She gave me every chance. I had kicked it all away.

And for what? To pursue a conniving fraud whose only interest in me was that I was an easy mark. I was a thousand times a fool. That was bad enough, but it utterly burned me that Yee was here to rub my face in the mess I had made of my life.

"I still don't understand, Mister Yee. How you know all these things—things the police don't know, things about the secret intelligence agencies of other countries, things about me I have never told anyone?"

Yee was not looking at me. He was peering at the bottle of Vernor's ginger ale he held with both hands in his lap. Perhaps he was gazing into its opening where dark mysteries swirled among the golden effervescent bubbles that only a Chinese wizard could divine. Maybe a genie from the Ming Dynasty was about to materialize.

"I said that we Chinese, because we endure, are suited to inherit the earth." He nodded and rolled his head around, indicating our surroundings. "If I were not suitably adept at what I do, Anthony, we would not be here having this conversation."

It occurred to me that I could simply open the door and walk away from all of this. But it was raining out there, coming down cold and hard like the facts about me I could not avoid. It was warm and cozy in the back seat of the Rolls.

Yee had explained that "facts" were only temporary, momentary rest stops for perspective. Perhaps in time that would give me comfort. Maybe the aromatic box resting on my thighs would comfort me too.

There was a third gift Yee had promised. I was by no means sure that I would want it. But I sure as hell wanted to know what it was.

Yee murmured, as if he were speaking to himself. "When I was a boy, I was enchanted with mathematics and the physical sciences. As a young man, I indulged all my appetites, gustatory and sexual. Later, I read much philosophy and literature, particularly of the classics. In my maturity, I became disenchanted with the shallow, selfish pursuits of people, with their intractable stupidities, vanities, jealousies, acquisitive desires and pointless ends. I retired to a Tamil monastery in Sri Lanka to practice asceticism and meditation.

"I came to understand that this 'now' we think of as concrete, this happening of everything—it all just dissolves, ripples away. Time sweeps it all downstream. I was paralyzed by the grandeur of my insignificance."

"Then one evening, as I was lying on a grassy hillside contemplating the immensity of the universe from its stupefying vast expanses to its inconceivably tiny fundaments, I awoke."

Yee turned to me. He was excited. He put a hand on my arm, the better to secure contact to transmit his current of ideas.

"One day you will wake too, Anthony. You will see, hear, taste, touch, and smell for the first time. It will amaze that you ever lived the life you presently live.

"This is my third gift for you: I offer you a new life. I will give you the opportunity to awaken, to be aware, to have a purpose. I want you to work for me."

"Work for you? You mean like Randy?"

Yee's laugh was like the yelp of a golden retriever. "Yawp! Yawp! Yawp!

"Randy Garch works for me only in the sense that a shovel works for a gardener. He spreads manure for me.

"Confucius wrote, 'People may be made to follow a path of action, but they may not be made to understand it.' Randy did not understand that I fertilized Liquid Avenue to grow weeds, unselected flora that stunt the growth of native culture and prepare the ground for the more suitable ideas to come."

I glanced at the inviting box in my lap. "This is fertilizer?"

"No, Anthony. That's what I smoke when I want to let my hair down.

"My employee here is Luis Alvarado. Luis may seem humble in his appearance and demeanor, but, like Carla, he is a brilliant professional under camouflage. Luis has a phenomenal memory for spoken words. He can recall anything ever said in his presence regardless of the language. He runs a network that collects information for me from dozens of service and delivery workers in the Tri-County area. He has people in place from the seaside hotels of Ventura and Santa Barbara to the strawberry fields of Santa Maria. Luis owns a home in Montecito and a ranch in Los Olivos.

"Through others I have contacts with the police, sheriffs and Highway Patrol. I am in touch with harbor watches, county seats, and courthouses. Information reaches me from the Chambers of Commerce, the Missions, the University of California and the local colleges.

"I learned about you from another of my seiners, Sen-Jie Worthen, who, you may recall, is married to your associate Herb

Worthen at Golden Sunset Publications. I considered recruiting you when that publisher dismissed you. At that moment in time, you were still involved with Rita Barron and unlikely to consider my employment offer, so, through Sen-Jie, I steered you to Robert Bellaire.

"Luis and Sen-Jie are but two of many such people who sift and filter the hurly burly for nuggets of value to me. And I am but one of many similar men and women whose purpose is to enable the world to become Chinese."

"You want me to help you make the world Chinese?"

"I want to make *you* Chinese, Anthony. From that it will follow as surely as a river finding its way to the sea that Chinese is the most suitable way to be."

"What is it you want me to do?"

"In addition to the collection of information, I also disseminate it. I have print shops in Santa Barbara and Ventura. I want you to move to Venice, where I own a small press. There you will meet a woman called Chin. She will find you a suitable apartment and arrange for your employment with a suitable salary as editor of a literary magazine called *Ideograms*. You will have complete discretion as to the content of the publication. From time to time Chin will submit pieces that you will publish without editorial scrutiny. These, of course, will contain coded directives for our agents.

"Ultimately, Anthony, you will have your moment of awakening. It will occur in due course, as it did with me, without any particular preparation on your part. All you need do is to live well and stay aware. Endure."

Yee set aside his bottle of ginger ale and leaned forward to push a button in the dividing panel between us and the front. The partition slid down. I was surprised to see that there was no one else in the car with us. I presumed there would be a chauffeur. Apparently, Yee liked to do his own driving.

He pushed himself off the back seat, reached into the front, and pulled out a satchel of brushed brown leather. He settled back into his seat and opened snaps on the satchel. He handed it to me.

I could not have bundled the money better myself. All the bills looked used. They were grouped with rubber bands not bank wrappers. All the currencies from singles through hundreds were abundantly represented. It was a generous pile of dough—money intended to make me "Chinese?" Was I about to be instructed to launder it?

"That should be enough to settle your debts here and get you started in Venice. Endure. Be suitable. Be Chinese. What do you say?"

Rita was gone. Liquid Avenue had evaporated. Santa Barbara was no longer a tranquil harbor for me. What else could I say?

"Suits me." I said.